COW CRIMES AND
the Mustang Menace

A Ruby Taylor Mystery

COW CRIMES AND
the Mustang Menace

Sharon Dunn

Kregel
Publications

Cow Crimes and the Mustang Menace: A Ruby Taylor Mystery

© 2005 by Sharon Dunn

Published by Kregel Publications, a division of Kregel, Inc., P.O. Box 2607, Grand Rapids, MI 49501.

Published in association with the literary agency of Janet Kobobel Grant, Books and Such, 4788 Carissa Ave., Santa Rosa, CA 95405.

Library of Congress Cataloging-in-Publication Data
Dunn, Sharon
Cow crimes and the mustang menace: a Ruby Taylor mystery / by Sharon Dunn.
 p. cm.
 1. Taylor, Ruby (Fictitious character)—Fiction.
2. Women detectives—Fiction. 3. Theft—Fiction. I. Title.
PS3604.U57C69 2005
813'.6—dc22   2005008349

ISBN 0-8254-2490-9

Printed in the United States of America

05 06 07 08 09 / 5 4 3 2 1

To Michael, who got second billing after our cats
and hardly complained, for your support of this and all my
writing endeavors. You are always a cattle rancher in your heart
even if practicality doesn't make it possible. I thank you for
being the inspiration for this book and for providing much
of the expertise.

Acknowledgments

There really is a potato festival in Montana, and I'm sure it's a sophisticated and dignified affair, not filled with the silliness of Potato Queens and lawn-mower races like my fictional festival. I'm grateful to all farmers and ranchers. Your respect for the land and for the animals, and your willingness to do hard, often unrewarding work, is an inspiration to me.

As always, I'd like to thank the American Christian Fiction Writers—for rejoicing over my successes and weeping with me when I wept. I would especially like to thank Karen, Tina, and Connie, who helped me understand the perils of multiple chemical sensitivity.

Bev and Joanna, thank you for being willing to read through the entire book when it was less than polished. Your comments helped more than you know. And to Linnae, your support and encouragement has meant so much to me.

I am deeply grateful to Ann at the Pioneer Museum for helping me understand how land ownership and sales were recorded way back when. Despite my muddled questions, you gave me exactly what I needed.

Finally, to my children, Jonah, Ariel, and Shannon—you inspire me to sit at the computer even on days when I don't feel like it. Thank you for making me a better person and for "playing nice" so I could write.

COW CRIMES AND
the Mustang Menace

Prologue

In 1902, some of Seb Van Kriten's closest friends and neighbors rousted him out of bed in the early hours of the morning. They tied his hands, put a pillowcase on his head, and forced him into the backseat of his hay wagon. With several people following on horseback, an unspecified number of them drove into a valley that contained a single, tall cottonwood.

Folklore about the incident says that Seb fought so hard, it took four of the neighbors twenty minutes to get him onto the back of a bay mare. At that point, the neighbors slapped the horse's flanks and unceremoniously hung Seb. The group drove or rode away, vowing never to speak publicly of what they'd done or to reveal who'd been there.

Seb's death was the last recorded incident of vigilantism in Colter County. At best, Seb Van Kriten gets a one-sentence mention in Montana history books. Most of the older residents of Colter County, those whose ancestors settled in and around the little town of Fontana, know this story. All of them tell a slightly different version, and none of them claim to be related to the unknown assailants who chose to take justice into their own hands one cold February morning.

The reason why Seb's neighbors turned on him is unclear. He was a wealthy man who owned a substantial amount of land. There was some question as to how he'd come into so much money. He was known to gamble and had very little respect for his own or anybody else's marriage vows. In other words, there were plenty of reasons to be angry at Seb. It only takes a sprinkling of bitterness for anger to become rage and rage to become violence.

A hundred years later, all of this would be ancient history, or just a good question for a trivia game, except that Seb's death determined the course of my life for the winter of 2003. I was held hostage by history—or my ignorance of it.

If only I'd looked closely at the newspaper my mother folded into a tight square that day in her car, I would have seen the article about Seb written by historian Martin Grant. That edition of the *Fontana Ledger* contained the announcement about the upcoming Potato Festival and the opportunity for single women to have a shot at being the Potato Queen in the spring.

But it contained a lot more.

In that Thursday edition of the *Ledger* were, in fact, most of the pieces of the puzzle for a series of seemingly unconnected events and crimes. I would have seen the police report describing the pattern of theft of liquid fertilizer from the farms around Fontana. The front-page story was about the robbery at Vern Mackafferty's car dealership—not only did Vern lose money and a '65 Mustang, but the thieves also took his favorite Charlie Russell sculpture. Had I skimmed through that paper sooner, I would have read Nathan Burgess's letter to the editor about the increased traffic on Old Gorman Road. And maybe, just maybe, I would have connected the dots faster. I could have saved myself a lot of grief—and at least one life.

Hindsight is a beautiful thing. Too bad it only happens after you learn your lesson, make mistakes, and experience pain.

I don't really know where to begin to explain how this all went down. I suppose it started the night that Georgia and I attempted a little vigilante justice ourselves. . . .

Chapter One

Mocha espressos taste better in the dark. The smoothness of the chocolate is more tantalizing on the tongue—the bite of the caffeine stronger. Had I not agreed to run a stakeout at Benson's Pet and Feed, I never would have made that discovery. But before we turned off the lights and slipped behind the counter, my boss, Georgia, mixed up two steaming 20-ouncers, complete with whipped cream and chocolate sprinkles.

I allowed the warm liquid to linger on my tongue before swallowing. Forget all those apologetics books; chocolate and coffee are the clearest evidence that God exists and that he loves us.

I pressed my back against the counter and felt along the shelf for the Ruger revolver Georgia had brought from home. My fingers touched cold metal then trailed over the smooth ivory of the grip. Right next to it was the cell phone. The plan was to call Wesley at the police station the second we heard a suspicious noise. I doubted Wesley would endorse our taking the law into our own hands, but the store had been robbed twice already, and even with my connections, the cops had done nil.

We were two women with a plan and huge cups of steaming coffee—a dangerous combination.

Georgia's neon "Closed" sign glowed in the dark. One lonely light across the street shimmered in a murky mist of falling snow.

The thieves were very directed in what they took. The two previous times they'd cut the bolt on the glass-front refrigerator and snatched all our vaccine. At $103 a bottle, it wasn't a lot of money.

But it was an irritation that they had popped in for a refill two Thursdays in a row. They'd also snatched all of Georgia's top-of-the-line horse clippers—five pair at $160 each. The losses were adding up.

This Thursday, Georgia had filled empty vaccine containers with milk and placed them in the usual spot in the fridge. She hadn't restocked the horse clippers. This wasn't our first day at camp.

I inhaled a healthy dose of the chocolate-scented steam. "I suppose all the sleep I'm missing is fair trade for this coffee."

"I think you're ahead on the deal, honey. Quit yer whining, Miss Pansy Butt." Georgia repositioned herself in the dark. One of her joints cracked.

"So I'm going to owe you money. Is that what you're saying?"

"You don't owe me anything, Ruby. 'Preciate you coming to help." Her hand slapped my shoulder, her version of being affectionate.

"Just keep the java flowing, woman. That's all I have to say."

I am not sure exactly how old Georgia is. My guess is somewhere close to seventy. Prior to my turning out the light, I'd witnessed her lowering herself to the floor to sit cross-legged next to me. Her cracking joints and swear words created a dissonant symphony as she moved herself into position for the stakeout.

To her credit, she didn't complain about her lumbago or bursitis once she was settled. I have no idea what those two ailments are, but I think it's a federal law that anyone over fifty gets to complain about them. Georgia was a rancher's wife for many years. After her husband died, she opened the store. We've never arm wrestled, but she'd probably beat me, even though I'm less than half her age. I've seen her heft huge bags of feed like they were pillows and toss them onto the backs of trucks.

"Store's going to go under if this keeps up." Georgia tapped the side of her cup with her fingernail.

"You've been in business for fifteen years." I spoke into the darkness, sensing rather than seeing where my boss was. "You're not going under because of a little theft."

"My whole life is in this store. Sold the farm to pay for it after Glen died. All I can say is those thieving jerks better come tonight."

"Third time's the charm." As my eyes adjusted to the darkness, I could just make out Georgia's curly brown head. "Besides, I'm busy tomorrow night. Wesley and I are going out to his brother's place to watch the kids."

"Kids? How many?"

"We'll be babysitting five. Zac and Julia have six kids. I've only met the oldest, Jason. He helped Wesley when he owned the roofing business. Jason doesn't live at home anymore. Zac and Julia need a weekend to themselves, so Wesley and I volunteered."

"How is the man of the hour?"

My fingers tensed around the coffee cup. "Things were good for a while. Then he kind of clammed up, started canceling stuff." I had the feeling his absence was work related, but he wasn't sharing any details with me. His silence had become so frustrating and confusing that I found myself keeping a journal and writing letters to him every time he canceled. They were letters that only the inside of my drawer would get to read, but they'd become a form of therapy. I had no claim on him. We weren't even dating. Yet none of that logical stuff stopped my heart from twisting into tight knots when he wasn't around.

Somewhere in the store, a cat yowled. Her Majesty, the resident Siamese, padded across the floor and jumped up onto the counter.

I could feel her staring at us from above, probably planning some strategic dive bombing on these two annoying people who kept coming into her store and moving all the comfortable beds.

"So that's what she does when we're not around." Georgia rested her head against the back of the counter. "Gets her nasty little fur all over my counters."

"Like you didn't know." I took another sip of coffee. "I'm always pulling little black hairs off the stuff people bring up."

"I'm just glad she lets us hang out in her store."

Both Georgia and I understood the pecking order. There was a reason the Siamese was called Her Majesty. In addition to demanding she be viewed as the queen, she had serious mood issues. Every time I reached to pet her, it was a gamble whether she'd scratch me or rub up against my hand and purr.

On the street outside, a large truck roared by. Both of us jumped, causing the wooden cupboards to vibrate. My panic systems switched into high gear. By the time I reached for the gun, my heart was jitterbugging in my chest.

Georgia lifted herself to peek over the counter. Light haloed the top of her head. "It's nothing. They drove on," she whispered, settling back down.

My hand moved from the gun to the phone. Maybe it's just my background—a childhood disrupted by my parents' embezzling and consequential incarceration—but sometimes I exhibit the survival instincts of a mercenary. *Mental note: reach for the phone first, not the gun.*

Mom and I probably seem pretty normal now. Mom became a Christian when she was doing time. God and Mom found me a few years after she finished her sentence. My father died in prison, and my little brother was recently sentenced for fencing stolen goods. And that's how we all became the Brady Bunch.

Georgia's fingertips tapped linoleum. If the thieves were coming back, they probably wouldn't use the front door anyway. We'd found the lock on the back door busted and the alarm system disabled. Would the thieves be dumb enough to come back on a third Thursday? Slick as their operation was, it seemed absurd that they'd stick to a robbery schedule. But maybe we'd get lucky. Didn't matter; the coffee was good.

The silence of a snowy Montana night augmented Georgia's gulps of coffee. I heard her set her mug on the linoleum. She sighed several times. "Can't stand quiet. Wish I could throw some Tammy Wynette on the turntable."

Georgia is pretty hip when it comes to coffee, but there are certain unspoken rules about what kind of music is played in here. First of all, a CD player is poison and can never come across the threshold of the store. I learned that the hard way. Second, we are not allowed to bring in any of that "long-haired, hippie, country-western music." I don't think Georgia can process terms like *rock and roll* or *Christian rock.* I must confess I was becoming quite a Johnny Cash fan.

Her Majesty paced across the counter. My eyes had adjusted enough to the darkness so I could see her jump to a shelf on the opposite wall. Napkins spilled all over the floor.

Georgia made a growling noise. "Why do I keep her?"

Her Majesty yowled before settling down on the shelf she'd just cleared.

"She keeps us. Remember the ground rules of cat ownership." My coffee had grown lukewarm but still packed a punch.

I listened to the ticking of the clock and rotated my cup in my hand. Outside, a few cars and trucks zoomed by. Georgia's store was on the edge of Eagleton, the last stop before you hit alfalfa fields, small towns, farms, and ranches. Wesley's family farm, where his brother and father still lived, was about an hour's drive from here, outside a little town called Fontana, the same area Georgia's ranch had been before she sold it.

Her Majesty purred with the intensity of a freight train.

"Must be past eleven by now." I couldn't stand the quiet either.

"Shhhhhh," Georgia advised.

I counted my fingers—ten in all—opened and closed my hands twenty times, tried to remember all of Psalm 40, and brushed my cheeks with a strand of hair. Yeah, I could go for some Tammy Wynette, too, or even some Donna Fargo. She really was the happiest girl in the whole USA.

Not only were sounds more distinct in the darkness, but I noticed new odors in the store. Georgia smelled like strawberries and hairspray. If I inhaled deeply, I even picked up an Italian spice smell. My own mother emanates lilac or rose with an underlying scent of vanilla.

I could detect three layers of smells in the store. Citrus-scented cleaner—which Georgia insists on using—was the most obvious. But beneath that was the smell of wood and varnish, and even below that the subtle aroma of straw and manure threaded the air. That third layer was probably a combination of all the farmers who milled through here and the pets that Georgia kept for sale, mostly farm orphans people brought in: rabbits, calves, cats, and the occasional goat or pig.

"Georgia," I whispered.

"What?" she whispered back.

"I need to make a potty run."

"Did you drink all that coffee?" she scolded.

"You gave it to me. There's nothing happening here anyway. I'll be right back." I found her shoulder in the dark and squeezed.

"Hurry back. You'll miss all the fun."

Instead of standing straight up and walking to the bathroom, I slithered in a crouch behind the counter, out of the line of sight of the door. The lyrics for "Secret Agent Man" ran through my head as I passed the far wall where the muck boots and flannel shirts were displayed.

Georgia and I had both dressed in black. Anyone who thinks women bond through quilting parties and sharing birthing and PMS stories has never tried a stakeout.

The bathroom was at the very back of the store. I slipped inside the room marked with a silhouette of a cowgirl, flipped on the light, and closed the door behind me. While I washed my hands, something bumped against the door. I pulled a paper towel out of the dispenser, staring at the door. My throat went dry. Muffled footsteps.

"Georgia?" I whispered. That's me, the ever-hopeful one. As if Georgia would toss things against the door while I answered nature's call.

When I tried the door, I couldn't open it. I shook the handle again. More muffled bumps outside. Blood drummed in my ears. I sucked in a shallow, ragged breath of air. They must have seen the light from underneath the door and heard the water running. Something told me screaming would not be a good idea. I slapped the door with my hand. The thieves had only had a second to move the obstructing object into place. How heavy could it be?

I found a piece of thin cardboard, turned the knob, and slipped the cardboard between the bolt and the door frame. I stepped back and charged at the door. Red-hot pain radiated through my shoulder as I slammed against wood. The door moved about three inches. I repeated the procedure two more times until I had enough space to slip out.

Utilizing the light spilling from the bathroom, I felt along the base of the door and found two, forty-pound bags of feed. I couldn't read the labels, but I suspected they'd grabbed the bags from the storeroom by the bathroom. If they'd taken a moment, they could have found something heavier.

I stood for about a minute, waiting for my eyes to adjust to the darkness, waiting for my tactile memory to kick in. Then I could feel my way along the counter and—I hoped—find Georgia in one piece with a phone in her hand. There was no light switch close by.

To orient myself, I stumbled toward the wall that was part of the hallway leading to the back entrance of the store. The hallway was dark. My hand touched the textured wall.

The only sound was the ticks of the wall clock. Her Majesty wasn't purring anymore. I would have expected her to yowl when she knew I was in the room. I'd made quite a bit of noise slamming into the bathroom door. Maybe I'd scared the thieves away in the middle of their heist.

Fixating on the lamp in the lot across the street, I willed my heart to quit pounding.

Something brushed past my arm. A tension tingled and pulsated at the back of my neck. My lungs deflated. This was the same paralysis I'd felt when I stumbled onto a moose and a young calf in the forest. Heat from another body radiated around me. I closed my eyes, held my breath, and stood very still.

Please, dear God, don't let him hurt me. Please, dear God, don't let him hurt me.

The subtlest rustling of clothes competed with the ticking clock. A moment later, the back door opened and closed almost indiscernibly.

With my eyes pressed shut, I whispered, "Georgia?" I barely mouthed the words. Engine noise, a large truck starting up, broke the quiet. My eyes shot open.

Two lights like eyeballs turned on in the empty lot across the street. A cracking sound split the air outside.

By that time, I'd found the light switch. I did a quick inventory of the room around me. A cut lock dangled from the fridge handle. The shelf where the vaccine was supposed to be was empty. All the muck boots, five pair, were gone.

Georgia wasn't behind the counter. I raced to where two coffee mugs lay on the linoleum. The phone rested on the shelf, but the gun was gone. My fingers curled into fists, and I stomped once. *Gun gone. Phone here. Oh no.*

Another crack reverberated outside. *Oh no. Oh no.* My leg and arm muscles tensed. I grabbed the phone and raced toward the door into the snow and darkness. A truck pulled out into the street. A single headlight pierced the darkness. A dark shadow came from my side of the street and jumped into the back of the truck before it zoomed up the hill. Melting snow glistened on the road.

Georgia stood beneath the lamppost across the street. I jogged to the street corner and angled the phone so I could see the numbers. I know two cops—Wesley and his friend Sevee Cree—so I dialed directly into the station and identified myself. Wesley was out on another call. Cree said he was on his way.

Snow fell in wet clumps, chilling my bare skin. I raced across the street to the empty lot. Georgia's curly brown hair matted against her face. The gun hung in her limp hand.

"They took Her Majesty." She shivered.

"What? Why? Are you sure?" I brushed melting snow from my eyes.

"Those dirty rotten . . . took my cat." Georgia readjusted her grip on the gun.

"Georgia, we need to get back to the store. The police are on their way."

"Took my cat. That crabby old Siamese isn't worth anything to anybody but me." She shook her head. "What are they going to do with a mean old thing like that?" Her voice quavered.

I patted her back. "Come on . . . I'll walk over with you. We need to get you back inside before you freeze."

Georgia looked at the gun, angling it sideways. "I wouldn't have shot at them. But they took my cat."

Getting Georgia across the street was going to require more diplomacy than I had anticipated. The loss of her beloved pet caused an inertia that made it difficult for her to perform even the simplest task.

"We'll get her back." I doubted it was true, but it seemed like an uplifting thing to say. I was still hopeful that Georgia was wrong about the catnapping. Stealing the vaccine and even the boots made sense, but why would anyone want a cat . . . especially that cat? Her Majesty could be sweet as molasses to me and Georgia, but she became all claws and hackles around other people. Muck boots and vaccine had some black-market value, but no one would pay a dime for that cat.

I pried the revolver out of Georgia's hand and shoved it in my waistband.

"I wouldn't have shot at them, but they took my cat." She sounded listless and dizzy—like all the fight had been drained from her.

"Come on, we need to get you inside and dried off."

A police car slid into the parking lot of the feed store. Two uniformed officers got out. I recognized Sevee's dark hair and medium build. The other officer—a tall, thin, slightly hunched man—was a stranger to me.

I wrapped my arm across Georgia's back and cupped her shoulder. Chilling moisture soaked through my clothes as I guided my friend across the street. Our feet made a sort of smattering sound when they hit the melting snow. By the time we got back to the store parking lot, we were drenched.

The younger officer had flipped back the lid of the dumpster and climbed in. Cop behavior has never made much sense to me. I waved at Sevee just as he clicked on a flashlight and surveyed the area around the store. He leaned over and picked something up.

Georgia swayed and stared at the ground. Officer Cree approached, holding a black rubber boot in his hand. Did I mention that cop behavior has never made much sense to me? The boot was a muck boot but not the brand we carried.

"I don't suppose you got a look at the vehicle." Cree wore a police-issue, black rain poncho that made rubbing-plastic noises every time he lifted his arm.

"Not really; it was a truck. I can tell you it has only one headlight."

Officer Cree waved the boot. "Ranch supply place might have

traceable chemicals. They dumped their over boots so it would be harder to use forensics to link them to the crime."

"The barefoot burglars," I joked.

Sevee gave me the cop look—straight-lipped, stone-faced. "They'd have shoes on underneath, Ruby. Officer Malmin is looking for gloves." His expression was the same unemotional look I'd seen when Wesley handed out parking tickets. Cops must practice it in front of the mirror.

He shifted the boot to his other hand. "Something must have scared them. It would have been smarter to dump the stuff up the road so it would be harder to connect it to your store."

"The something that scared them was Georgia trying to get her cat back." I pulled on the hem of my blouse, which was plastered against my stomach. My clothes weighed an extra five pounds. A chill snaked its way toward the marrow of my bones. I'd be soaking in a hot bathtub for days before I warmed up. "At least that explains why they took all our muck boots. They're planning on another robbery."

"Found them," Officer Malmin yelled from the dumpster. He tossed several gloves out onto the wet ground.

"This snow is going to wreak havoc with our evidence. Did you see anything at all?" Illumination from the flashlight revealed water trickling down Cree's face.

I didn't think he needed to know I'd spent the entire burglary in the little cowgirl's room. "They weren't in that store more than five minutes. One of them must have gotten delayed. He brushed against me. He had a chance to hurt me, and he didn't."

"Not violent, huh?" Holding his flashlight in his mouth, Cree took a small notebook out of his back pocket and flipped it open.

The page darkened as melting snow bled all over it. He rolled his eyes and closed the notebook.

I crossed my arms to keep out some of the cold. "They knew exactly what they wanted. Just like the other two times when you guys didn't catch them." My tone was a little accusatory. I stomped my feet to stave off the chill in my legs. None of my aerobics warmed me up.

"We're working on it, Ruby." Cree leaned a little closer. Even in the dimness of night, I could see lines in his forehead.

"Sorry." I knew from what Wesley had told me that the Eagleton police force was stretched thin. Crime and population were increasing. Funding was not.

Georgia lifted her head and huddled beside me. The glazed look had left her eyes. "They took my cat." She shivered violently. Prisms of water sprayed from her hair when she shook her head. "They had small lights. Four of them . . . I think. Her Majesty ran up to them. I heard her hiss. That precious thing was trying to protect the place."

Tossing one final glove on the ground, Officer Malmin climbed out of the dumpster and ambled toward us. When he wasn't soaking wet, Malmin probably had blond curly hair. As he was, his most dominant features were buggy eyes and distinct cheekbones. He couldn't have been more than twenty.

Malmin lifted his chin and squared his shoulders. It's hard to look dignified and authoritative when you've just crawled out of a dumpster. "Odd number of gloves. Only three."

Cree slapped Malmin on the back. "I think their plan got thrown off a bit. They may be dumping more items up the road. Check the dumpster again just to be sure."

Malmin rolled his eyes and trudged back to the dumpster

"So are you training him just like you did with Wesley?"

"He'll ride with me for twelve weeks before he finishes up at the academy."

"Must be nice to have someone else to do the dumpster diving."

"Just a perk of the job." Cree grinned. "I'm going to put the word out to have highway patrol look for trucks with a missing headlight. I know it's late, but you guys need to make a statement while things are fresh in your mind."

"I hope it won't take long. I need sleep. I'm going out to Zachary Burgess's place to watch kids in eight hours."

Cree planted his feet. His head tilted slightly. "With Wesley?"

"Yeah, with Wesley."

"Zachary's farm is over by Fontana, right?" Cree stared long enough for me to feel uncomfortable.

"Yes." I took a step back. He was looking at me with his police interrogating eyes, not his I'm-your-friend eyes.

"Was it your idea or his?" Cree stepped a little closer and studied me without blinking. His dark brown eyes narrowed.

I inched away. He seemed totally unaware that he had moved into cop interrogation mode. "It was his idea. We're just watching their kids so Zac and his wife can have some time to themselves." Placing a hand on my hip, I shifted my weight. "Is there something I should know?"

He turned slightly so I couldn't look him in the eye. "No, no. Nothing you should know."

Cree had never lied to me, but I guess there was a first time for everything.

"Are you sure about that?" I pressed.

"Why don't you guys go inside and get dried off? We'll meet you down at the station house. Malmin can take your statements."

Which meant, if my guess was correct, Cree wouldn't even be around by the time Georgia and I got there. I wouldn't be able to question him further at the station house. Now my planned weekend with Wesley had even more frustration connected with it.

I wrapped my arms around Georgia. We trudged through the wet parking lot to the store and the espresso machine that provided fresh brewed cups of life. If the temperature dropped past freezing, the soggy snow would turn to chunky ice by morning. Beyond the city lights, I could just make out the dark silhouette of the mountains that surrounded Eagleton. My eyes followed the highway leading out of town. Her Majesty was out there somewhere. "I'm going to miss that old cat."

"Me, too." Georgia moaned.

It was going to take a lot of mochas before Georgia and I felt like we were back in the land of the living. As we slipped into the store, I glanced across the street and wondered where someone would hide a cat in need of a Prozac prescription—and how long they'd put up with her.

Chapter Two

*D*ear Wesley,

Since your abandonment of me, I have been taken prisoner by a tribe of midgets. They are a peculiar little people who delight in causing me pain. Throughout the farmhouse where they are holding me captive, they have laid land mines of Legos. Nothing produces a cacophony of laughter faster than if I step on one of those wretched toys, howl, and jump on one foot. They run from other rooms to watch me bounce around in pain. If I hit my elbow or head, that is cause for the little people to roll on the floor, holding their stomachs and kicking their legs while they giggle and point at me. Obviously, putting my shoes on would prevent much of this torture. If only that were possible. They have taken my shoes and hidden them somewhere devilishly clever. I am sure there must be women's shoes around this house somewhere, but my captors' torment is relentless, and I have not had a free moment to look for them.

All day long, since you left me without explanation, I have been wearing a pair of large rubber boots to go outside. The boots are caked with manure and are at least a size fourteen, so wearing them inside is out of the question. I suspect the foot gear belongs to your brother, the one the midgets called "Papee." I have only a vague memory of him. He and the one called "Mamee" left the house so quickly when you and I arrived. Their faces are a distant blur. I do remember Mamee shouting as she raced toward the car, "Thanks for watching the kids for us. See you in two days."

I must confess I have never seen a car accelerate quite that fast down a gravel road.

There are five in the tribe, two females and three males. With the exception of the tall one, the one called Josie, they follow me around from room to room, often attaching themselves to my legs. Height seems to have something to do with the pecking order in the tribe. The shorter you are, the more power you have.

I have seen the smallest one, the one they call Boady (although I don't think that is his real name; one of the characteristics of their language is the absence of the letter r. When they say my name, it comes out "Ooby"), control the other midgets through a series of howls and squawks. During one screaming episode, I witnessed a stunning display of ritualistic sacrifice as the others threw boxes of toys and bags of candy at Boady's feet in an effort to stop the squawking. Their homage quieted him only momentarily. The others seem almost afraid of Boady and will do anything to prevent his high, shrill keening. He is like a miniature monster that they must constantly feed and appease.

I had no idea taking care of children would be like this. I should have realized that Boady would be the most dangerous of all of them when Mamee kissed him on the forehead before she left and said, "Now you be good for Ruby and Wesley, Mr. Naughty Naughty."

Wesley, if you had stayed here in Kidletland, you would have had a chance to read the three pages of handwritten instructions that Mamee left to aid us in dealing with the little people. Number four on her list states, "We are working on having a sugar-free household. The children are allowed one small piece of candy after dinner." If only I had been able to abide by that prescribed behavior. If only.

About an hour after you disappeared in your Jeep, the midgets found the bags of candy. I was upstairs trying to locate my shoes and rewind toilet paper onto a roll. The toilet paper trail started in the bathroom and led from bedroom to bedroom. I could not have been upstairs more than ten minutes. It was the heady silence coming from downstairs that alerted me to trouble.

When I came into the kitchen, only the skeletal remains of the candy wrappers and packages were left. All four of them (Josie was up in her room reading, which is where she spends most of her time) had telltale chocolate stains around their mouths.

Once the sugar high kicked in, they jettisoned themselves off the porch into the snow screaming, "I can fly! I can fly!" I chased after them in my oversized boots, putting hats and coats on repeatedly. The next five hours were a blur of flailing arms and legs—of me trying to prevent freezing and injury. They whirled around me at warp speed, chanting their strange mantras: "um ver um ver, you're going to get it when Mom gets home, you started it, no you started it, um ver um ver."

At one point, one of them, the short female called NeeNee, climbed a tree in the yard. She sat on the branch, shivering, but refused to take the coat we handed up to her. None of my coaxing worked until Josie brought out a kitten and told NeeNee she could hold the cat if she came down.

When she is not reading, Josie has been quite helpful. She seems to understand the others' language and strange rituals and is willing to serve as a translator. Of all the members of the tribe, I am most intrigued by her. Though she is reluctant to go beyond the bare minimum of communication, she is quiet and bookish, which reminds me of myself at that age.

Wesley, where are you? Where have you gone? And where is my mother, who was supposed to come out and chaperone our nights at the farmhouse? She knows more about little people than I do. This is not the weekend I had planned.

I didn't tell you this, but I saw this weekend as a sort of test. Spending time with your brother's kids was supposed to be a chance for me to see how you were around children. Yes, Wesley, it was a test to see if you would be a good father. I haven't told you this because we haven't really even had our first date, but thoughts of marriage and children with you keep popping into my head. Ain't that just so old-fashioned of me? I can't help myself when I look at you.

But now, something has changed, and you won't tell me. I am afraid for you, but you have shared so little with me, I am not sure what I am afraid of. Even before this, I sensed you pulling away.

Maybe your abrupt departure has something to do with

your work. Cree certainly wasn't excited about us coming out here. Or (and I hesitate to even write this) maybe you sensed that I was testing you and didn't appreciate my pushiness. I thought I was hiding it well. This is all new to me. I grew up in an era where marriage and children were a little thing you did on the side. The big important career was where you put your energy. If nothing else, this weekend has shown me how all-encompassing motherhood would be.

I don't know what compels me to write these letters, though I have a dozen of them in my drawer at home. There are so many things I want to say to you. Fear of hurt or an inability to trust makes me pour my feelings into these stupid lined pages instead of saying them to you. I have a master's degree in English, for crying out loud, and I can't even tell you how much I care about you.

What makes me write these letters and what makes me sound like a bad television adaptation of a Jane Austen novel in them? I don't know. Why can't I just say these things to you?

Maybe I will work up the courage to give you the letters someday. But I can't do that if you don't come back.

Ruby

I folded the letter and shoved it in the pocket of my down coat. The wood beam of the porch railing felt firm against my back. It was only five o'clock, and already the sun, shrouded by clouds, rested low on the horizon. In the distance, snowcapped mountains surrounded Eagleton. The terrain around Fontana was more rolling hills and prairie. Snow covered the yard and the field beyond the gate. Julia's barren lilac bushes, coated with ice, looked like they were made of crystal.

Wesley had taken the obvious transportation, his Jeep. Maybe there was a farm truck somewhere I could get started if there was an emergency. Still, I had a sense of complete aloneness—total isolation. I zipped my coat to the neck. Mom wasn't even answering her phone.

NeeNee, barefoot and dressed in an oversized T-shirt, came to the door of the farmhouse. "Awex is painting wif peanut bucker."

"He is, huh?" I didn't even move from my perch on the railing. At the beginning of the day, I would have jumped right up to stave off such an impending disaster. Now after almost a full day with the tribe, I realized such thinking was unrealistic. Disasters would come and disasters would go, no matter how hard I tried to prevent them. The only price I had to pay for such a blasé attitude was a knot of tension invading my neck and spreading to my shoulders. I had reached a very important conclusion. I wasn't very good at this parenting stuff.

Josie came to the door and touched her little sister's shoulder. "It's okay. I got it away from him." She addressed me. "I put it on the top of the fridge. That's where Mom puts stuff when the boys aren't supposed to have it." Part of Josie's long blond hair was clipped back in a barrette. She had high cheekbones and a narrow face. Every time I looked directly at her, she bent her head and covered a pimple on her cheek.

"Thanks, Josie. For all your help." I wanted to tell her that I only noticed the pimple when she touched it. But I was afraid such a comment, a vocal acknowledgment of the imperfection on her preteen face, would only cause a flood of tears. She was at that age.

Inside, I found Boady, whose real name was probably Brody, asleep in the dog bed with two fluffy kittens curled against his little belly. Tormenting your siblings uses up a lot of energy. I hauled Brody to his bed, and the rest of us had peanut butter and jelly sandwiches for dinner. Not the spectacular meal I had envisioned making with Wesley. Cooking has never been my forte. I wasn't sure why I thought things would change when I came out here. Forget about Wesley passing the parent test; I was the one with a D minus.

Getting the kids to bed was a two-hour process because they kept jumping up and running around the house. After some trial and error, I concluded that the best tactic was to let them run until they collapsed and then carry them to bed.

Once everyone was asleep, I wandered through the quiet house, massaging the back of my neck. My head throbbed. Chocolate as a means of relaxing was out of the question because the tribe had eaten it all hours earlier. I had noticed a claw-foot tub in the downstairs bathroom. . . .

Water gushed out of the faucet and steamed up the mirror. I eased into the tub with hot water up to my chin then placed a washcloth on my eyes. My muscles relaxed, and the stress and worry melted off.

Then I heard the voice.

"Why woo not have toys in tub?"

Tightness crept into my neck muscles. I peeled the washcloth off but hesitated in opening my eyes. With a deep breath, I opened the left eye to see a blond head, NeeNee's head, very close to my face. "I don't want toys in my tub. Go back to bed. I'm relaxing."

Eyes blinking rapidly, she pulled her head back. She stared at me for a long time, twisting her finger in her nose. "I get in the tub wif you?"

"No, NeeNee. Go back to bed."

She sat on the closed toilet and swung her legs back and forth. "I keep woo company."

"NeeNee, just go to bed."

"I have Stupeman on my unwear." She stood up and pointed to the pair of boy's jockeys she had on. I guess you end up wearing boy's underwear when you have three brothers. Her face beamed with delight, and her lips were drawn into a tight rosebud shape.

I closed my eyes. "That's great NeeNee."

She stood there, breathing, for some time, then her little feet pitter-pattered on the tile. I took a deep breath and sank deeper into the tub. The cords of tension had nearly untwisted when footsteps padded rapidly toward me. She ran so quickly I didn't even have time to open my eyes before a bunch of somethings showered down on me.

NeeNee giggled. "Toys."

When I opened my eyes, naked Barbies, plastic cars, and boats floated on the surface of my "relaxing" bath.

Satisfied, my blond tormentor disappeared. But when I came out into the living room, wrapped in my bathrobe, she was waiting for me. She held a stuffed animal that I suspect at one time had been a mouse. Now it had no ears and only one eye. Its tattered tail looked chewed on.

"You need to go to bed, NeeNee." I collapsed onto the couch. I had no fight left in me. Even the walk up the stairs to the bed where I was supposed to sleep seemed overwhelming.

NeeNee crawled up beside me, cuddling into my armpit. She stroked the arm of my velour bathrobe. "Woo look boofo, Ooby. Woo do." Then she wiped her nose on my bathrobe and fell asleep in my arms.

Her downy hair touched my chin and lips. I listened to her breathing while her tiny hand rested on my wrist. We seemed to be almost expanding and contracting together in our breathing. My heart felt tight in my chest. In that moment, as NeeNee drifted off in my arms, I thought about the little girl I'd given up for adoption thirteen years ago. I held NeeNee tighter. Was that little girl my only chance at motherhood? Nobody knew about her, not Mom, not Wesley.

I nuzzled my face against NeeNee's silky hair. I was a stranger in a strange land, but I could get used to the little people and their language and customs. I could get used to the magic of holding a child while she slept. Although I understand you have to cook if you're a mom—that concerns me a little. I'm kind of domestically challenged.

I touched the worn upholstery and thought that Wesley should be sleeping here on this couch. That had been our plan. Me upstairs and him down here. Mom here to serve as a chaperone. Really, I felt like we were beyond sexual temptation. We both knew what a destructive force that can be, so why did it feel like our relationship had stalled out? I just wanted Mom around so she could be impressed with how good Wesley was with children. So much for all my fantasies.

I leaned back against the couch. My eyelids felt weighted. Holding NeeNee had eased all the tension out of my neck better than the bath. *I want a tribe of my own,* I thought. *But maybe I've wasted too much time living by the world's rules. Maybe I blew my one chance at motherhood with that little girl, wherever she is.*

In the seconds before I fell asleep, I glanced out the dark window and prayed that Wesley was okay.

Chapter Three

There's Wesley's Jeep." I pointed through the window of my mom's Caddy. The Jeep was parked in a snowy field by a metal building.

Mom leaned toward me, placing her fingers by her lips. "Oh dear, I hope he is out there."

"Me, too."

She returned to reading the Fontana newspaper she'd picked up at Zachary and Julia's house. Shortly after the kids had found every blanket in the house and hauled them into the living room, my mother had shown up even if Wesley hadn't come back at all. She'd been delayed because friends of ours, Laura and Brian, had had a baby, and she'd lost the phone number for the farmhouse. Everybody I knew seemed to be having babies.

Mom pointed at an article in the newspaper. "They're calling for entries for this cooking contest at the Potato Festival in Fontana this spring. Anyone residing in Colter County can enter. You have to come up with an original recipe using potatoes."

I rolled down the window. The Caddy's powerful heater had made it downright humid in the car. Chilly air wafted in, cooling my cheeks and neck. I didn't see Wesley anywhere, just the Jeep. "I don't want to enter a cooking contest, Mom." The large metal building stood on the crest of the hill about a hundred yards from the vehicle. No road led to where Wesley had parked. Black parallel tracks through the snow revealed the erratic path he'd driven— like he'd been in a hurry.

Mom chimed, "They're also having a Potato Queen pageant.

You could enter that. You're young and single." She leaned toward me, pointing at a black-and-white photo of last year's winner, a busty blond with large teeth and a cowgirl hat.

"I am old and single, Mother. It is only a matter of time before I'm wearing big-people diapers and have dark hairs sprouting on my upper lip. I don't want my claim to fame to be that I was the Potato Princess of Colter County." I really wanted to get an up-close-and-personal gander at Wesley's Jeep. "Aren't you worried about Wesley?"

"Potato *Queen*—not princess," she said softly. "And yes, I am concerned about him; it's just that—" Mom did that thing where she dropped her chin on her chest and blinked three or four times, her version of worrying. She pointed at the article again. "I think this recipe contest would be good for you. You're judged on your support and knowledge of agriculture. Your job at the feed store would help meet that criteria."

"I don't want to be spud royalty."

"You get to ride in the parade," she enticed.

My mother is about as subtle as an ice-cream headache. I knew exactly why she was bringing up this Potato Princess stuff. "Mom, don't push. I know I'm domestically challenged." I fidgeted with the door handle. My longing for closure on this issue was not going to be fulfilled today.

"Domestically challenged?" A tinge of pink spread across her cheeks. She patted her salt-and-pepper hair, which was twisted around her head in elaborate braids. "Ruby, you wrote 'over-achiever' in red ink a hundred times by Proverbs 31."

I gripped the steering wheel. Ever since she'd found my Bible open to that passage, she'd been buying me craft books that showed how to make furniture from coffee cans and old shoes. "That commentary was for God's eyes. We're working on it." Not too long ago at a church potluck, I got trapped in a conversation where two women were talking with great enthusiasm about attachments they wanted to get for their mixers. I tried to nod and show interest. But I've just never been excited about mixer attachments, which makes me think there is something wrong with me.

"You don't have to be the Potato Queen. I don't know why I suggested it." Mom folded the newspaper into a tight little square. "I saw anger in that red ink. I just think entering this recipe contest would be good for you."

"It wasn't anger in the red ink, Mom. It was fear. Who could live up to that standard? Especially someone like me, who has no frame of reference or preparation for it." I'd spent the first thirty years of my life living from relationship to relationship, getting a master's degree, and setting myself up for a big important career. The relationships never worked out, and I discovered I liked clerking at the feed store. Even with my slower pace of life, I still hadn't found time to learn how to make five fascinating and attractive meals out of a single chicken.

Mom sighed so deeply her floral-clad chest heaved up and down. "I don't know, Ruby. It was just an idea."

"I don't think Proverbs 31 even applies to me. That woman is married and has kids." Maybe that was why I felt such a longing for a tribe of my own. Being single in Christendom felt too much like waiting for my life to start. "I'm not married, Mom. I don't have kids." And no matter how hard I try, my heart rate never increases when I think about mixer attachments.

She sucked in her cheeks and stared at the car roof. Her fingers touched the top button on her old brown wool coat. Her eyes glazed.

I hadn't meant to make her sad. If I wasn't a mom, she wasn't a grandma. I thought again of my little girl out there somewhere. "Tell you what. When we get home, I'll make a peanut butter and jelly sandwich and put a potato on top of it." I winked at her.

Her mouth twitched, but she didn't laugh.

I patted her shoulder lightly. "I've got to go find out if Wesley is out there." I unclicked my seatbelt and leaned into the door. "Coming with me?"

"I'll just wait in the car." She crossed her arms. "I hope he's close by," she said.

After sliding across the worn leather seat, I pushed the door open. I'd pulled over to the side of the gravel road so the car was at a slant—half on the road, half in the ditch.

Pebbles crunched beneath my feet. Most of the snow had blown off the road.

I caught a glimpse of my mother through the windshield as I headed toward the grassy ditch. Streaks across the glass made her image murky, but I could see her smiling at me. She tried so hard. What a curse to have me as a daughter. She needed someone who could turn old socks and fabric scraps into duvet covers. I had only a faint notion of what a duvet cover was.

I didn't know any potato recipes either. While I tried to picture red russets with a patina of crispy dark chocolate on them, the winter breeze caught my already tangled hair and twisted it even tighter. I have very fine hair that tends to knot up easily. I gave up trying to comb through it years ago, so it looks like I tease my hair as a style choice when actually it's an accident.

The barbed-wire fence snagged my down coat when I crawled through it. I slipped out of my parka to prevent further damage. A million tiny swords of cold air stabbed through my sweater. A few down feathers floated away on the breeze. After untangling torn nylon from the twisted barb, I straightened up, shaded my eyes, and assessed my surroundings.

Clumpy western wheat grass, sticking through the snow, populated the field that led to Wesley's car. White hills behind the metal building rolled up toward the sky. Off in the distance, about three fields and two barbed-wire fences away, a three-story brick house towered. Piles of dirt covered in a thin layer of snow surrounded the mansion. The structure looked new, obnoxiously huge, and out of place. Most of the farms around here were tidy but old.

Other than the metal building and a rusty, older-model tractor, I could see nothing but open field. The house that the metal building belonged to must be out of sight over the hill or farther down the road. I doubted it belonged to the mansion.

Ranches around here are large, into the thousands of acres, so it wasn't unusual to find a building that seemed to belong to nothing out in the middle of nowhere. Ranchers often built equipment sheds and calving barns miles from anything.

My red and turquoise cowboy boots dislodged small rocks as I trekked toward the Jeep. Wind pressed on my ears. Several sets of footprints—some of them only concave impressions, others more recent—were evident in the snow.

My theories about where Wesley had gone for the last two days ranged from the paranoid to the totally paranoid: he was spending time with another woman, or he was working deep cover for the FBI, locating rural meth labs. I actually preferred the second theory to the first.

Behind me, a car door slammed. My mother buttoned her brown coat as she walked to the barbed-wire fence. She wore yellow rubber boots that slipped over her shoes, and she'd put her red ear muffs and gloves on. I waved at her, turned, and walked a little faster. Still no sign of Wesley. No sign of anyone or anything—not even a cow. I broke into a trot to keep from thinking about the tightening of my rib cage. My feet sunk down into the crunchy, dry snow.

By the time I got to his car, I was breathing hard. I clicked open the driver-side door. Wesley's rifle was not in the rifle rack. The rest of the Jeep was clean. I leaned in and twisted open the jockey box, which contained the usual insurance and proof-of-ownership papers.

It wasn't until I stood up that I noticed the stain on the driver's seat. Then I saw the dark liquid circle on the nylon of my coat. I swallowed and touched two fingers to the wet spot in the Jeep. I sniffed my red fingers. My throat constricted in reaction to the coppery smell. A vinegary taste rose up in my mouth and nose as my imagination went into overdrive.

I stepped back from the Jeep and did a 180 all around the prairie. Tall grass sticking out of the snow rippled like ocean waves. To the west, the sun rested about forty-five degrees above the horizon. I checked the ground around the driver-side door. When I kneeled down, I found a few drops of blood on the grass and a distinct footprint. I traced the waffle pattern left by a hiker's boot. Wesley's boot. I knew him so well, I even knew what the bottom of his footgear looked like. I wiped the blood on the grass, stood up, and walked to the front bumper of the Jeep. A set of tracks—not Wesley's—was fresher than the others. I also noticed what looked like horse tracks. Where the snow thinned, the less distinct people tracks faded, but they were pointed in the direction of the building. The horse hoof prints led away from the building, up over the hill.

Mom had crawled through the barbed-wire fence and made her way toward me. The skirt of her yellow dress with the tiny blue flowers rippled in the wind. She held her obnoxiously big purse in the crook of her elbow with her fist resting on her shoulder. The purse was a quilted job she'd made from fabric scraps. Mom had everything in that purse.

The wind was too strong for my voice to carry any distance. I waved at her and pointed toward the metal building.

She waved back.

I trudged up the gradual incline toward the building, trying to keep my mind from creating scary scenarios. Why would Wesley's car seat have blood on it? *I'm sure there's a logical, non-violent explanation.* I just couldn't think of what it could be. Wesley had met an injured gopher and allowed it to drive his car? Wesley had shot a deer out of season and dragged it across the driver's seat as part of some ancient male hunting ritual?

Wind whipped around me and blew snow against my jeans. My eyes watered. I pulled a tangled strand of hair out of my mouth. I really needed to think about investing in a scrunchie. I edged closer to the metal building to get out of the wind, running my hand along the corrugated metal. The long end of the building ran about sixty feet. I turned the corner and faced the short side of the building, which featured a big, garage-size door and a smaller, people-size entrance.

I glanced around at barren rolling hills. A series of blown-over tracks probably made by ATVs created snake-like patterns up the hill. I walked toward the people-size door and twisted the knob. The door eased silently open. It wasn't unusual to find buildings around here unlocked. Wesley's father, Nathan, had explained the unwritten rules ranch people abided by. To put bars on a window or to lock a door was a huge insult to your neighbors 'cause it suggested you didn't trust them. For the last hundred years, such a rule had probably worked just fine. But now, since Montana had been "discovered," neighbors were often people you didn't know and couldn't trust.

My boots touched dirt floor.

Though the wind lessened when I stepped inside, the place was hardly airtight. Metal groaned and clanged. Wide beams slanted down from the pointed roof like a giant rib cage. Six straight beams ran perpendicular to the dirt floor. Light and wind threaded through the open space between the wall and the roof.

"Wesley?" I croaked.

Three pieces of farm equipment populated the middle of the storage shed, two side delivery spreaders and one rotary tiller. The only reason I knew the names of the things was because I'd helped Wesley and his father repair similar-looking stuff as prep for spring planting. This equipment was hosed down and clean. It probably wouldn't be taken out again until the ground thawed in April. On the other side of the tractor was a car underneath a cover. When I lifted the vinyl, I saw the metal silhouette of a horse on the grille.

In one corner of the shed, a baby crib slanted against the wall with a bassinet and stroller beside it. I hoped Zachary and Julia's five little tater tots were doing okay after two days with me. Zachary had taken off down the road to look for Wesley. We'd left Julia to deal with the carnage that two days of my ineptitude with children produced. She hadn't seemed too bent out of shape about the peanut butter hand prints on the kitchen wall or the pile of blankets in the living room.

I walked the twenty paces to where the dusty bassinet stood. When I touched the plastic ruffle on the cover of the tiny crib, my stomach tightened like someone had dropped a hot rock in my belly. I bent over from the rush of emotion. What if something had happened to Wesley? Darn him anyway. Here I had spent the weekend with visions of having children with him and growing old together, writing him sappy letters, and now he goes and falls off the face of the earth. The nerve. I'd kill him when I found him. I just hoped someone hadn't beaten me to it.

I shuddered and kicked the dirt with my boot. *Hold it together, Ruby.* When I reported the abandoned Jeep, it would probably be enough to alert law enforcement. I had the feeling that Sevee Cree knew something about this. Maybe he wouldn't be so evasive with his answers now that Wesley was missing.

"Ruby?" Mom stood in the doorway. "I saw the . . . I saw the blood. Now, I'm really worried."

My teeth clenched. I should have called the police the second Wesley left the farmhouse. But with each hour I thought that within the next hour, he'd come back and offer a reasonable explanation for his absence. Wesley was a former Marine and a cop. It wasn't like he couldn't take care of himself. Still, I worried.

"Ruby?"

"Yeah, I know. The sheriff for Colter County lives in Fontana. We can tell him about the Jeep." I had only seen Sheriff Reslin at a distance. I hadn't met him yet. Fontana, population five thousand, home of the Potato Festival and, of course, the Potato Queen, was about five miles up the road. Fontana had sprung up close to the Jefferson River as had most of the surrounding ranches. The river divided the Burgess property. Julia and Zac lived in the old farmhouse, where most ranch operations were, while Nathan had a trailer on this side of the river.

I touched the picture of a little bunny painted on the crib and pretended like my chest wasn't straitjacket tight. "We've got to get ahold of Julia, too. Let her and Zachary know. Maybe Wesley is at his Dad's house. We can swing by there."

I trudged toward my mother and the open door. Fine, dry dirt formed dust clouds around my feet. I didn't see any of Wesley's footprints in the barn.

"Wesley didn't say anything to you before he left?" Mom readjusted her earmuffs.

"No, nothing." Irritation colored my voice. We stood close to the open door of the building. A funnel of dust swirled in the beam of light created by the late-afternoon sunshine.

Mom touched my back. "We need to pray."

"I don't want to pray. I want to worry and run worse-case scenarios through my head." Visions of disaster fast forwarded through my mind. Wesley lay somewhere, bleeding to death, with coyotes circling him. Or Wesley was already dead. Magpies got out their napkins and carving knifes while his body lay lifeless in the snow. "I just don't feel like praying."

Mom wrapped her arm around me. "How very human of you. We'll pray when we get back to the car."

We stepped out into the wind. I closed the door behind us. "I don't even know whose farm this is. Maybe if we find the farm-house this shed belongs to, they might have seen him."

Off in the distance, a backhoe dug into the earth beside the new brick mansion. The mechanical arm arched as the toothy bucket angled into the ground. A dump truck rumbled away from the house toward the main road where Mom's Caddy was parked.

"Building in the winter." Mom crossed her arms over her chest with her purse hanging from her forearm. She shook her head. "That house looks really out of place around here. Too big."

"It screams money, doesn't it?" Two newer-looking cars, one of them a Lexus, were parked in front of the house. "Probably some East or West Coast escapee who doesn't understand about blend-ing in." Wealthy people were buying up family farms and ranches in droves. Georgia called them fake farmers because they thought ranching was a quaint, romantic activity, not a hard way to eke out an existence. She was short with them when they came into the store.

When I'd first come out to help Wes and his dad with ranch stuff, Wes had pointed out a tidy farm with old trucks parked by the barn and a nice but simple house. "Those guys are the top-ranked Angus breeders in the nation. They get thirty, forty thou-sand for their best bulls. But they still work, putting up hay every fall, right beside their hired hands and sons." Wesley's words were spoken with a tone of admiration. The message was clear: even if you had money, you didn't make a big show of it and you didn't sit on your butt counting your cash and viewing your art collec-tion. The code was something most outsiders didn't understand.

Whoever lived in the big house was obviously not from around here. Piles of rock, brick, and wood were stacked outside the colossal structure. The house looked close to finished; the bulldozer must be doing some last-minute landscaping, a tall and expensive order considering the ground was probably mostly frozen.

With the hum of heavy machinery at our backs, Mom and I slipped around the corner of the shed.

When we stepped out into the open field, a man holding a rifle was sticking his head through the open door of Wesley's Jeep.

Chapter Four

I didn't see the man's face right away, but I knew it wasn't Wesley. Different build. I yelled, "Hey!" He yanked his head out of the Jeep. Black wavy hair fell past his shoulders. He held the rifle in a nonthreatening way, stock in one hand and the barrel resting in the crook of his elbow.

"That's my friend's Jeep," I shouted as I ran toward him. With Mom trotting to catch up, I got close enough to see that the man wore a tweed jacket. Yes, I said tweed. "That's my friend's car," I repeated. His jeans were new enough to make him walk stiff legged, and his cowboy boots were so shiny I could have seen my reflection in them if I angled my head right. I gave myself one guess as to which house was his.

"Where is your friend?" He touched his lacquered hair.

I shrugged. "I thought maybe you'd seen him."

He reminded me of those shirtless men on trashy novels at checkout counters of the supermarket. Except this guy buttoned his shirt all the way to the top. He had the same "pretty boy" look.

"I was out setting up targets when I noticed the Jeep." The man pointed with his rifle in the direction of the mansion. "Over on my property."

Bingo, score one for the home team. "Is this your place, too?"

"No, it belongs to the Campbells over the hill." Drawing in the rifle closer to his chest, he held out his hand. It was smooth, no calluses. "I'm Lance Kinkaid—just moved here eight months ago."

I almost sputtered. Lance Kinkaid? That had to be made up. It sounded like a character on a soap opera.

Mom's footsteps pounded behind me, growing closer. I pulled myself free of Lance's strong handshake. Mom brushed my arm when she came up beside me, out of breath and clutching her purse.

"I don't suppose you've seen my friend? Tall, muscular, dark blond." The wind whipped my hair around, and I had to pull a strand out of my mouth.

Lance shook his head. "I haven't seen anybody." He pointed the barrel of his rifle toward the open door of the Jeep. "There's blood on the seat."

My straitjacket of anxiety cinched up another notch. *Why did everyone have to point out the obvious?* "I know," I sputtered as another strand of hair got caught in my mouth. Despite the increasing intensity of the wind, Lance's hair didn't move at all. I was impressed with the level of follicle stability he exhibited.

Mom dug through her purse. She pulled out a barrette, grabbed my hair, and twisted it. "We're going straight to find the sheriff in Fontana if Wesley isn't at his father's place," she said. She continued to twist and style my hair and yank it at the roots while she chatted. My job was to stand still while Vidal Taylor did her thing. "Wesley's a policeman over in Eagleton," she announced.

Lance raised his dark eyebrows. "Oh really. What was he doing out here?" He leaned toward me.

When he got close, I expected to get a whiff of strong cologne, but Lance had no smell at all—not hairspray, not soapy cleanness, or even deodorant—nothing. Weird.

The barrette clicked at the back of my head. My mother was

giving away too much information, and I didn't like the way Lance's interest antennae perked up when she mentioned Wesley was a cop.

I squeezed my mother's arm in that special place just above the elbow, home of a thousand nerve endings.

"Mom and I really have to be going." I could feel my mother resisting, planting her feet. I squeezed a little harder in her tender spot. This was actually a trick I'd learned from her.

"Have fun shooting and eating whatever you shoot. Nice meeting you, Lance . . . Kinkaid." I stifled a giggle when I said his name.

"Actually, I only shoot targets and trap. I don't think I could ever kill anything."

"We have to be going, don't we, Mother?" Mom finally moved her feet, but not before twisting her elbow out of my grasp.

When Lance was out of earshot, Mom leaned close and shout-whispered in my ear. "Honestly, Ruby, you could have left a bruise." She massaged the tender spot above her elbow.

I glanced back at Lance, who swaggered across the snowy field with his rifle slung over one shoulder.

"I don't think Lance needs to know details about Wesley." Dry snow crunched beneath our boots.

"I was just being friendly."

"Something is up with Wesley. He could be hurt . . . or something. We don't need to be blabbing about him to every Tom, Dick, and Lance."

"He seemed like a nice young man." Mom touched the under-side of her chin. "Not everyone in this world is up to something, Ruby." She stopped for a moment, crossed her arms, and narrowed her eyes.

About a hundred yards across the snowy field, Lance leaned his rifle against a fence post and crawled through the barbed wire. "I'm not paranoid, Mom, just cautious."

She placed a hand on her hip. "I suppose we should go over to Nathan's house. Too bad I didn't bring my cell. We could just call." She touched my shoulder. "I'm sure we'll find Wesley there."

Wind blew gusts of snow against our legs as we trudged across the field. After slipping through the fence, I separated the barbed wire by pressing a boot on the lower wire and pulling up on the higher one so Mom could inch her way through.

When we got to the car, I resumed my place behind the steering wheel and clicked the key in the ignition. Mom buckled herself into the passenger seat. She glanced briefly at the tightly folded newspaper and then shoved it in the jockey box.

"Application deadline for the recipe contest is the middle of March," she said faintly.

"I'll keep that in mind." I really didn't want to make anything out of potatoes, not even a duvet cover. But that worried look on Mom's face made me sad. I slipped the Caddy into drive, pressed the accelerator, and lunged forward. I had been coming out to Wesley's family farm since the end of December. Now a month and a half later, I'd finally gotten used to navigating without street signs. Only the main roads were marked. Landmarks like trees, abandoned cabins, outbuildings, and close attention to the odometer were the means of getting from one farm to another.

Mom opened her purse and pulled out a small bottle of lotion. She dabbed a few drops on her palm and rubbed her hands together. "Want some?"

I held up my right hand. She squeezed droplets on my palm

and rubbed the cool lotion in. A subtle rose scent wafted up to my nose.

"I'm worried about Wesley." I placed my right hand on the wheel and pointed my left hand toward Mom so she could put lotion on that, too.

Mom massaged my hand and then moved her fingers over my knuckles and down to my fingertips. "Two days without getting in touch is a long time." She shook her head. "And that blood." Mom worked the anxiety out of my system via my fingertips. "You've fallen in love with him, haven't you?"

I stared at her long enough for the car to veer to the wrong side of the road. She grabbed the steering wheel, straightening the tires before we ended up in the ditch.

"I didn't mean to upset you. I just see the way you look at him . . . the way spending time with him puts a spring in your step."

"Coils in your shoes? Is that how you know it's love?" I put my hand close to my nose so I could smell the rose scent and allow warm fuzzy thoughts about Wesley to flood my system. "It's just being with him . . . spending time with him. He's been decent to me." Over a year ago, Wesley and I had hiked into the woods to find his missing friend Brian. I had anticipated that we'd sleep together—that his intention in inviting me had been sexual. He turned me down. I was the only woman in a big wide forest, and he turned me down. It was the first time a man had respected me enough not to use me. "I have no idea what love— real love—looks and feels like. I like being with him, helping him with ranch stuff. I thought this weekend would be a step forward."

I turned off on another side road marked by a single dead tree in the field. The terrain transformed from rolling prairie to steeper hills. As we rounded the top of the first hill, we saw a heavy plume of smoke hanging in the sky, rising up from near Nathan Burgess's homestead.

My mother gasped. Her shoulders bunched toward her ears, almost a flinching motion.

The hills blocked our view of Nathan's trailer and barn, the corral and outbuildings behind it. "He could just be burning stuff in his yard." Tongues of smoke held a foreboding message. Even as I offered my logical explanation, my neck muscles tensed.

I pressed the accelerator a little harder. The Caddy's huge engine surged. Tires melded to the dirt road. I maneuvered through curve after curve. We ascended and descended one hill after another, keeping our eyes on the rising column of smoke.

My waist felt like someone had put a belt around it three notches too tight. "Yeah, he could just be burning something in his yard ... big pile of brush or old wood or something." Winter was a good time to burn things. Less fire danger.

Mom tugged at her coat collar. "He's old, isn't he?"

"Seventy plus. He was past forty when Wesley was born." It seems funny for Mom to ask me if someone is old. She's past sixty, so I think of her as old.

Mom laced her hands together and placed them on her purse. "Does he forget things? Leave the stove on?"

"Mom, stop it." The Caddy rounded another hill. The acrid smell of smoke drifted through the window. "Nathan Burgess might be a little paranoid, but he's not senile. Wesley and Zachary wouldn't let him live alone if he was."

"Doesn't he have a wife?"

"She died when Wesley was a teenager."

"He's by himself." She smoothed over the lace trim on her purse.

"Ma, stop." By now, the smoky smell was so strong I had to roll up the window. Can you say *denial?*

We came to the top of the final hill. Looking down into the valley that sheltered Nathan's property, I saw first the dilapidated gray barn halfway up the hill. Then I saw the newer metal building. All of this I viewed through a haze of thickening smoke. The front bumper of the Caddy pointed down, and the final building, Nathan's trailer—or what was left of it—came into view. I pressed the brakes on the Caddy and stared down at chaos.

Nathan's trailer looked like a melted milk jug trapped in parts of a blackened, metal frame. I recognized Zachary's older-model Buick and saw four blond heads racing around the property. The fifth little head, Brody, was in his mother's arms. Several other cars I didn't recognize were parked around the smoldering mass. One of them had the sheriff's insignia. I saw Zachary's distinctive balding blond head as he sprayed what was left of the trailer with a garden hose. I scanned the area around the trailer, looking for two more family members.

Nathan should have been easy enough to spot. He shuffled more than he walked, and his shoulders were hunched. He had puffy, white, cotton-ball hair and was in the habit of wearing red shirts and blue jeans.

I let up on the brake. Our car drifted down the hill. The sound of the Caddy's wheels rolling over dirt was deafening. Still unable to find Nathan or Wesley, I continued to search the area around the trailer, then farther out to a corral full of Angus heifers ready for calving.

Mom shook her head. Her forehead was a sea of furrows.

Josie, with her blond hair streaming behind her, ran through the snow toward the forest that bordered one side of the property. Tension drained from my muscles. Nathan sat crumpled beneath an evergreen. His neck curved downward, and his legs stuck out straight in front of him, but he was alive.

Where was Wesley? My throat constricted, and all the tension returned when I glanced back at the trailer. What if Wesley had been in there?

Nathan raised his head only slightly when his granddaughter came and sat beside him. Josie leaned against his shoulder, and he slumped even more, resting his face in his hands. A huge orange cat sauntered over to them and curled up on Nathan's outstretched legs. He wrapped his arm around his granddaughter and lifted his head. She hugged her grandpa. I really liked that kid.

Again, I surveyed the people milling around the fire. Wesley had a distinctive walk that was almost a swagger. On a clear day like today, the sun would catch the golden highlights in his hair. He was ten years younger and much leaner than his brother. I had a sort of radar where he was concerned. My rib cage tightened. None of the people in the whirlwind below were Wesley.

With our windows rolled up, we'd been separated from the noise that would have drawn us into the panic. It was like watching a silent film. Now even through the tightly closed windows, shouting and smoke seeped in. Mom coughed. My eyes watered. The yelling increased in volume. I brought the Caddy to a stop beside the sheriff's car.

A few small flames shot out from the smoldering debris. Men doused them with buckets of water—a seemingly pointless activity.

Nathan's home was gone. Maybe it made them feel better—like they were doing something to help the old man.

Nothing at the front of the trailer was recognizable, but at the back, part of the frame with a window remained, along with a blackened dresser. A gauzy, singed curtain blew back and forth in the light breeze.

Mom kept shaking her head.

I opened the door and stepped out. Heat, oppressive and thick, pushed me back against the car. The high temperature made the air seem like smears across eyeglasses. Already, beads of sweat seeped through my pores despite the winter cold.

My worry over Wesley and the disaster in front of me weighed on my shoulders and chest. With each step, I felt like I was sinking into the ground.

Caught up in the frenzy, no one had even glanced at us when we pulled in. In addition to Zachary and his family, four or five grown men, two women, and a skinny teenage boy in oversized clothes wandered around the disaster area. The skinny kid hung close to a muscular man—Sheriff Reslin. I knew who he was though I'd never been introduced to him.

Some of the people had stopped bringing water from feeding tanks in the corral and sat on the grass with their empty buckets beside them.

Julia, with Brody in her arms and the other two boys bouncing around her, noticed us. NeeNee, whose real name was Nellie, carried a plastic bucket that belonged in a sandbox. She got within a hundred feet of the blackening mass and dumped her little pink pail of water before gamboling back to the feeding trough.

Julia waved me over. Sweat trickled past her temple as Brody yanked on one of her long brown braids. "Poor Nathan." She wiped her brow. Brody nuzzled into her neck.

"What happened?" I unzipped my coat.

Julia shrugged the shoulder that wasn't bearing Brody. "We're not sure. The whole thing went pretty fast. I saw the smoke from across the river. Sheriff Reslin and his son, Hayden, got here a little after the kids and me. Zac and everyone else showed up within minutes."

From what I could remember, Nathan's living room had been filled with lots of paper and books—a virtual tinder box. The elder Burgess kept an eye on the registered Angus that had been brought in for calving, but he spent most of his days reading newspapers and history books.

Brody squirmed out of Julia's arms and ran in circles around her, along with his older brothers. Julia spoke above the bantering play of the boys. "This is all so terrible." She shook her head. "But the blessing is that Nathan was out making his daily trip to the Fontana library when the fire started."

"I'm glad he's okay." Black, paper-thin debris fell from the remaining frame. It seemed someone from every close farm was there. They'd seen the smoke. Why hadn't Wesley come to help his own father? How far away was he?

"Any sign of Wesley?" she asked tentatively.

She must have read the worry on my face. I really needed to sit down. My legs felt like boiled macaroni and wouldn't hold me much longer. "No." I swallowed hard. "Just his Jeep over by the Campbell place." I really didn't want to get into the blood news again.

"That doesn't make any sense." Julia gazed at me with her round brown eyes. "He's got to be somewhere. How far could he get on foot?" Brody bounced and held his hands up, making pleading noises. Julia gathered him into her arms again. "Sheriff Reslin is right over there. The guy with the—" She touched her upper lip. "He might be able to help."

She pointed at Reslin, who had graying sideburns and a large handlebar mustache. He'd rolled up the sleeves of his denim shirt and stood beside Zachary. The sheriff's teenage son must have wandered away.

"I know who he is," I said. "I've never had a reason to talk to him . . . until now."

Almost everybody but Nellie had stopped throwing water on the trailer. One of the men stomped out some flames that had spread to the grass around the trailer. The rest collapsed onto the snow or onto the hoods of their cars.

Julia positioned herself so her shoulder touched mine. Both her arms were wrapped around Brody, who had stopped bouncing and was resting his face against her chest. I appreciated the gesture of proximity even if Julia couldn't wrap her arms around me.

Julia wore her shoulder-length brown hair in two braids. On the day she and Zachary had gone on their date, I had seen her quickly twist it up into a loose bun. No one would label her as stunning. She had even, nondescript features: brown eyes, not too close together or far apart, symmetrical eyebrows, and thin lips—a sort of sturdy prettiness. Though not overweight, the pear-shaped body was probably a result of having birthed six children.

She gazed out at what remained of Nathan's house. "I don't know what we'll do with Nathan until we can get another trailer moved out here. The farmhouse is crowded already. I can probably make room for him on the couch."

"Or the dog bed," I said. "The children seem to find that quite comfortable."

Julia laughed while Brody brushed the end of her braid over his cheek.

"He's coming to stay with me." We both turned to look at my mother, collector of orphans and misfits. "He can stay on the extra bed in my sewing room." The bed had most recently been occupied by my little brother, before he got sent to jail. Before that, my friend Maryanne had used it when she came to town to hunt down a husband who'd cleaned out her bank account.

"Julia, I don't think you've met my mother."

Julia swayed back and forth while Brody sucked on his fingers. "Are you sure that would be okay?"

"He can't be alone. Not after what he has been through." Mom reached out and touched Brody's sleek blond head. "I can get some clothes for him down at the Senior Citizens' Center. What does he like to eat?"

Though she'd known my mother for only two minutes, Julia must have been smart enough to sense that when Mom set her jaw and drew her mouth into a straight line, you didn't argue. Nathan Burgess was about to be adopted by my mother, and no one was allowed to question her decision.

"All right . . . Zachary and I can keep an eye on the heifers. Maybe move them and Nathan's bull a little closer to our place across the bridge."

Mom and Julia loaded Nathan into the back of the Caddy, accompanied by all his worldly possessions—a leather saddlebag and a large orange cat with a singed tail. Meanwhile, I found Sheriff Reslin kicking smoldering rubble with his boot.

His rolled-up sleeve revealed a Semper Fi tattoo on his muscular forearm. The huge handlebar mustache drooped a bit in the intense heat. His large nose was thin at the top but blossomed into a round ball at the end. His light blue eyes and thick lashes looked like they belonged on a doll.

He kicked a pile of feathery black debris that had probably been newspapers. "Darn shame, Nathan losing his home." He took a bandana out of his back pocket and wiped the sweat off his forehead. "Guess he's pretty shook up."

"He's in good hands. He's got a place to stay."

The skinny teenager came and stood beside Sheriff Reslin. He had his father's features, the same long eyelashes and blue eyes.

"And where is that?" Reslin twisted the bandana and then drew it taut.

Why was everybody such a nosy body around here? At five eleven, I towered over the sheriff by about four inches. But his broad shoulders, gruff bass voice, and tendency to lean toward people when he talked intimidated me . . . a little.

I squared my shoulders and stared down at him. "He's staying with my mother."

Reslin nodded while he touched the curly end of his mustache. He stared at me beyond the social etiquette time limit.

Perspiration trickled down my back. I slipped out of my coat and pulled feathers from the barbed-wire tear. "I need to talk to you about Nathan's son, Wesley."

Realization spread across Reslin's face. "I know who you are. You're his girlfriend. I've seen you out with him doing winter feeding." He pointed to his head. "Your hair's easy to see a long ways off."

Okay, so there were no secrets in an area as sparsely populated as this. "I'm just a . . . I'm just a friend. Not his girlfriend." The gossip network around here must be quite efficient.

The sheriff crossed his muscular arms and looked out toward the forest that bordered Nathan's property. His son took on the exact same stance.

"I wouldn't worry too much about Wesley. I'm sure his brother and father have told you Wesley was pretty wild when he was a teenager." The sheriff shifted his weight. "I went to school with Zac—he's the level-headed one. I'm glad to help you folks out. But Wesley's probably just returning to his old habits."

My teeth clenched. "He's not a teenager anymore. Wesley's an Eagleton cop." Reslin was the sheriff for the whole county. He must know that. His dismissing my concern made my toes curl. "I found his Jeep over at the Campbell place. There was blood on the passenger seat."

"Whoa . . . whoa there, lady. I didn't make him disappear." He held up his hands, creating a wall to diffuse the emotion I threw his way. "I can have the vehicle brought in if that would make you feel better."

His sympathy reminded me of someone patting an upset puppy on the head. And his lack of reaction to the news about the blood was disturbing. "That would help." My throat constricted. "But you need to find him." I raised my voice enough that a couple of men craned their necks at us.

Reslin put his hand on my shoulder. His tone and demeanor said, "Now calm down, you silly flighty woman."

"Look, Miss Taylor. Law enforcement will handle this. Wesley is probably at his home right now in Eagleton."

"Don't you think I thought of that? I phoned there a dozen times. Something has happened to him."

"If the two of you had a tiff . . . maybe he has Caller ID. He's just not answering the phone when you call."

"Maybe he just doesn't want to talk to you." Reslin's son echoed.

My teeth clenched so tight that it took considerable effort to speak. "We did not have a 'tiff.' Something has happened to him. Ask his brother."

"We'll look into it, Miss Taylor." He dragged my name out, emphasizing the *s*'s and the *r*'s. "The law will handle it."

I crossed my arms. "Thank you." I did not like being condescended to.

He stared at me for a moment before sauntering away. His son, hiking up his baggy pants, followed on the sheriff's heels. Reslin put an arm around the kid.

I could feel the press of the sheriff's gaze as I walked toward the Caddy. Sevee Cree knew more about Wesley's strange behavior than he was telling, and I had the feeling that Reslin did, too. Maybe that's where the calm-down-you-dumb-little-woman routine came from. Reslin wasn't half as alarmed as he should have been. Like he'd already known about the Jeep. Why did it feel like there was this giant conspiratorial vat of information about Wesley that I was not privy to?

Mom had left the driver's seat of the car vacant. Nathan Burgess's snowy head was barely visible above the backseat. I clicked open the door, slid behind the wheel, and turned the key.

I glimpsed at Nathan in the rearview mirror as I backed the car out of the field. Sweat glistened on his mottled pink and white skin where charcoal smears were evident.

Nathan whispered from the backseat, "Persistence is gone. They've taken Persistence." The old man rocked back and forth, staring at the floor of the car and clutching the saddlebag. The orange cat meowed. "Persistence is gone," he mumbled.

"You'll get your persistence back," I said. "Ranchers are tenacious. We'll get you back on your feet, Nathan."

"Persistence. Persistence." He shook his head.

This was not the articulate Nathan I'd come to know. I looked over at my mother for an explanation.

She shrugged then patted her braided hair by her temple. "He's been through a lot. We'll get him cleaned up and rested and fed. He'll be better."

Mom was talking about Nathan as though Nathan wasn't in the car, always a sign that people think you've gone off the deep end.

She gave Nathan a reassuring nod. "He'll be right as rain."

Nathan patted the saddlebag he held. "I've got evidence."

I put the car in drive and pressed the accelerator.

The old man leaned back against the leather upholstery and closed his eyes. If anyone could bring Nathan back to the land of the living, it was my mother.

I pulled out onto the rutted dirt road.

The car rolled up and down hills. Nathan snored from the backseat only slightly louder than the purring cat on his lap. My mother looked droopy eyed as well. She sighed deeply several times before offering me a faint smile.

Dusk comes early this time of year, around dinnertime. We pulled out on the gravel road, and I turned the car toward the setting sun, Eagleton, and the surrounding mountains.

Chapter Five

The foam on Officer Sevee Cree's soy latte had become an object of great fascination and a cause for continual investigation. I watched as he poked the bubbles, tilted the cup, licked his finger, and did everything else possible to avoid answering my question.

Cree wiggled on his stool at the gym's juice bar. A platinum-haired twenty-year-old posed behind the counter, and threw scary-looking stuff into a blender. She claimed she had "smoothies" for anyone with two bucks. The woman wore a white sports bra and workout shorts. Her tan was even enough to suggest that she hadn't gotten it from the good old-fashioned sun.

Behind us, men and women grunted and groaned and stood for long periods, staring at themselves in the floor-to-ceiling mirrors. They angled their bodies this way and that so the light hit their muscles just right.

The gym was maybe fifty by thirty feet. It was laid out so the free weights and treadmills were placed against the nonmirrored walls of the room. The workout equipment you strapped yourself to was in one central torture area in the middle of the gym.

When Cree's buddies at the police station had told me I could find him at the gym, my chest had instantly tightened. The thought of having to hang out with athletic sweating types caused me great anxiety and brought back a wash of bad junior-high school memories. Images flashed through my head as I drove to the gym—being hit in the face with a basketball and placed so far in the outfield that I needed binoculars to see the pitcher.

As a dedicated egghead, I consider walking up and down stairs the height of my athletic ability. I'd hoped that Cree would respond to my inquiry quickly so I could get back to an environment I felt more at home in. But it didn't look like that was going to happen.

I repeated my question and added another for good measure. "Where is Wesley? You know, don't you?"

"Look, Ruby, I want to find Wesley as bad as you do." He took several gulps of latte and tossed the cup in the garbage. "I just don't know how much to tell you." Cree had sweat stains on his T-shirt around his neck and armpits. After he slipped off his stool, he hooked his hands together over his head and bent from side to side.

"Tell me what you know. Where's Wesley, Sevee?" The woman behind the counter pressed the button on the blender. Grinding sounds made it impossible to be heard. While Cree bent to the floor and grabbed his ankles, I waited for the noise to stop. The blond turned off the blender. I leaned over and angled my head so Cree and I could have something resembling eye contact. "At least tell me that he's safe."

"I don't know where he is exactly." Sevee had jet black hair, dark skin, and angular features that suggested Native American ancestry, though he'd never mentioned a tribal affiliation. Sevee had never talked about a wife or any family, either. Really, I knew very little about him other than he was a Christian and he had helped train Wesley as a probationary officer over a year ago. "I can't say if he's safe or not."

I straightened up, swayed a bit, and slumped back onto the stool. My little workout had exhausted me and caused all the blood to rush to my head. I blinked my eyes a hundred times until the floating white spots faded.

Sevee stood up and craned his neck so it made cracking noises. "Are you okay, Ruby?"

I nodded.

"Gotta finish my workout while my muscles are warmed up." He turned away from me and headed back toward the grunting people and gym equipment.

I slipped off the stool and glanced around at the intense faces, then followed Sevee into testosterone land. He was doing that cop thing where he wouldn't give away any info and acted like no one could be trusted. I trotted after him. "Come on, Sev. It's me. Ruby. I care about Wesley."

Sevee glanced side to side, assessing the other people in the gym.

There were only two other females working out. One was an extremely muscular woman in a one-piece workout suit that looked like it had been ordered from a lingerie catalog. She moved deftly from one free-weight exercise to another, paying little attention to the men who sneaked glances at her. The other lady trudged on the treadmill; her red round face was shiny with perspiration. She wore a T-shirt and sweatpants and was maybe eighty pounds overweight. Even though I'm tall and skinny, I felt a greater affinity with her than with the other woman. What an act of courage it was for her to come here and hang with the muscle-bound crowd.

Sevee stood beside a machine that resembled a medieval torture device. The air was pungent with perspiration and cologne. I waited with my arms crossed, feeling conspicuous in my jean jacket and broomstick skirt. Some of the men had glanced in my direction. They probably weren't used to seeing a woman with most of her clothing on.

Cree leaned over and pulled a metal pin out of the stack of weights. When he straightened up, he looked at me, as if taking an assessment. "I'll tell you what I know," he said in a low voice. "There's been a series of thefts from farmers in Colter County around the Fontana area." He shoved the pin in a different slot and stood up straight. "Sheriff Reslin is a little overwhelmed and ill equipped. There's only one deputy out there, and he has a two-hundred-mile radius to cover. Even though Reslin lives in Fontana, he's got to deal with crime county wide."

"So Wesley's helping Reslin?" That was why Reslin had dismissed me and the news about Wesley so quickly.

For almost a minute, I waited while Sevee gripped a bar, pulled it to his chest, and then straightened his arms. He let out a heavy gust of air. "Wesley's from there, and he understands farm people. He's not an outsider. People are more likely to trust him. He was just supposed to be taking reports and helping farmers make their equipment more secure. Farm equipment isn't like cars. There's no national registering system. You can steal a one-hundred-thousand dollar tractor in Montana, load it on a truck, and sell it to a farmer in North Dakota without much trouble."

Everyone except for me was either strapped to a machine or lifting free weights.

I leaned against the contraption Sevee was using so I blended in a little better. "What kinds of things are being stolen?"

"Farm equipment, fertilizer, tack, even livestock. Olsen over by the river lost his prize sheep dogs. It's an organized group doing the stealing."

"A group of guys." I watched Sevee's biceps bulge and unbulge. "Like Georgia's robbery."

Cree gritted his teeth. Strands of muscle were visible in his jaw and neck.

"Georgia's robbery breaks the pattern. Same MO, a group of thieves, but all the other robberies are in a twenty-mile radius around Fontana and just on farms."

"What are they doing with the stuff they take?"

"We noticed the fertilizer disappearing last spring. It contains anhydrous ammonia, a key ingredient in meth. A thief can take a couple of gallons out of a tank parked in a field or left in a barn. Farmer might not notice it missing until months later.

"Reslin thought it was just a drug thing, but then the thefts kept on even after the fertilizer wasn't around. Same farms kept getting hit over and over. Most of the stuff being taken has black-market value."

"But you don't know why Wesley has disappeared?"

"Two months ago, we caught seven guys loading a tractor onto a semi. Some of them were career criminals from Eagleton, couple of teenagers, a drifter. Once they were all in jail, the thefts increased instead of stopping."

"So whoever set up the thefts just recruited more punks."

"My guess is Wesley got a lead on whoever's behind all this." Cree ambled over to a metal rack that contained folded white towels. He swathed his face and tossed the towel in a bucket next to the rack. "He didn't say or do anything unusual while you guys were out at Zac's farm or on the way there?"

I shook my head. "Nothing. He had his cell with him. Someone could have called him."

"It's Reslin's jurisdiction out there. I don't want to step on toes. He's got to send the blood sample out of the Jeep to the state lab."

"So you heard about that." It had been my experience that there wasn't much cops didn't know about. Their gossip network was more elaborate than the coffee klatch at a quilting party. "The Jeep was parked on the Campbell place next to that big house with all the construction going on."

"Lance Kinkaid's house." Sevee sauntered to a corner of the gym where mats were laid out. He flopped down and performed a series of body contortions that I can only assume were part of cooling down.

I trotted after Sevee and stood at the corner of the mat, talking down at him while he practiced his audition moves for Cirque du Soleil. "So Wesley did say something about him. I thought the guy was a little strange. Doesn't his name sound . . . like . . . totally made up? Like he got it off a soap opera? And he has no smell."

Cree wrinkled his forehead at my olfactory comment but continued. "Wesley just said that there were large groups of people coming and going. The Kinkaid guy moved in about the time the thefts started last spring." Sevee twisted sideways and touched his cheek to his leg. "At this point, Kinkaid's nothing more than a person of interest."

"Oh really." The gears were already turning in my head. *Maybe I should pay Mr. Lance a little visit.* I plunked down on the mat, tucking my legs and skirt around me.

"Yes, really." Cree straightened out his legs. Instead of touching his toes, he leaned toward me and grabbed my wrist. "You be careful. These are not dime-store thieves."

The warmth from Cree's touch seeped through my pores. His

grasp and the steeling of his eyes meant he was serious. "I know. 'Let the police take care of it. Blah, blah, blah . . .' I hear it from Wesley all the time. I just want to find Wesley, that's all."

Cree let go of my wrist and rose to his feet. "I'll let you know the second he gets in touch with me."

"Thanks." I leaned forward on my hands, preparing to put my weight on my knees and stand on my feet. It was a simple enough plan: girl stands up on the mat, says goodbye, gracefully exits stage left. Somewhere between propping myself on my knees and standing, my skirt caught on my boot and set me off balance. My left foot landed on the edge of the mat and twisted sideways. Instantly, fiery pain detonated in my ankle, threaded into my calf muscle, and seared the ligaments in my knee. Arms jerked and fluttered like a bird attempting take off. Midst my twirling and twisting, a firm hand clamped around my forearm.

"Are you okay?" It was Cree's voice.

My gyrating came to a standstill. A smeared kaleidoscope of color washed over my eyes. I bent over.

"Ruby, are you okay?" Cree patted my back.

When I stood up, searing hot pain pulsated through my ankle. "I . . . I think I . . . my foot. I twisted my foot."

Cree hollered for an ice pack. My vision cleared, but I remained bent over—not because that lessened the pain. I dreaded having to make eye contact with all the buff individuals whom I just knew would be staring at clumsy me.

I've twisted my ankle and other body parts plenty of times. But once, just once, I wish I could have an injury that was connected to a glamorous story: "Yeah, I tore up this ligament doing my triple Salchow at the Olympics." Or, "Yes, that's right, my broken leg is from climbing a brick wall to rescue a child from a burning building."

But, "Why yes, I twisted my ankle trying to stand up," just doesn't cut it.

"Here you go, honey."

I lifted my head. The lady from the treadmill held an ice pack out for me.

The rest of the people in the gym continued to grunt, groan, and gaze at themselves in the mirror. Their own shapely bodies held way more interest than my awkward one.

Treadmill woman leaned close and whispered, "I've done the exact same thing." She patted my shoulder. "Those full skirts are pretty, but they can be a hazard."

"Thank you." The ice pack chilled my hand.

Cree squeezed my other shoulder. "Why don't you sit down and get some cold on that ankle?"

Treadmill woman returned to her torture device of choice.

"I'll just prop it over my ankle while I drive. I really want to get out of here."

"Okay, Ruby, if that's what you want." Cree must have noticed color rising in my cheeks. Considering I'm a light-skinned red-head, I probably resembled a bloated strawberry by now.

I took a step forward on my injured foot and nearly buckled all over again. Cree gripped my arm at the elbow and helped me across the gym floor. To a cacophony of motorized exercise machines and clicking and clanging of steel weights, I hobbled toward the door.

Cree stayed with me all the way to my car, wrapping his arm across my waist as I hopped through the parking lot. At no time did his touch become sexualized. He was just a Christian gentleman helping a woman in need.

When I got to the car, I freed myself from his arms and leaned on the hood of the car for support. "Thanks, Cree. I'm glad Wesley has you for a friend and coworker."

Cree actually blushed at my compliment. "Make sure you keep that ankle iced." He planted his hands on his hips and stared at the asphalt.

I clicked open the door, tossed the ice bag in, and positioned myself behind the wheel. Then I rolled down the window. "Cree, the second Wesley gets hold of you or anyone in the department, let me know."

"He's a big boy. He can handle himself."

I clicked the Valiant's push-button shift and spoke over the sputter of the engine. "I know, but I'm a woman. I worry. It's my job."

Cree waved at me as I pulled away. The chill wind must have been cold on his arms, but he didn't return to the gym until I pulled out onto the road.

I'd left the ice pack on the passenger seat. I could work the brake and gas with my right foot, affording my left foot the luxury of sitting inert and flaming with pulsating pain.

I drove back home to get ready for work, changed out of my skirt, and taped up my ankle. I steeled myself to deal with Georgia, who'd entered a funk I couldn't shake her out of since the loss of Her Majesty.

Chapter Six

After a long day at work, I hobbled up the stairs, past the porch swing, and into our house. Fortunately, Georgia hadn't dropped in on my shift. Instead, she phoned several times, not saying much, just sighing heavily. I'd give anything to get that cat back.

The salty aroma of bacon frying and other spices greeted me when I opened the door to our house.

"Ruby, supper's almost ready. I'm trying a new potato recipe," Mom hollered from the kitchen. She showed remarkable restraint in that she didn't suggest I should be coming up with recipes, too.

Using the wall for support, I dragged myself through the living room and into the kitchen. The air was steamy and moist. I slumped down in a chair. Nathan sat kitty-corner from me, still clutching his saddlebag and staring at the floor with glazed eyes.

Mom had combed his hair so it lay flat against his head. He wore a short-sleeved button-down shirt and men's business slacks. Mom probably couldn't find something more his style at the Senior Citizen's Center on such short notice.

"Can you grab some ice for me? I've twisted my ankle." I turned one of our wooden chairs slightly and rested my foot on it. After pushing my shoe off with my other foot, I leaned forward and unwound the tape. The area around my shin and ankle was soft and swollen.

Mom pulled the frying pan off the stove and opened the freezer. Her cheeks were flushed from cooking. She was a petite woman, fragile looking, like Audrey Hepburn. And she had given birth to me, the six-foot, redheaded mutant.

Honestly, I don't think anyone would look at the two of us and think we were related. I have orangey red hair and am tall, thin, and flat chested. She's short and curvy with salt-and-pepper hair, which had been almost black when she was younger. The red hair and tallness came from my dad's side of the family.

Mom dropped the ice into an empty bread bag, bustled across the kitchen, and placed it gently on my ankle. "Am I allowed to ask?" She stood up straight, lacing her hands together and pursing her lips.

"Nothing super dangerous, just stupid." I tugged my pant leg up and readjusted the ice bag. "I tripped on the corner of an exercise mat." Wouldn't it be nice if I could say it was a skateboarding accident or that I'd hurt myself roping a steer?

Nathan shifted slightly in his chair but didn't say anything. His orange cat had made itself at home. I'd seen the feline resting in the laundry basket in the living room when I'd walked through. We have three other cats we inherited from my brother, Jimmy, while he does his time in prison.

Did I mention that Mom and I are not your standard-issue Christians?

Mom crumbled up the bacon bits and sprinkled them on a steaming casserole that rested on the counter. "I'm excited for you two to try this." Hopeful expectation sparkled in her eyes.

My line at this point would be to say, "I've been mulling over several potato recipes myself. I'll don my apron right after dinner." But that would have been a lie. The coming events of the Potato Festival were the furthest thing from my mind right now.

Salt and cheese aromas rose up from the casserole behind her. My stomach growled. My mouth watered. I wasn't going to get any food until I threw her a nibble of hope. "I can't enter the Potato Princess contest with a bum ankle, Mom."

"Potato Queen." She set the salt and pepper shakers on the table. "And it's not until April. Your ankle will be fine by then. You don't have to be walking at all to enter the potato cook off."

"I'll think about it." Mind you, I didn't say I'd *do* it. I said I would think about it.

Satisfied, my mother grabbed her potholders and placed the casserole on the table. "I think this is the winner. See if you can beat this one." She patted my shoulder.

There was a layer of crusty yellow cheese on top of the potatoes. Mom spooned a pile of the casserole onto Nathan's plate.

Nathan picked up his spoon. "They've taken Persistence."

Mom whispered in my ear, "He's been saying that all day. I don't know what it means." She situated herself opposite Nathan, unfolded her napkin, and placed it on her lap. "I'll help you with your recipe if you like, Ruby."

I shoved a spoonful of potato-bean-cheese-bacon-bit casserole into my mouth. It tasted salty, warm, and comforting. "Okay." I chewed. "Though it's gonna be hard to compete with this, Mom." Mom's domestic talents dwarfed anything I could come up with. She's like Betty Crocker in hyperdrive. Maybe that was why I was reluctant to even try. What's the point in doing something if you know you'll be bad at it?

Mom glowed. "Well, thank you." She leaned forward, chin lifted. "Nathan, are you doing all right there?"

"They've taken Persistence." Nathan repeated between bites. His saddlebag rested on his lap. I hadn't seen him without the saddlebag since we took him from the burned-out trailer. Did he sleep with it?

Mom shrugged almost indiscernibly and glanced at the ceiling.

I took another bite. "Yep, I think you've got a winner here. Now all you have to do is come up with a catchy name."

We spent the rest of the evening eating dinner and dessert and watching an old black-and-white movie Mom had rented. Nathan mentioned losing persistence a few more times. He pointed to his saddlebag and said, "I've got evidence."

Because of some previous strange conversations I'd had with Nathan, I feared the "evidence" he spoke of might be connected to Area 51 or crop circles. I didn't dare press him for details.

After the movie, I limped to my bed, pulled on pajamas, and slipped beneath my comforter. Worries over Wesley danced in my brain. Maybe Lance Kinkaid knew where he was. I needed to get out there. Sleepiness flooded through my muscles. I heard Mom instructing Nathan about extra blankets and pillows, like she'd done every night since he'd been here. My eyelids were heavy, so heavy. . . .

Pulsating in my ankle woke me. When I turned slightly, it hurt even more. I reached over and turned on my nightstand lamp. The clock glowed 4:00 A.M. I swung my feet to the wood floor and groped my way to the bathroom to locate some ibuprofen—or a noose—to put me out of my misery.

Tingling vibrations of pain made my toes numb, and I could feel a tightening in my calf. Gripping the bathroom sink, I opened the medicine cabinet and grabbed the Advil bottle. I fussed with the childproof cap for a full two minutes before reading the illustrated instructions on the side of the bottle. I still couldn't get it open. Where was a kid when you needed one? I'm sure any seven-year-old could get the top off.

After I made two more attempts, the lid gave up its death grip on the bottle. I popped the pills into my mouth and drank from the faucet. Wiping my lips with my sleeve, I sank back down on the toilet and closed my eyes. My ankle still throbbed. The thought of the long journey back to bed overwhelmed me. The only thing that sounded like a worse idea was falling asleep on the bathroom floor. I needed rest. We'd made plans to go to early service at church.

In the kitchen, a cupboard slammed shut. I heard the hum of the refrigerator being opened. Feet shuffled across the linoleum.

I hopped down the hall to see if it was Mom or Nathan getting a late-night snack.

I found Nathan in the kitchen, spooning Mom's casserole into a plastic container. The light above the stove glowed and spilled halfway across the kitchen. Nathan was fully dressed in a brown polyester three-piece suit. Mom had confiscated his smoke-stained farm clothes almost as soon as he got in the door. In the suit, Nathan resembled a car salesman or a preacher.

In order to take the weight off my hurt ankle, I leaned against the wall that led into the kitchen.

Nathan glanced at me. His hair was a fuzzy ball again. "Might be gone awhile. Need to eat. This is a good casserole."

"Gone?" I hobbled into the kitchen. "Where are you headed? It's four o'clock in the morning." I had a sinking feeling I wasn't going to make it to church.

Nathan smoothed down his hair. It sprung right back up. "I've been telling you. They've taken Persistence. I've got to go get him back."

"Persistence is a guy?" I crumpled into a chair.

"A bull—a prize registered Angus. Most of my herd came out of Persistence."

Despite the throbbing in my ankle, I was suddenly very tired and having a hard time processing information. "Somebody took your bull?" I hope that soon the anti-inflammatories would kick in, and I'd have the coherence of mind to realize this was all a dream.

"Kidnapped—held for ransom."

Nathan Burgess could be the most rational, intelligent person in the world, except for one thing. He tended to see conspiracies in everything. I mean everything. Since I'd met him, I learned that the Mafia controlled the cheese industry, that a shadow government had existed in San Francisco since 1860, that the militia movement was a fabrication of the media, and that crop circles and cattle mutilations were the meat-packing industry's way of keeping ranchers in line. He claimed he had evidence for all of it. Which I was now beginning to believe he had in his saddlebag.

So when he suggested that his bull had been kidnapped and held for ransom, I heard *Twilight Zone* music in my head, and assumed yet another conspiracy would spill from his lips.

"Maybe you should just go back to bed, huh, Nathan?"

"Can't." He tapped his watch. "Ransom drop is at six. Need to get there before they do." He pressed the cover onto the plastic container that held Mom's casserole.

I doubted Emily Post had written a chapter on etiquette at a ransom drop, but apparently it was good manners to show up early. "And how are you going to get there? Your car is back at your place."

Nathan held up a set of keys, my keys. "Thought I'd borrow yours."

I rose to my feet and limped toward him. "No way." I reached for the keys.

With a swiftness that was surprising for a man his age, he shoved the keys in the pocket of his sports coat and shook his finger at me. "Uh-uh, you can't have them."

I detected a teasing twinkle in his eyes as he shook his head at me. It was the same twinkle I'd seen in Wesley's eyes a thousand times. He was in the habit of holding things over his head, making me jump for them. It was a stupid game we played so I'd have an excuse to touch him, to be physically close to him. When I saw that same expression in Nathan, the rising ache of missing Wesley was almost unbearable.

"Come with me if you want." Nathan had already rounded the corner and was headed into the living room.

"Wait." I grabbed a sticky note and a pen from the little caddy Mom had on the counter. I scribbled as I talked. "I gotta let Mom know where we are." The shock of the fire must have sent Nathan off the deep end. He needed a babysitter. I spared Mom the strange details and simply wrote that we'd gone out to Nathan's property and that she should go to church without me.

"When will we be back?"

Nathan shrugged.

I had no idea how long a fictional ransom drop would take. I wrote that we'd be back in time for lunch.

Nathan strode toward the living-room door.

"Wait. I'm in my pajamas."

"No time," said Nathan. "Want to get there before the kidnappers."

I grabbed my down coat off the rack and slipped on some shoes that wouldn't hurt my ankle. "I'm driving, Nathan." I spoke while hopping up and down. "You can't drive my Valiant." Maybe it was just because the anti-inflammatories hadn't kicked in yet, but this whole scenario suddenly seemed rational—like it was what I was supposed to be doing—following Nathan around at early hours of the morning to make sure he didn't get hurt.

When I got outside, Nathan was sitting in the passenger seat of the Valiant with the saddlebag on his lap. He wore a polyester-looking dress coat Mom must have found for him. We drove through the older residential neighborhoods and turned onto Main Street.

Traffic lights flashed yellow at this hour, and all the downtown businesses were dark. Plenty of parking available at this time of day. Too bad nothing was open.

I slowed down when we got close to Benson's Pet and Feed. All the lights were turned off. There was no ominous truck parked across the street or in the lot. No shadows lurked by the dumpster. Georgia had installed a new alarm system.

I accelerated as we got to the edge of town. "Okay, Nathan, where are we headed?"

Nathan unbuckled his saddlebag and pulled out a folded piece of paper with a burnt corner. "They left this note on the gate." He unfolded the paper and read out loud: "If you want to see your precious bull alive, bring ten thousand dollars to the Gorman Bridge at 6:00 A.M. Sunday."

I inhaled a deep breath of conspiracy-laden air. Nathan held the note up. The large shaky scrawl was not Nathan's handwriting. Now the old man had physical evidence for a fictional kidnapping.

Curiouser and curiouser. I felt like Alice after she fell down the rabbit hole. "Nathan, do you have ten thousand dollars in that saddlebag?" Given the circumstances, it seemed like the most logical question to ask. "Is that why you've been watching it so closely?" He was the type to stash away cash in a mattress somewhere or bury it in a coffee can in the backyard.

Nathan clutched the saddlebag tighter. "I'm not giving those good-for-nothings any money."

"So you're serious. Someone took your cow—"

"Bull," Nathan corrected. "Registered Angus. Straightest back in three counties. Persistence will give you heifers with bags bigger than mountains. Fatten up a calf faster than you can say Joe's your uncle."

Now we were talking about the size of cow udders. Special. "Are you sure your bull was really kidnapped? Some kid could have left that note as a joke."

Nathan shook his head. "No joke. Persistence was in the north pasture separate from the heifers."

"Maybe he jumped the fence."

"Bulls don't jump fences; they bust them down. Persistence wasn't a fence buster. They started the fire to distract me." He punched the word *they,* bloating it with conspiracy.

I was too afraid to ask who *they* were. "Nathan, that whole trailer was a pile of kindling."

"Ah." He raised a gnarled finger. "But where did the initial spark come from?" Nathan sucked in his lips and nodded his head as though that one bit of evidence clinched the deal. "They were gunnin' for 'im."

I turned off the highway and onto the frontage road. The sky was still a gray gauze. Snow-covered fences and fields clicked by as the paved road became asphalt and the asphalt turned to gravel. Nathan directed me—"turn here" . . . "left just past the cattle guard" . . . "just around the corner."

We parked in a grove of trees and brush close to the river. I killed the engine of the Valiant. Even though most of the branches were bare, thick foliage hid us from view. At least this wasn't boring. I had nothing better to do but sleep and think about how much my ankle hurt.

I checked my watch: twenty after five. I had a couple of theories on how the next hour would go down. The most ideal one was that we'd wait around until twenty after six, nothing would happen, I could drive home and get a couple hours sleep, and maybe I'd catch late service at church. Zac would call later in the day and say he'd found Persistence wandering the countryside, theorizing that the bull had been spooked by the fire.

The second theory would be that some kid would show up dragging the bull with a piece of rope. The kid would say he was sorry, that his hoodlum friends talked him into it. Blah, blah, blah. And then he would beg us not to turn him in for stealing.

Those were my theories, my projections into the future. After thirty-one years, you think I'd learn that nothing ever turns out the way I plan.

I crossed my arms and slumped into the seat. "How exactly are we going to get this bull home?" Our car faced east. The sun became a sliver on the horizon, glinting through the trees in star shapes.

Nathan's jaw dropped. "I hadn't thought of that. Should've brought a trailer. He's a real sweet-natured bull. We can probably just tie him to the bumper. We're not that far from my place. Course I'll have to keep watch on him."

I got out of the car and sat on the hood so I could see the countryside a little better. A sloping hill covered in snow was visible through the bare trees.

I heard the car door slam, and Nathan came and leaned against the bumper. He had the container of Mom's casserole in his hand.

"That's where they hung Van Kriten in 1902." Nathan pointed to a single, ancient cottonwood midway up the hill.

"Didn't they usually have hangings in the town square?"

"Not if it's your neighbors stringing you up." Nathan scooped up a pile of casserole. "Everyone says that's the tree anyway. Doesn't seem like it should still be alive a hundred years later."

"Folklore. The whole story is probably distorted. The real tree probably died or got cut down."

"Yer Mom makes good casserole." He offered me a bite by shoving the plastic container toward me.

I shook my head and opted for the piece of candy I had in my coat pocket. "Just make sure you get that container back to Mom. She's weird about her plastic storage things."

Nathan nodded and continued to chew.

"Don't want to come between a church lady and her Tupperware," I said. "I've seen her wrestle other women to the ground for it."

Nathan chuckled. "That's what Wesley likes about you. Your sense of humor."

"He told you that? Did he . . . say anything else about me?"

"Said he likes that you can take care of yourself. That you're not clingy."

This was fun. Hearing what Wesley said about me to other people. Glowing embers burst inside me like Fourth of July sparklers. "Anything else?" I was going to milk this for all it was worth.

Nathan leaned over and patted my hand. "He likes you."

I stared out at the landscape through the trees and brush. If he liked me, why did I sense him pulling away in the days before we went out to Zac's? "Where is he, Nathan? Where has Wesley gone?"

Nathan scraped the bottom of the plastic container with his spoon. He shook his head. "Don't know. Wesley was kind of a wild teenager. That boy had extra angels assigned to him. It was hard for him losing his mama when he was so young. Maybe those angels are still around taking care of him." He touched his chest. "Don't know what I'd do if something's happened to him."

Me either.

We sat in silence, watching the hills and road around us. The sliver of the sun became a half circle. The temperature rose maybe ten degrees. Magpies showed up for their morning performance. Glints of sunlight angled through foliage, brightening the icicles on the bare branches of the deciduous trees. The forest looked like it was made of crystal. The hood of the car warmed, and we waited.

When I checked my watch at five to six, I started to think that my first theory about possible outcomes was about to transpire.

Then I heard the awful rumbling.

Chapter Seven

The racket seemed to be coming from over the hill. It continued for some time, grew louder, and then stopped abruptly.

"Why don't you stay here, Nathan?" I slipped off the hood of the car. "I'll see what's going on."

"I'm coming with ya." Nathan stepped in front of me.

"What if the kidnappers come with Persistence, and you are not here?"

"What if Persistence is over the hill?"

He had me there. I had no idea what was over the hill. But I didn't want to be responsible for an old man getting hurt. Right now, the safest place seemed to be far from whatever had made that noise. "You should stay here, Nathan."

The tightness of his expression told me he wasn't going to stay behind no matter how long we argued.

"Okay, you can come with me, but you have to keep up." This was my new plan. I'd run really fast up the hill. Nathan would have a hard time keeping up and head back to the safety of the car. My ankle still hurt, but I thought maybe I'd be able to outrun a seventy-year-old man.

"I think you're the one that's going to have trouble keeping up with me, little missy."

"You're on." Branches clicked in the wind as we bolted up the hill. Because of my ankle, I sort of hobbled and sort of skipped.

Nathan kept up with me. He didn't run. Instead, he took big, deliberate steps. Halfway up the hill, I glanced at that lone tree where some friends and neighbors were supposed to have lynched one of their own.

Nathan and I crouched behind some brush that ran parallel to the tree line. Sweat glistened on the old man's red face. I was out of breath as well, and my ankle was back into rock-and-roll drum-beat mode.

I stared out at the ragged tree. Ghostlike images flashed in my mind—a man with a rope around his neck. "So why did they hang him?"

"Guess he owned quite a bit of land. His kids and widow lost most of it after he died. None of his kids had a head for business like Seb. Hard to get the story straight. People around here don't like to talk about it. Some of them are descended from the murderers. My folks didn't get here until 1920."

"People had to be pretty mad at a guy to hang him like that."

Nathan pulled his coat off and slipped out of it. "I hate polyester." He tossed it to the ground.

"I'm sure Mom will find you something more your style."

"I like cotton. Cotton in the summer. Wool in the winter."

A two-fabric fellow. Nathan Burgess was not a complex man. I wondered how he'd managed to raise such a complicated son. Wesley was more of a wool-cotton-poly-spandex blend kind of guy.

I patted him on the shoulder. "Doing okay?"

"Keeping up just fine. You're the one huffin' and puffin'."

With my ankle throbbing, I rose to my feet. "You had to go and point that out, didn't you?"

We headed the rest of the way up the hill. As we drew closer to the top, a chorus of men shouting and the engine noise of ATVs grew louder.

Nathan darted ahead of me and found cover behind a juniper tree. By the time I got up to the tree, the noise down below was oppressive, like I'd walked from a library into a factory.

Two long horse trailers pulled by powerful trucks were parked below. That explained the rumbling. Heifers, some with calves gamboling after them, some still pregnant, were being herded into a portable corral by four men, one on an ATV and three on horses. Two other men leaned against the corral; one opened and closed the gate. Something about the way the men shouted at each other suggested a level of panic.

"Some rancher is rounding up cattle for sale?" I speculated. The scene below had a menacing feeling to it. Maybe it was just the time of day and the furious level of activity.

The breeze rippled through Nathan's cottony hair. "Ain't the time of year to take them to market. Half the heifers haven't calved out yet; the other half aren't weaned. New ones aren't branded yet."

"Then what?" The buzz of the ATV stopped. The man swung off the four-wheeler and pointed at the sunrise. A calf bawled.

Nathan shook his head. "Something else is wrong. Near as I can figure, this is the backside of the Thurmans' land. Those cows have a lazy SN bar brand, the Spences' brand ten miles up the road."

"Cattle rustlers? Get out of here, Nathan. That doesn't happen anymore. Even I know brand inspectors would catch them when they tried to sell them."

"Not if they avoid the highway. Brands are registered state by state. A buyer in South Dakota or Wyoming might have a similar brand or be able to alter it so it looked like his."

"But he'd know the cows were stolen."

Nathan shrugged. "Some guys don't care. Or you could just butcher the cows and sell the calves. Spence paid for the hay and went through the heartache of calving and wintering them." Nathan's hands curled into fists. "And he's not seeing any of the profit."

The men below were in a frenzy of activity, some of them glanced at their watches or at the sun inching above the horizon. Something told me that whatever the plan was, they were behind schedule.

Even though we were pretty remote—I couldn't see a single farmhouse or outbuilding—the plan had probably been to have everything loaded up by dawn. The older men yelled and pointed at the younger men. The younger men shook their heads and cursed.

An older model Ford truck came up over the hill and parked by one of the trailers. A very large bull was tied to the rails in the truck bed.

"Persistence." Nuances of affection surrounded Nathan's word. He rose up above the cover of the tree. I yanked him back down by pulling on his polyester vest. The old man furrowed his white eyebrows at me. "They got my Persistence."

"We can't just go down there and get him. Those guys are probably armed."

The man hauling Persistence got out of his truck. Another man in a black cowboy hat strutted over to him

"Besides, we're outnumbered," I whispered.

Nathan sucked in his lips and crossed his arms.

"I want to get your bull back, too, Nathan, but I don't want to die."

"I want my Persistence back. Ain't right."

"I know. I know," I soothed.

Most of the activity had quieted down. Circles of dark tracks stained the pristine snow.

The man in the black hat shouted something about a "stupid idea" and then pointed at Persistence.

I couldn't hear much of the other man's response, but I did hear the phrase "easy money." The man in the black hat shook his head and walked away.

"Looks like they aren't feedin' him right," Nathan whined.

"They've had him for less than a week, Nathan."

One of the trailers was lined up with the corral gate, and half the cows were herded up the trailer ramp. A stocky man returned to the ATV while the other trailer was lined up and loaded with the remaining cattle. As though the whole thing had been choreographed, men dismantled the corral and loaded the pieces into truck beds.

"I got to get him back." Nathan rose to his feet. His head was visible above the short juniper tree. A man closing up the back of the second trailer glanced up the hill.

"Nathan, no."

I thought I heard noise behind us in the forest, but with the buzzing sputter of the ATV, I couldn't be sure.

Realizing the error of his impulsiveness, Nathan crouched back down. It was too late. The man by the trailer had alerted an older-looking man, and they were headed up the hill. The first trailer and ATV were already on their way over the hill, away from the us.

I squeezed Nathan's shoulder. "I think we better get going."

"But Persistence."

The men were halfway up the hill. One of them slipped on the snow but didn't fall.

"Later, Nathan. Come on, we know what that guy's pickup looks like." I squinted through the juniper branches but couldn't make out the license plate.

I hadn't noticed any of the men carrying guns. I could see a rifle rack in the back of the truck. No indication they were violent—standard issue equipment for a truck in Montana.

Nathan's shoulders stiffened. He shook his head.

"Nathan, please. We don't have any way to get that bull home other than pulling him. Do you really think we're going to get away if our top speed is five miles an hour?"

"Guess I didn't think this through." Nathan set his jaw. "We could take the truck."

I pounded my forehead with my palm. "Then we'd be guilty of stealing the guy's truck." Just my luck: I have to end up with a criminal mastermind. "We're outnumbered. I don't want to take that kind of chance."

The men were about forty yards away. Thick juniper bushes provided us adequate cover. Even though the men moved slowly—stopping and glancing around a lot—they were making a beeline for us.

I surveyed the flora and fauna behind me. There was enough tree and underbrush for us to stay hidden if we dived into the thick of the forest before they got closer.

"Nathan, I'm going. Meet me back down at the car. I'll wait five minutes." That was a lie, of course. I would wait until he showed up even if it meant being caught. I said what needed to be said to shake him from his fixation on that bull.

I dashed into the trees. I use *dashed* lightly. Because of my twisted ankle, I took one strong stride followed by one weak step. When I glanced behind me, the old man had already risen to his feet. My motivational speech had worked. Anthony Robbins, eat your heart out.

I couldn't see the other two men through the brush. If we were lucky, they'd decided the movement was a wild animal or the wind and gone back to their vehicles. They must be anxious to get away from their crime scene.

Because it was my hiney I was trying to save, I erred on the side of caution and zigzagged my way deep into the forest. Sticking close to the tree line would be faster and more direct, but I'd be too easy to spot.

The way I had it figured, if I headed in a general downhill direction, I'd come to my green Valiant eventually while remaining out of sight of the thieves.

I jumped over a dead log. Tree growth was thick enough to cut visibility to about ten feet. I heard branches breaking to the side of me and assumed it was Nathan.

By summer, this place would be a forest fire waiting to happen. The dead undergrowth was a foot deep in some places, covered by a thin layer of snow. I pushed myself deeper into the forest. Again, I heard breaking branches. *Come on, Nathan. Stay with me.*

Blood drummed past my ears. I couldn't exactly run because of the mushy dead fall on the forest floor. My pajama leg caught on a branch. I bent over to assess the damage. My green and pink flannel pajama bottoms had an eight-inch gash in them. Beads of blood formed on the scratch. My hand drifted down to my swollen ankle. The adrenaline coursing through me had masked the pain of the injuries for a moment. But now, my leg felt like it was on fire.

Blood from the scratch stained my pajamas. I stood up, and the forest spun around me. My stomach rolled. I had planned to simply head downhill, knowing that would bring me back to the Valiant. The ground I stood on was flat. Hopping, I pivoted in a half circle as the dizziness subsided and the trees came back into focus. Winter cold cut through me.

The gash in my leg pinched a nerve on the inside of my knee joint. How stupid was this? Running from criminals with a bum ankle. I took several steps in one direction and then changed my mind.

I heard footsteps and breaking branches. But when I surveyed the trees, I detected no movement.

All the trees looked the same. White bark with black marks on them. Most of the trees were close together, and none of them were more than six inches in diameter—the effect was one of prison bars.

I'd only had half a night's sleep, my muscles were swimming in anti-inflammatories, my ankle was all but screaming for me to take the weight off, and now my leg was bleeding, and the air felt suddenly colder. Against my better judgment, my muscles totally relaxed. All I could think about was falling asleep in a warm safe bed.

I trudged forward, heading in a direction that I was sure would take me downhill. If I could get to the road, I'd be able to orient myself back to the car. Thousands of paranoid thoughts raced through my head. What if the cattle rustlers got to the car first? What if they hurt Nathan? I'd counted on them giving up and returning to their vehicles. I assumed if they saw no further movement, they'd turn around.

I should have stayed with Nathan. I should have made sure he got back to the car safely. *God, please keep that old man safe.*

I stumbled through the clearest path I could find, pushing the low-lying branches out of my way. My ankle throbbed. I tried hopping and ended up crashing into a tree. I rubbed my forehead where I'd hit the trunk. At least the new owie on my head was severe enough to take my mind off the pain in my ankle and calf. Another branch broke. I couldn't discern what direction the sound came from. Someone was in this woods with me. I hoped it was Nathan. And that he was just as scared to cry out my name as I was to call out his.

I staggered into a small clearing where there was a large flat rock. I slumped down on the rock, sitting far enough back so that my foot was elevated. Birds cawed in the higher parts of the trees. Branches, covered in ice and snow, created a web that let only patches of blue sky through.

I listened for a moment, hoping to hear the rumble of a vehicle so I'd know where the road was. There wasn't much traffic on the road, but something had to go by sooner or later. The wind lifted my hair. I closed my eyes. Whatever I had done to my ankle on the exercise mat, I'd made worse by running up and down the hill and scraping up my leg.

When I readjusted my foot, hot needles shot through to my bones. Once again, I'd hurt myself pretty badly, and I didn't even have a glamorous story to go with my injury—an exciting story maybe. If I'd hurt myself skydiving or barrel racing, that would be glamorous. I pulled my shoe off to have a closer look at my injury. Frigid air sliced through my thin sock.

When I pulled up my pajama pant leg, a stream of dried blood from the scratch formed a perfect arrow pointing at my swollen ankle.

Birds fluttered suddenly out of the tree tops. The flapping of their wings faded. No branches creaked in the light breeze. Quiet settled like a shroud on the forest.

A single black crow swooped down and landed on a lower branch of an aspen. He cocked his head and leaned toward me, readjusting his feet for balance.

I'm not carrion yet, buddy. Quit looking at me like that.

A second and third crow lighted on the branches around the first bird. They all danced on the tree limbs, staring at me with their beady black eyes. How Hitchcockian.

With a wary glance at the crows, I pulled my shoe back on my foot. How much farther could it be to the car? I was sixty percent sure I was headed in the right direction.

I scooted to the edge of the rock and planted my feet on the snowy dead branches that littered the forest floor. Favoring my injured ankle, I pushed myself to my feet. The trees above me were still incredibly quiet. I tilted my head. Patches of blue that sneaked through the web of limbs looked like a mosaic.

One of the crows flapped its wings and dived to the forest floor about ten feet from me. His staring made me shiver.

I tilted back my head, took in a deep breath of clean air, and closed my eyes. Summoning the energy, I hoped this would be the last spurt to the car.

I hadn't realized someone else was in my personal space until his rough, smelly hand slipped over my mouth.

Chapter Eight

A flutter of wings filled the air. Branches vibrated where the birds had just taken off. My attacker slammed the back of my head against his chest. I got a full-screen view of blue sky and tree limbs. Almost involuntarily, I closed my eyes. His body pressed against the back of mine. When I tried to twist away, he cinched his arm around my waist and made a shushing sound.

This guy was being way too friendly in his body language.

His hand smelled of dirt and leather. *Just my luck, I have to end up with an assailant in need of a bath.* Layers of perspiration assaulted my nose. My eyes watered. If he didn't remove his hand soon, I was going to pass out.

What were the vulnerable parts on an attacker? All those self-defense shows I'd watched and I couldn't remember a single one. While I was trying to twist free, something about the groin and the shin flashed through my head. In the course of my struggle, I aimed for the vulnerable area above his ankle. My shoe crunched something.

The assailant didn't make any noise, but he let go of me. I spun around. He was dirty and had several day's growth of dark beard. But now I understood why my attacker had seemed so chummy in his body language. I knew this guy.

"Wesley!"

Wesley took time out from hopping, grimacing, and holding his foot to put his finger to his lips, signaling me to "be quiet."

I rushed over to him. "Wesley, Wesley. Where have you been? Why didn't you at least get in touch with me?"

"I thought I was getting in touch with you—just now," he whispered and slumped back down on the flat rock. "Until you broke my foot." He unlaced his hiking boot and tore off his footgear and thick sock.

"Attacking me from behind is your idea of getting in touch? Have you ever heard of a phone?" I was unbelievably happy to see him. I didn't know why everything I was saying came out angry.

Again, he put his finger to his lips. "They're still tromping through this forest," he whispered.

I searched the trees for the real assailants before sitting beside Wesley on the rock. His unwashed odor wafted up. I covered my nose delicately with my fingers. "Why didn't you just come up to me?"

"I was trying to keep you quiet so you wouldn't scream." He touched a red spot on his foot. "I had no idea you'd beat me up."

"Sorry. Better put your sock on before your foot freezes." I leaned a little closer to him, a real sacrifice on my part, considering he was one of the great unwashed. I whispered, "Cree clued me in on what's going on with the ring of thieves."

"I'm glad he did."

"Why did you go? Why did you leave Zac's place?"

"I saw a flatbed semi on one of the roads. The thieves have been stealing farm equipment—the kind you haul out on a flat bed. I thought maybe if I followed the truck, it would lead me to whoever is engineering the thefts."

"Why didn't you say something to me?"

"I was in hurry, Ruby. I'm sorry. I meant to call. Things were happening so fast. I thought I could get this wrapped up."

"And where have you been since then?" Obviously, nowhere near a shower.

"Following the truck led nowhere. They saw me coming before I got there. I started watching Lance Kinkaid's house."

"I found your Jeep with blood on it."

He touched his five o'clock shadow. "It's cow's blood. After I gave up on the flatbed, I found the remains of a butchered cow. It probably ended up in someone's freezer."

"I didn't know that. I was afraid for you. Why did you leave the Jeep there?"

"I thought maybe if I could be quieter, I could catch them. I had Reslin bring me a horse. He was supposed to arrange to take the Jeep over to Zac's."

That explained why Reslin hadn't been bent out of shape about Wesley's disappearance.

Wesley slipped his sock and boot back on, lifting his gaze in the direction of the most recent cattle-rustling episode. "They're getting bolder and more organized. Before it was a cow here and a cow there. I'm sure we're going to have more reported losses when ranchers bring in wintering cows to calf out."

"Why didn't you go to Zac's and at least call me and . . . take a shower."

"I thought the trail was hot." He pulled keys from his pocket. "Ruby, I need your help. I need you to go to my house and get my Glock. My rifle is too cumbersome to haul around."

"Your police firearm? They are just thieves, right?" It felt like a hundred spiders with frozen legs crawled up my back. I shivered. "They haven't killed or hurt anyone, have they?"

"Not yet." He dropped the keys into my hand and then pulled a cell phone from his back pocket. "I'll call you on this," he said, placing the phone in my hand. "I have another cell. Be careful; someone might be watching the house."

He had two cell phones and found time to give Reslin an electronic holler. He could have called me. I had a feeling his evasiveness wasn't about work. Work was the excuse. When I viewed watching the kids as a test, I'd pushed. I pushed—and he pulled away. "So now I get to be part of your cops-and-robbers games." Of course I couldn't say what I felt; it came out in anger code. "Please, this is getting way too conspiratorial." I stood up and took a couple of limping steps. "You sound like your dad."

"Just 'cause I'm paranoid doesn't mean someone isn't after me." His gaze fell to my feet. "Why are you limping?"

"Injury. Kayaking accident." I squared my shoulders. I so wanted to have a glamorous story to go with my injury.

Wesley grinned with only one side of his mouth curling up. "Rivers run awful cold in February."

I slumped back down on the rock. "I was trying to stand . . . just trying to stand. An exercise mat jumped up and tripped me."

He kneeled down and gently pulled my shoe off. My sock had gotten wet in the snow. Warm hands touched my shin. "Pretty swollen." He pointed in the direction I had been moving. "Your car's about a hundred yards that way. Dad should be there by now. Can you make it?"

"You mean you aren't going to carry me?"

"I'd love the opportunity to be chivalrous, but I need to get out of here. My horse is tied up over the hill."

"Wow. Just like in an old cowboy movie."

Again, he gave me his crooked grin. "It's quieter than an ATV."

He continued to rub my injury, massaging my sole and then the top part of my foot. Lifting the torn pajama leg, he narrowed his eyes at my bloody scratch. When he looked at me, he must have noticed the bump on my forehead. "Jeepers, Ruby, you're pretty banged up." His voice was filled with concern.

"I'm okay. Really I . . ."

He rose to his feet so he was standing over me. Leaning, he touched my forehead lightly with his fingers. "Gonna be a little bruising there." His hand slipped down to my cheek. He lifted my chin.

I relished his touch. He leaned over and kissed my forehead. I closed my eyes. His inhaling and exhaling surrounded me. A long moment passed before he straightened up and I opened my eyes. I could have done without his unwashed aroma, but I wasn't about to complain.

Even in this unkempt state, he was handsome. His five o'clock shadow and dark eyebrows contrasted with wheat-colored hair. And his concern for me now almost made up for him not calling me . . . almost. "I really missed you." There, I said it. My real feelings were out on the table, naked and vulnerable.

He gazed down at me. In the early morning light, his green eyes had a soft quality to them.

Come on Wesley, you can do it—just say you missed me, too.

"You'll get the pistol for me?" He angled his body slightly away from me.

I tightened my back muscles so my shoulders wouldn't slump. "Sure," I said. That was me, the dutiful assistant. I'd really stuck my heart out there with the missed-you thing. "You must have recognized some of those people who rustled the cows." Back to a safe topic—work. "They have your dad's bull."

"I know. I'll have to look at his trailer closer. Maybe the fire wasn't an accident."

That was a scary thought. Nathan's conspiracy theory might be true. "Why don't you just arrest the rustlers and come out of hiding?" Already, disappointment had corrupted my emotional database. *Why can't he say he missed me? Why? Why? Why?*

"That was our first thought. I know some of them—petty criminals from town, some farmers' kids." He leaned over and stroked the top of my foot while gripping the arch with his other hand. I was grateful. While his lips were dancing across my forehead, my foot had become quite the frozen little appendage. The warmth of his touch was the only thing that kept it from turning blue in the morning chill. That marvelous tingling sensation that created a hum inside of me was a nice bonus.

Weird. He wouldn't say he missed me, but he'd touch my stinky foot tenderly.

"But I need to figure out who set all this up and why," he continued. "That's the only way it will end."

"Now you really sound like your dad. You mean there *is* some big conspiracy network headed by a kingpin? I know that's what Cree said. But it just seems . . . out there."

A look of confusion crossed Wesley's dirty face. He stopped massaging my foot. "This is serious." He picked my shoe up off the ground where he'd dropped it.

"Sorry . . . an organized crime ring just seems so improbable for around here. So who do you think is behind all this?"

"I'm not sure, but I have my suspicions." Gently, he slid the shoe back on my foot. "The thefts started about the time that Lance Kinkaid guy moved in."

"I met him. He's a little strange."

Wesley nodded. "During the time I watched, I noticed a lot of people coming and going from his place. Other than a trip to the Fontana library almost every day, he doesn't seem to have a job. No clear explanation where he'd get the money to build a house like that." Wesley rose to his feet. "He's new to this area. That's not enough to arrest him yet, but I can't imagine someone from around here doing this kind of thing. It could be financially devastating to the farmers and ranchers. People raised in this country don't do this to their neighbor."

Voices—two men shouting as though they were some distance from each other and from us—rang through the silence of the forest.

"Gotta go." Wesley held out his hand and pulled me up off the rock. "You need to get down the hill." He kissed me on the cheek. "Watch that ankle."

I wrinkled up my face in response to Wesley's pungency. "Do one thing for me. Next time I see you, get a shower first."

"Picky picky. It's not like there's a shower under every cottonwood tree. I'll call you and tell you where to bring the Glock. Don't tell anyone you saw me."

"Not even Cree."

"Cree's okay." He gazed at me long enough for the moment to become uncomfortable. "You better get out of here."

I turned and limped back down the hill. Wesley hadn't told me where in the house to find the gun. When I turned back to ask, the clearing was empty.

Nathan was waiting at the car when I came to the edge of the forest. Other than his hair being a white fuzz ball and his cheeks having turned red, he was none the worse for wear. "You made it. Did Wesley catch up with you?"

"He found me. We better get out of here."

I slid behind the steering wheel and buckled my seatbelt.

"They're still beating the bushes for us," Nathan said.

My Valiant was green with gray showing through where the paint was chipped, which sort of camouflaged it. That was probably why they hadn't found the car.

The whole ride back to town, Nathan lamented that we may have lost our only chance to get Persistence. He talked about that bull the same way a doting parent talks about a child. At one point, his eyes misted up.

"We'll find a way to get him back," I said. "We know what the truck looks like. It's got to belong to someone around here. You didn't recognize it, huh?"

Nathan shook his head. "Lotta new people moving in. It's like you don't know your neighbor anymore."

"We'll get him back." Getting the bull back was down the line on my to-do list. First, I needed to get Wesley's gun for him, and I was seriously considering paying Lance Kinkaid a visit.

Nathan looked off into the distance. His lower lip stuck out.

Poor guy. I needed to find a way to cheer him up.

When we came into town, I noticed Georgia's car parked outside the feed store. We weren't open on Sunday, but Georgia had probably come in to catch up on something.

Nathan leaned forward in the passenger seat, moaned, and put his face in his hands. An idea blossomed in my head. I slowed and pulled into the feed store parking lot.

After she got home from church, Mom would be gone, teaching

craft classes most of the day, leaving Nathan alone in the house. Why not get Nathan and Georgia together so they could relive fond memories of missing pets? Maybe if Georgia had someone to console, she'd get her mind off her own sorrow.

"I gotta get a bandage on this scratch and get cleaned up. Georgia usually has that kind of thing. Then maybe you can hang out with Georgia while I take care of some stuff."

"Why?"

"She could use your help."

Nathan shrugged. "Okay."

When we went inside, Georgia was standing at the counter, pushing the buttons on an adding machine and working her way through a pile of papers.

"Georgia, you remember Nathan, Wesley's dad."

Nathan stood up a little straighter and ran his hand over his fuzzy fine hair.

Georgia barely lifted her eyes. "Yeah, I remember him." She gazed forlornly at the shelf behind the counter where Her Majesty used to perch.

"Georgia, Nathan's prize bull got stolen when his trailer caught on fire."

Georgia tilted her head. "Really." She nodded for several seconds.

Nathan placed his hand on his heart. "Sure do miss my Persistence."

Georgia's shoulders straightened a bit. "Sweet-natured thing was he?"

"Walk right up to him. Not a fence breaker. Never gave me a bit a trouble."

Georgia strutted over to the other side of the counter and slid onto one of the stools. "I know they're just animals and you try not to fall in love with them."

Nathan chuckled. "Yes indeedy."

Half an hour later, Georgia and Nathan were restocking shelves together and laughing. Even if the rest of my day fell apart, I'd done a least one thing right. I'd gotten two people together who understood each other.

By the time I got most of the blood cleaned off my leg and rewrapped my ankle, my eyelids felt heavy. "I need a nap."

"Go on home and get yourself one." Georgia and Nathan stood shoulder to shoulder, arranging buckskin gloves, a job that didn't really require two people. "I'll bring Nathan home when we're done."

I drove home, ate lunch, and collapsed in bed. When I woke up, it was 4:30. All this trauma to my body was causing exhaustion. The house was still quiet. Nathan and Georgia must be getting along really well. In the kitchen, I found a note from Mom saying she was at the church helping with some kind of decorating thing. I changed out of my blood-stained pajamas and headed across town to Wesley's.

The sky grayed up. This time of year, sunset came around suppertime—about five. A fluffy layer of white clouds shadowed the mountains surrounding Eagleton. The town itself nestled in a valley between two ski resorts and lots of national forest.

I drove downtown. Older brick buildings populated Main Street. Most of the businesses were art galleries, overpriced clothing stores, and restaurants that catered to the tourists and the new money in Eagleton. The location attracts a lot of telecommuters and people with family money or who invested in the stock market at the right time—a rich leisure class. The middle class consists of mostly business owners and people employed by the university. Most of the other people around Eagleton serve the leisure class, barely keeping their heads above the poverty line.

Wesley lived five blocks from Main Street in the older part of town. His house stood between a boxy white cottage surrounded by a chain-link fence and a tall pastel-purple Victorian. A thin layer of snow covered the brown grass. The skeletal remains of what would probably be raspberries in the spring jutted out of the flower bed by the house.

I fumbled through my purse for the keys Wesley had given me.

"Excuse me. That's Wesley's house."

The voice startled me. A forty-something woman sat in a wheelchair parked on the sidewalk. Soft brown hair created a halo around her squarish face. Her purple overalls matched her purple house. A thick book rested in her lap.

"I'm a friend of Wesley's. He asked me to check on his place." I found the key in my purse and pulled it out.

"Where's he at, anyway?" She maneuvered the wheelchair down the sidewalk and up Wesley's walkway. "He sure has a lot of people checking on his place."

"There've been other people here?"

"They sit across the street in a car for a long time, then come up and try the door or look in a window. Thought it looked a little funny."

"Do you remember what they looked like?" Wesley's conspiracy theory gained a little momentum.

"Young teenagers, early twenties. Different every time." She craned her head toward the street. "There was an older man once.

I don't have much to do but sit and watch the world." She angled the wheelchair sideways before pressing a gloved hand on the brake. "Where's Wesley at, anyway?"

"Out of town."

"Nice guy. He helped me put my tulips in last fall." She leaned forward. "I'm not real good at bending over anymore."

"Wesley does do sweet things like that."

She narrowed her eyes at me. "I know who you are. You're Ruby. The red hair gives you away. He talks about you."

"Good things, I hope."

Her mouth dropped slightly. She readjusted the book in her lap and glanced into the other neighbor's yard.

"I hope he has something nice to say about me." Why did it feel like I was slipping down a steep mountain?

"Oh . . . he does. He does. He likes you. It's just—" She touched her palm to her forehead. "I shouldn't have opened my mouth. He told me things in confidence. He comes over for coffee in the morning. Don't worry. There's nothing between us. I think he just feels sorry for me. I'm alone a lot since the accident."

A heaviness settled into my heart. So Wesley was giving a mixed review to his confidant about me. I was tempted to press her for details but decided I'd had enough disappointment on my plate.

"I really shouldn't have opened my mouth. He likes you. I think the issues are more on his end then on yours . . . his history with women." She eased her chair back a few inches. "Look at me, I've got nothing better to do but gossip and spy on other people."

I shrugged. "Doesn't matter." Of course it mattered. I felt like having a big long cry over the whole thing. I stuck the key in the slot and twisted. "Nice meeting you. Thanks for keeping an eye on the place." Wasn't I just Miss Suzy Perky Pants?

"No problem." She rolled down the walkway.

I pushed the door open and stepped into Wesley's living room. His house was simple on the outside. He'd remodeled the inside in an "I love natural wood" theme. Wood floors, rough pine chair and a couch with leather cushions, and walls paneled in wood.

I wish he'd told me where to find his gun. It didn't look like there was any place in the living room to put a pistol. One small table with no drawers stood by the couch. A Bible rested on the table. A wooden shelf that contained a CD player and CDs was fastened on the wall that led to the kitchen.

I glanced into the kitchen. A sliver of setting sun shone through the window above the sink. Except for a coffee cup in the drying rack, the dishes were done and put away. Wesley's whole place screamed former Marine—clean, orderly, with only the bare minimum of material possessions. I thought of my own room with its week's worth of clothes scattered across the floor. Books, magazines, and Bibles stacked, piled, tossed, and kicked all over the room. I'm a chronic reader and often use it as a way of putting myself to sleep. Photographs and other mementos clutter my dresser.

If we were married, I'd probably make him nuts. We were a mismatch in so many ways.

I decided to forgo checking all the kitchen drawers. His bedroom was a more logical place to put a gun. I sauntered into a room with bare, off-white walls. I could probably bounce quarters on the precisely made bed.

A bedroom is such private territory; I felt a little strange entering

Wesley's. I checked the closet where his uniform hung—no shoulder holster, no gun. Wesley had three dress shirts and two pairs of dress pants. A plain tan bedspread covered his queen-size bed.

Several photographs stood on a large antique dresser. One was of him and Zac on dirt bikes. Wesley looked like he was barely thirteen. He had a picture of me and Mom at a wedding. Mom and I had our arms around each other, heads together.

The wedding had been Brian and Laura's. Over a year ago, Brian had been kidnapped and we'd tromped through the woods looking for him. Now Brian and Laura were married and had a new baby. Everyone seemed to be moving forward in their lives except me. Mom looked pretty—a pink flower comb in her salt-and-pepper hair and a soft smile backlit by sunshine. The other photo was a yellowing picture of a woman. She was standing on the porch of what was now Zac and Julia's house. Her clothing was a seventies pantsuit, and she held a baby in diapers in her arms. An older boy of about ten leaned against her leg.

Zac and Wesley's mother had died when Wesley was in his teens. I picked up the photograph. Fold lines and wrinkles were evident in the picture. It had been scrunched up and flattened back out. I imagined a teenage Wesley crumpling the photo but not being able to bring himself to throw it away. Eventually, it had gone back into its place of respect in the frame.

Two pictures that I would have expected to be on display were absent. He had no photographs of himself in either his policeman's or Marine uniform. He'd chosen two professions that, in addition to requiring uniforms, were very black and white in their regulations and purposes. Wonder what that meant in the psychology rule book?

I opened each drawer of the dresser, moving the clothing care-fully to look for the gun. I made several discoveries. Wesley wore boxers not briefs. There was something reassuring in discovering that he didn't own Sponge Bob underwear or a pink and black heart print. His were all gray, white, and burgundy. Also, he owned a well-worn copy of the *Sonnets of the Portuguese. How do I love you, Wesley? Let me count the ways.* Beside the book was a flat wooden box. I flipped it open. Inside were two Glock magazines—one full, one empty—and three boxes of unopened bullets. Of course, Mr. Safety would keep his ammo separate from his gun. I set the box on top of the dresser and continued my search for the pistol.

In the bottom drawer, I found a ratty old teddy bear and a child's metal John Deere tractor. One of the wheels on the tractor was wobbly, and some of the green paint was scratched off. Next to the toys was an envelope with the word *Ruby* printed in neat, pre-cise letters.

I turned the letter over. It was unsealed. My intention had not been to snoop. He'd asked me to find a gun, and I was looking for his Glock. In the process, I felt like I was getting a virtual tour of the part of Wesley I never saw. I could bring none of this stuff up to him. I put the letter back in the drawer.

I sat down on the bed. Either he stored his Glock on the high shelf in the closet, which would require me getting a chair from the kitchen. Or he put it in the nightstand drawer by the bed.

I opened the drawer. The gun, secured in its shoulder holster, was inside. Mission accomplished. *I should go. Yep, I should be go-ing.* I glanced at the dresser. *Just tootle right out of here.*

I gave a sidelong glance to the drawer that contained the letter addressed to me.

It did have my name on it.

I lifted the shoulder holster out of the nightstand drawer and placed it on the bedspread. I stared at the drawer with the letter in it. Sort of like trying to resist a bag of potato chips after I'd had the first nibble.

With no clear memory of traversing the distance from the bed to the dresser, I opened the bottom drawer and took out the letter—my letter. I stared at my name on the envelope for a long time—touched his handwriting.

After pulling the paper out of the envelope, I unfolded it and read.

Chapter Nine

The letter was dated February 18—two days before we'd gone out to Zac and Julia's to babysit and Wesley had run off. He'd written my name six times on the first line and then penned over it so much he created Braille-like indentations on the backside of the paper. The second line began in his precise, slanted script:

I am not sure why I am writing this. I don't know why I can't just come out and say these things to you. I want to tell you how much these last few months have meant to me. I have gotten to know you better than I have gotten to know any woman. That's not saying much. Ruby, from the time I was fifteen, girls threw themselves at me. I slept with them because they made it so easy. I'm not blaming them. I should have said no. After I slept with them, they started putting these expectations on me like we were going to do stuff together. In their minds, sex was supposed to seal the deal in our relationship.

A woman gives her heart to the man she sleeps with. It's different for guys.

Sometimes I would try being the boyfriend for a while because I thought that would make it right. Even now, I can see you tighten up your face if I were to tell you this. I know I was a sleazebag. I am the first to admit it. Not a day goes by I don't regret the way I lived. The regret eats at my gut.

You didn't know any better; I understand why you made

the choices you did. But Ruby, I grew up in a Christian family, and I still messed up. I had a million excuses, Mom dying, feeling like I was in my perfect brother's shadow, Dad being so old when I was born.

The truth is, those women I was with disgusted me. Weird how desire turns to disgust when you step outside God's boundaries. When I looked at them, it reminded me of my sin. I know that now. I didn't know it then. That's why I pushed them away. That's where the disgust came from.

When I look at you, it reminds me that I am capable of obedience. We are good together. Sometimes when I am bummed, I close my eyes and think about that day we went out into the far north field to feed Zac's herd. It cheers me up.

I open my mouth to say these things, but when I see that look of hope on your face, I crumble. Maybe I can say it this weekend. This letter is practice for me saying how I feel.

I know that there were expectations on both our parts about these last few months. We both want more than just a friendship. I know that you want to be married. Sometimes, I think I want to move forward. But then I think I'll just mess things up. That seems to be my gift.

I get to thinking it might just be better for me to stay single and work on being the best cop I can be. Work on making sure my nephew Jason and other kids don't make the same mistakes I did. When I am working patrol, I feel like I hit a groove and I am where I am supposed to be, where God wants me to be. Enforcing the law is all so clear. It makes perfect sense.

Caring about you, being with you is confusing.

When I am away from you, I crave being with you, think about you all the time. When I am with you, I see you look at me like you think I'm an okay kind of guy, and I am afraid.

I'm not dumb. I know that this weekend at Zac and Julia's is a test, Ruby. You will be watching me to see how I do with kids. In a way, it's kind of cute.

I don't want to hurt you. If we started working toward marriage, I fear disappointing you. I'll probably just mess up again. I knew better. I grew up in a Christian home, and I still messed up. Before you, I never had anything resembling a relationship with a woman. Uncommitted sex doesn't count. Maybe I should just tell you that you are wasting your time so it would free you to meet someone else. Am I being cruel by allowing you to hope? I know you didn't invest this time to stay friends forever. I think that, and then I think about how much I miss you when we are apart. Does this make any sense at all?

Wesley

The last paragraph I read through wet eyes. With my heart aching, I folded the letter and sat on the edge of the bed. Wesley hadn't brought the letter with him to Zac's. He hadn't intended for me to see it. I had violated a trust, and now I would have to bear the burden of knowing this about him without ever bringing it up. Wesley had two sets of standards: one for people who grew up in Christian homes and one for people who didn't. Apparently, if you grew up in a Christian home, you were supposed to be perfect.

I slipped the letter back into the envelope and placed it next to the toys in the same position I'd found it. I needed to keep my word and get his gun to him. Now I understood why he worked so obsessively at his job. My weekend test with the kids scared him, and he retreated to his work. Saying that regret ate at his gut meant he hadn't gotten the memo on that whole grace thing. His work was clear cut; it made sense to him. I confused him. Too, it seemed like working so hard was a sort of penance for the past. He was a good cop, and he could do good as a cop. So what was I supposed to do? Help him with his work, or scream "quit that" a thousand times?

I grabbed the gun, the magazines, and a box of bullets. I flung the holster over my shoulder and put the magazines and ammo in my coat pockets. I placed the wooden box where I'd found it and skedaddled out of the house, making sure to lock the door behind me. I'd keep my word and get this gun to Wesley. The whole thing with Lance Kinkaid had sparked my curiosity. But after that, Wesley was on his own.

No suspicious-looking vehicles were parked on the street as I walked over to my Valiant. The sky had gotten even darker.

After shoving the gun and its holster in the jockey box of the Valiant, I checked to see that I had Wesley's cell. He hadn't said how long it would be before he called. Probably best to leave the gun in the car so I could get it to him quickly. I called Mom and left a message saying I wouldn't be home for dinner but that Georgia had promised to drop Nathan off. I spared Mom the details of my plan to find out about Lance Kinkaid, simply saying that I had some business to take care of around Fontana.

I drove through the residential streets and turned on to N. 15th, driving past banks and box stores, past houses that had been converted into attorney's offices and antique shops. When I drove by Benson's Pet and Feed, the windows were dark and the "Closed" sign was turned on. I stopped at a convenience store at the edge of town to gas up and grab a reasonable facsimile of food for dinner. I wolfed down a hot dog, which settled like a rock in my stomach.

I took the ramp off N. 15th onto the highway that led to the farms and little towns surrounding Eagleton. Stars twinkled above me in the night sky. Yellow lane markers clipped by. Only a cone-shaped view of the highway was visible in the bands of illumination created by my headlights. A few cars passed me headed back into Eagleton. Except for the guy who rode my bumper for twenty miles, no one else was on the road to Fontana and beyond.

I really didn't have a clear plan as to what I was going to do when I got to Lance's house. Probably just talk to him and see if I found out anything that would be helpful to Wesley. I could at least ferret out where he got all the money to build such an obnoxious "look at me" kind of house.

Was finding out more about Lance feeding into Wesley's compulsiveness about work? Maybe. My own curiosity was getting the better of me anyway. My alter-ego, a sort of geriatric Nancy Drew, wanted to know who the real Lance Kinkaid was.

A chilly breeze blew in through the driver-side window of my Valiant. I didn't have the window rolled down by choice; it was jammed again. One of the things Wesley and I had done together was get my car running a little better. Now the engine didn't make a *chug-chug* sound after I got it up to fifty miles an hour. Wesley had done most of the repairs. I'd just handed him the wrong tools and hung out with him while he gave me a hard time about not knowing the difference between an Allen wrench and a Phillips screwdriver. The memory made me smile. Now the window he had fixed was jammed again.

I veered off the highway and onto a frontage road. After taking several turns and driving beyond where the gravel roads had marked names, I approached Lance Kinkaid's house. The yard was well lit. About ten cars were parked outside. Maybe Lance was having a little meeting with his gang of thieves. All the bulldozers were inactive. Piles of dirt covered in a layer of snow surrounded the three-story brick house.

I parked on the side of the road, maybe a quarter mile from his house. If there was something going on, I didn't want to call attention to myself by showing up in a loud car.

I thought for a moment about taking Wesley's Glock but decided against it. I knew how to use a gun, but something about strapping on the police-issue holster intimidated me. It would probably get Wesley in trouble with his department anyway. I decided to just have a look around, maybe take down some license plate numbers. I walked on the gravel road until I got to the Campbell place. The large metal building that stored their equipment, baby stuff, and a Mustang rested on the horizon. A crescent moon shone in the night sky.

I climbed through the barbed-wire fence that ran north-south and made my way across the field. Tall grass brushed against my jeans. Lance had mounted a huge floodlight about ten feet above his front door.

The door of the house opened, and a bundled-up person, maybe a woman, ran out to a car, opened the back door, and crawled in.

When she emerged from the car, she held something in her hand that I couldn't make out from a distance. The woman ran back to the house.

I crawled through a second fence that ran east-west. The place was quiet again. I didn't see any signs of activity outside. A row of saplings with their roots still wrapped in bulbous burlap bags blocked some of my view. Those trees wouldn't make it through the winter. Toward the front of the house, untarped rocks and bricks created half a moat around the mansion. From the looks of it, Lance had some elaborate landscaping plans. All of which would have to wait until spring.

When I got within a hundred yards of the place, I could see that the area around the house had been leveled. Someone had placed roundish flat stones in the entryway. Piles of topsoil and gravel stood on the outer perimeter of the property. The air was still—breezeless and cold. Judging from the visibility of my breath and the tingle on my exposed skin, the temperature hovered around freezing.

Among the dozen or so vehicles parked outside the house, one of the trucks mentioned a real estate company on the driver-side door and another had a reference to organic farms. Other vehicles offered no similar printing that might suggest professions or income levels. Some were beat up, older, and dirty, and others were newer, bearing only the dirt they'd probably accumulated on the drive out. Voices, increasing and decreasing in volume, drifted from an open window. I thought I heard a guitar strumming or a CD playing, but I couldn't be sure. The noise sounded more like a party than people planning their next crime spree. How strange to keep a window open in the dead of winter.

The front door creaked. Voices and laughter increased in volume. I bolted toward the side of the house to avoid being seen. Several people stood in the front yard, talking in muffled tones. Though I couldn't distinguish any words, the ambience of the conversation suggested they were not leaving anytime soon. I'd have to get license plate numbers later.

I circled around to the back of the house. My hand touched the rough brick exterior of the mansion. A Bobcat was parked where the yard had been flattened. A half-circle berm of dirt surrounded the future backyard.

When I tried the back door, it was locked. After taking a step back, I tilted my head up to an open window on the second-floor level. A gauzy red curtain hung in the window. A metal trellis void of vegetation ran past the open window. What was it with Lance and the open windows? It was the middle of winter.

When I glanced down the length of the house, I saw four more trellises. None of them had plant life on them. Lance hadn't been here long enough to allow the ivy to grow. The aging Nancy Drew in my brain goaded me, *Go ahead; climb up and have a look around inside. The people are probably all downstairs.*

I shook my head and whispered, "They just make it way too easy for me, don't they Nanc?" Before Nancy had a chance to answer, I was on the third rung of the trellis. My leather gloves gripped the metal. In the process of stepping up, I stretched the muscle on my injured ankle. A simmering but sharp pain reminded me that it hadn't completely healed.

Heavy-duty steel rings secured the entire trellis into the brick. This trellis wasn't going anywhere unless they took a wrecking ball to the house. I thanked Lance for using such high-quality materials and continued to climb. About ten rungs up, I realized my bulky coat with the magazines and ammo in it impeded me. Hanging by one hand, I slipped out of the coat and let it fall to the ground. With a turtleneck and cardigan on, I was only a little chilled.

I had to readjust my purse, a little tapestry job Mom had sewn up for me. If I'd known I was going to be climbing a trellis, I would have left the purse in my car. If someone stole it, I could probably recover from the loss of the three dollars and forty-two cents I had in it. But Wesley's cell was in the purse, and I didn't want to miss his call.

As I climbed through the window, the wood frame scraped against my stomach, and I had a moment of mental clarity about Wesley. Here I had just vowed not to feed into his workaholism, yet I was anxiously awaiting a call that would basically be all business. Was I reduced to pining for even that level of attention from him? Did I think being supportive of his work would help him give more emotionally? In a lot of ways, Wesley had already made the choice he'd been mulling over in his letter. He was making his job his priority over me. Blah, blah, blah. I just hate pop psychology.

I slipped through the window. My hands touched green tile. Because of the angle of my body—I was in a push-up position with my legs higher than my head—all the blood flowed to my brain. I pulled my legs free of the window frame and rolled over onto my side. I leaned forward to touch my throbbing ankle. The pain wasn't as extreme as when I had first twisted it, but it still hurt.

Glimmering gold spots floated past my eyes. My whole head tingled while my stomach tightened and churned. I blinked several times, but not from the Tilt-A-Whirl my body had just been on. I wasn't sure I was seeing clearly.

The first thing I saw was a life-size model of Charlie Chaplin. Only he was dressed in a white, polyester sequined suit like Elvis wore during the Vegas years. The green in the wallpaper matched the green of the tile; ivy surrounded huge, almost cartoonish roses.

Voices from downstairs came through an open door. I rose to my feet. One entire wall was bookshelves, and another wall contained framed newspaper articles. A shelf by the Charlie Chaplin Elvis displayed a collection of cowboy hats with flashy bands. Vague, expressionless eyes of Styrofoam wig heads stared back at me. When I walked past the pool table in the middle of the room, I noticed that the balls in the triangle were hot pink, bright yellow, and lime green psychedelic patterns.

Curiouser and curiouser, this rabbit hole. I examined the books on the shelf. They were eclectic in nature: coffee table books about celebrities and exotic places to travel, natural health books, theology books, and a section by an author named Martin Grant. Looked like Martin Grant wrote history books. The framed newspaper articles were by him, too. Lance must be a fan.

Usually, I can figure out quite a bit about people by looking at their stuff. But I could get no clear picture about the person who had put this room together. There was an incongruent blend of the flashy and shallow with the intellectual.

A burst of noise from downstairs flooded through the open door. I tiptoed to the door and peeked out. A hallway with a banister bordered the upstairs rooms. The ceiling was thirty-feet high, and secured to it were long, gauzy pieces of material that draped to the first floor. The fabric was not the weirdest thing attached to the ceiling. A swing, like the kind trapeze artists use, hung from a thick wooden beam and hovered about four feet off the floor.

The front door opened, and people filed out. A voluptuous, platinum-haired woman stood at the door, giving people goodbye hugs. I slipped down on my knees and surveyed the hall. Nancy Drew had been right. Everybody must be downstairs. I crawled out and peered through the slats of the banister.

Lance stood behind the kitchen counter, waving at people as they left. The last person exited, and the woman closed the door. She must live here, too. Lance's wife, maybe. But why hadn't Wesley said anything about her? Vehicles started up outside.

Lance wore a red and black plaid jacket and a belt buckle that was visible because it had neon lights flashing around it. His black hair was shiny with styling products, reminiscent of the pictures of Superman I'd seen in comic books.

I peered farther over the banister. Tile on the first floor was arranged in a sunburst pattern. The flooring in the hallway was wood. These people did not like carpet. The platinum blond stepped across the orange and red tiles and mounted the swing. Lance stepped out from behind the counter and flicked a switch on the wall. He crossed his arms and watched the woman as the swing rose to about twenty feet off the ground. With her back to me, she pumped for some time until she got up a good speed. I wasn't surprised when she readjusted herself on the swing and began to do somersaults and twirls around it. I doubted she would notice me while she did her routine. But Lance could easily glance up in my direction, so I slipped back into the room and watched the circus act by peering around the doorway.

The woman positioned herself so she hung upside down with her knees bent over the bar. She swung toward me, coming within two feet of the banister and hallway. I turned away from the fascinating, odd performance and pressed my back against the wall in the fascinating, odd room. The swing continued to creak. I heard a blender running, and at one point, Lance applauded and said, "Good job, Starlight."

Starlight? What a strange name. But given what I'd seen so far, it would be absurd if her name were Jane. I really needed to get out of here. But I couldn't resist one more glance at the strange world down the rabbit hole.

I turned and peered through the open door with one eye still hidden. Starlight stood in the upstairs hallway. She had landed so softly I hadn't even heard a thud. She tilted her head, much like a bird of prey does right before it dive-bombs the mouse.

The rodent, that is, me, smiled up at Starlight. What else could I do? I was caught. Nowhere to run, nowhere to hide. No explanation that made any sense at all. I had trespassed on their private property. That wretched aging Nancy had made me do it.

Starlight placed a hand on her hip and blinked about twenty times.

From my kneeling position on the green tile, she appeared extremely tall.

Her mouth was puffy, like she had overdone it with collagen injections. I watched her bulbous lips part to reveal perfect, bright white teeth. She leaned a little closer to me. "Well . . . hello . . . there," she said, taking a deep breath between each word.

Chapter Ten

Starlight bent even closer, narrowed her eyes, and repeated her greeting. "Well, hello there." Despite her torso being at a forty-five-degree angle, her white blond hair remained in place as if it were carved out of wood rather than grown from actual follicles. *She must use a gallon of hairspray to create a do that stable.* I was impressed.

I braced myself for a well-deserved reading of the riot act and threats of lawsuits and arrest. Instead Starlight responded as if she'd encountered a stray kitten or bird who had wandered into the house, rather than a stranger who'd invaded her home.

I had expected an interrogation about why I, a stranger, thought it was appropriate to come into her house and spy on her. Starlight's kind response made me ashamed that my curiosity caused me so blatantly to disrespect their privacy.

"I came in through the window." I lifted a trembling hand and pointed over my shoulder. "I'm sorry."

"I forgot that was open." She fanned herself. "I don't know if it's menopause or medication, but I get really hot." I detected a slight southern accent. She tilted her head as I cowered on the floor. "Through the window, huh? I thought you were left over from the meeting."

"The meeting?" Was she talking about the group of hoodlums who'd been planning their next raid on the agricultural community?

Starlight straightened and placed her hand on her slender hip.

She wore a pair of black yoga pants and a modestly cut leopard-print leotard. "The church meeting. I thought you were someone who came with someone else, and I just hadn't met you yet." She held out her hand. "I'm Starlight Dawn."

I rose to my feet and shook her hand. Church meeting? Montana was Mecca for off-center, New Age religions. Lance had shown a fondness for hairspray, too. Visions flashed through my head of a bizarre cult where the members were required to wear excessive amounts of hair products. I pictured them lighting incense and chanting before an industrial-size can of mousse.

Starlight looked like a walking ad for plastic surgery. In addition to the puffy lips, the skin on her face was pulled so tight that any expression other than surprise would take substantial effort. And there was no way her bust line was a product of genetics. It was interesting, though, that she had no makeup on. Like Lance, she had no smell—no perfume despite the overdone hair-do.

When I glanced down at her hand in mine, I got an eyeful of clean, unpolished nails, a few brown spots, and thinning skin. Hands are the one body part that will always give away age. Starlight was probably in her late forties, maybe even early fifties.

She held my hand for a long time, gripping it securely. There was nothing fake about her clear blue eyes or her handshake.

"Believe it or not, Starlight is my given name." She let go of my hand. "I always say my mom named me after the hotel I was conceived in. But let's not go there. I think I've worked through the whole mother issue. Dawn is my stage name."

I kept waiting for her to condemn me for coming into her house, but she never did. Starlight just seemed delighted to have someone to talk to. "Stage name? Were you a trapeze artist?"

"Female wrestler. Lance—" she tilted her head toward the downstairs "—was my manager before he became my husband." She turned and leaned over the banister. "Hey, Lance, get up here. I have someone I want you to meet."

Something about Starlight's welcoming demeanor and lack of condemnation gave me the go-ahead to quit cowering. My fear that she was part of some weird cult lessened just a little bit. "Female wrestler. That was my second guess."

Starlight turned toward me and rested her elbows on the banister. "We weren't highbrow like the WWF. I've wrestled in every semi-solid you could imagine, but let's not go there. That was my old life."

Lance came up the stairs, walked with sort of a swaying stride down the hall, and put his arm around his wife.

"Lance, this is—"

"Ruby Taylor." I held my hand out.

"I know you. Out in the Campbells' field the other day. Did you find your friend?"

"Sort of but . . . let's not go there," I said.

"She came in through the window," Starlight said matter-of-factly.

"Oh," said Lance. There was no disdain in his voice either. "Like in the Beatles' song."

"That was the bathroom window, dear." She sang the first few bars of the song. "Ruby came in through the library window."

Is that what that room was, a library?

Lance nodded. "You're right, it was the bathroom window." He turned back down the hallway. "I've been mixing up soy smoothies downstairs. Would you like one?"

My throat constricted in response to the idea of a soy smoothie, and my stomach screamed, *No, no, please, no.* Something about this couple's welcoming eyes made me say yes anyway.

My initial impression of Starlight and Lance were that they were a little off center. But I couldn't picture them organizing raids on surrounding farms or even singing incantations to hairspray. Despite their strangeness, they had this utterly vulnerable and naive quality—like children. The warmth of their personalities didn't match the plasticness of their appearance.

Lance grabbed Starlight's hand as they walked in front of me and down the stairs to the kitchen. She leaned against his arm and turned her head so I saw her profile. Adoration for her husband glistened in her eyes.

The kitchen was decorated like a fifties-style diner. Stools, covered in hot pink leather, lined the counter. Pink gingham curtains surrounded the large window above the sink. I slipped onto one of the stools. A little white Pomeranian rested on a dog bed done up in a pink-checked fabric.

While Lance poured purple sludge from a blender into a milkshake glass, Starlight opened the large metal fridge. "How about some goat cheese and crackers with that?"

Goat cheese? I fought off a gag response.

Lance set the purple sludge in front of me on the counter. "That sounds good, babe."

I stared down at the semi-solid in my glass and wondered if Starlight had ever wrestled in a soy smoothie.

Lance must have noticed my hesitation. "It's made with mixed berries." He spooned globs of stuff out of plastic containers on the counter and tossed them into his blender.

I took a sip of the cool liquid and turned slightly on the stool. The swing and the gauzy material falling from the ceiling were the only things in the center of the living room. A piano and guitar were pushed into the corner of the room along with a bright yellow leather couch. I took another, bigger sip of the smoothie, which wasn't that bad—kind of gritty but sweet.

"We have folding chairs and pillows we bring out for the worship service." Starlight set a wooden serving plate with cheese and crackers neatly arranged on it in front of me.

"Worship service?"

After killing the button on the blender, Lance poured another smoothie into a glass. "Starlight has multiple chemical sensitivity. A church service is filled with perfume and other toxins. So we've been inviting people over to worship the Lord with the understanding that they don't wear anything that might cause an attack." He set the smoothie on the counter.

So much for this being the First Tabernacle of the Holy Hair Product. Starlight and Lance were my brother and sister in Christ. What a delightful gene pool God draws from.

"The MCS makes it hard for me to leave the house." Starlight took a sip of her smoothie and licked the excess off her puffy lips. She ran her finger around the rim of the glass.

Lance stopped wiping down counters long enough to wrap his arm around his wife's waist and give her a kiss on the cheek.

I wondered where they got the scentless hairspray they wore.

Starlight rubbed her husband's chin before addressing me. "I did all this—" she touched her chest and lips "—before I became a Christian. I'm so sorry I can't undo it. I'm sorry I can't bring back the babies I killed." She touched her stomach.

Lance kissed his wife's cheek. "Starlight and I were in to some pretty ugly stuff. If it hadn't been for Charlie the Chameleon, we would've never known that Jesus loved us." He shoved a cracker in his mouth.

I had to ask. "Charlie the Chameleon?"

"He was part of our tour. He's upstairs in the library. The wax figure."

"Oh." I nodded as though everybody kept wax figures of ex-wrestlers in their library. Life down the rabbit hole sure wasn't boring.

Lance took a sip from Starlight's smoothie and continued. "Charlie wasn't his real name, but he had a face like Charlie Chaplin. He would dress up like Elvis or the rhinestone cowboy for the matches. Charlie never preached at us. I just knew there was something different about him; he almost glowed when he walked into a room." Starlight nodded in agreement with Lance's comments. "He was always giving the glory to God any time he won a match."

Starlight picked up the story. "One night, Charlie dressed up like Jacob from the Bible, and he wrestled three brawny angels. Afterwards, some local TV station interviewed him in costume, and he shared the Jacob story and talked about how God had brought him out of an abusive family and alcoholism—"

Lance chimed in to clarify, "We'd driven Charlie to the TV station that night. He had a terrible sense of direction. Always got us lost when it was his turn to drive the tour bus."

"That Charlie couldn't find his way out of a paper bag." Starlight half sniffled and half laughed. "Lance and I gave our hearts to the Lord right then and there, standing offstage next to camera two."

"Right next to camera two," Lance repeated, nodding his head at the memory.

The story had a rehearsed feeling to it—like they'd shared it before. At the same time, it seemed sincere. They didn't know they were suspects for the thefts, and they didn't know I was a Christian. There was no reason for them to fake their beliefs to win favor with me.

We sat for a long time not saying anything, sipping the smoothies. I thought about how someone like Charlie cared enough to go into Lance and Starlight's world when so many others would have dismissed them.

Starlight had boxes of strawberries and apples strewn across her metal countertops. The air smelled vaguely of ripe fruit and sugar. In an effort to keep from tearing up over their story, I changed the subject. "What's with all the fruit?"

"I'm trying to learn how to make jam. I keep messing up." Starlight touched her wooden hair. "My mother never taught me how to cook. I am trying to be more like the woman in Proverbs 31."

My teeth clenched involuntarily. *Her again,* I thought.

Starlight continued, "I'm going to enter that potato recipe contest. Have you heard of it?"

I nodded. "Yes, I've heard of it."

"Lance will have to take my recipe in and answer the judge's questions. I don't know if I can risk being in a crowd like that." She bit one of her fingernails. "Maybe it's better I can't leave the house. Lance says people aren't very friendly anyway. Most of the people who come to our worship service are people who are doing work for us." She pursed her lips and gazed at me. "I don't know what we're supposed to do to make friends."

I tilted the purple sludge back and forth in my glass. How do you explain Montana xenophobia? I chose my words carefully. "People aren't used to outsiders around here." Lance stepped away from the goat cheese. He laced his fingers together, leaning close and listening in earnest. "And then when you indicate that you have lots of money by building big houses and stuff . . ." The words were hard to form. I was staring my own prejudice in the face. Wesley's biggest reason for suspecting Lance was that he was a newcomer. And I'd gone along with his assumptions, never thinking that I might have a Savior in common with rich outsiders. Lance's neon-light belt buckle caught my attention. "You just might want to . . . tone it down a bit."

Both of them nodded.

"Tone it down a bit." Lance repeated. I wasn't sure he fully understood.

"We want to fit in," Starlight grabbed my arm, and her eyes grew round, "to be a part of the community. That's why I am doing the potato recipe." Her face suddenly brightened. "Maybe we could do a recipe together. You could stand by our casserole dish for judging. Lance could film it."

It seemed a strange suggestion, considering I'd only met her twenty minutes ago. Was I the closest thing to a friend for her? Guilt washed over me. I had automatically labeled all the rich newcomers as the enemy. "Maybe."

She let go of my arm. "If you're too busy . . ."

"No, it's not that. It's just that, well, I'm . . . I'm a really bad cook."

"I don't care if I win. It just sounded like fun."

I shrugged. "Okay."

Starlight bounced and squealed. "I'm so glad you dropped in." She giggled. "Or climbed in."

"Me, too, Starlight."

We talked for about an hour more, and I shared that we had a Savior in common. By then the sky had gotten even darker outside. "I do need to get going," I said. "I have an hour's drive back into Eagleton."

"I understand." Starlight grabbed a Post-it from a basket on the counter. "I'll write down our phone number, and we'll start working on recipes. You don't smell like you use lots of perfume. If you can shower before you come by, and don't put deodorant on or anything."

"Sure, okay." I took the Post-it and headed toward the door.

Starlight walked with me. She seemed to be looking for an excuse to keep me here, even if it was only a few seconds more.

I took a piece of paper out of my purse and wrote down my phone number. "We'll figure something out."

She held the paper with my phone number like it was a diamond necklace.

I stepped out into the dark night, closing the door behind me. A billion stars twinkled in the sky. I shivered. The temperature had dropped twenty degrees, and I'd left my coat in the backyard.

All the cars were gone, and only a Lexus and newer-model lime green Volkswagen bug remained.

"Do you need to borrow a coat?" The voice came from high up.

Turning, I tilted my head to the third-story window. Starlight's hair showed up distinctly in the darkness.

My down coat was probably a purple Popsicle by now. "Yes, thank you."

Her head disappeared. Moments later, a shiny object cascaded out of the window. I caught the sequined coat and waved up at Starlight, who had popped her head back out.

"It has a fur lining. It should keep you warm, and the purple will look nice with your red hair."

"Thanks. I'll bring it back."

"Keep it. It's too flashy. I'm trying to tone it down, remember."

"Thanks, really. I mean it."

"I can see most of the countryside from here." She rested her arms on the window frame. Her platinum hair was so distinct in the darkness that it almost glowed. The rest of her face was in shadow.

"We'll work on the recipe together." I slipped into the coat, which felt like a heated down comforter. I couldn't resist touching the sparkly sequins on the sleeve.

"Okay." Starlight waved. "See ya." She slipped back inside. Worship music spilled from the open window. A bluesy version of "Amazing Grace" filled the air as my feet crunched on the gravel of the yet-to-be-landscaped yard. I ran to the back of the house and grabbed my frozen coat.

I drank in the cool, clean air of the country. The music grew dim as I headed straight toward the road instead of sneaking across the Campbells' field. Whatever Lance and Starlight were, they were not criminal masterminds. Wesley's xenophobia had led him to suspect them. I still didn't know where they got the money to build such a big house. A wrestling career that wasn't highbrow like the WWF probably hadn't made them rich. Maybe they'd been intelligent about investments.

The Valiant came into view, parked at a slant with two tires in the ditch and two on the road. I felt downright glamorous in my sequined coat. The thought made me prance a little bit, walk on tiptoe, do a couple of twirls in the middle of the gravel road. Was this how Miss America felt? Did it only take the right clothes to feel pretty? For one moment, I flirted with the idea of applying for the Potato Queen contest. Maybe all you needed to win a pageant was big teeth—I did have that. I shook off the impulse and trotted toward my car.

When I was within twenty feet of the Valiant, my purse rang.

Chapter Eleven

I pulled out Wesley's cell phone from my purse and pressed the button.

"Did you find it?" His voice sputtered.

"No 'Hi, Ruby'?" I said, "'how are you?'"

An audible sigh came across the line.

"Yes, yes, I have your gun." The sound of his voice brought back the memory of his letter. All that private stuff I wasn't supposed to know. "It's late. Can I bring it to you tomorrow?"

"Ruby, I'm holed up in Dad's barn."

"I have to work early in the morning." This was an old coping mechanism. When I'm up against a difficult emotional situation, I run away.

"I need it now." Static distorted his voice. "I need the gun now." His voice warbled. He sounded so far away.

"You're breaking up." I opened the door of my Valiant but didn't get in.

"Just bring it. I'm in Dad's barn behind what used to be his trailer. Please."

"Okay." I relented. Something in his tone indicated desperation. "I'm not far from there."

"When you get close, turn off the lights. Someone might be watching." He must have heard my heavy sigh because he added, "Just 'cause I'm paranoid doesn't mean someone isn't after me." He chuckled nervously.

"Stay put. I'll be there." I clicked *End,* tossed my frozen coat in the car, and slipped behind the wheel of the Valiant. Wesley's secret-agent-man games were a little troubling. I worried that he'd taken up his father's hobby—assuming there was a conspiracy behind everything. Nathan claimed he had evidence that the Mafia controlled the cheese industry. I was really looking forward to the day Wesley informed me that Elvis and Marilyn ran the black-market Chia Pet syndicate.

I started the Valiant and pressed the accelerator. Then again, Wesley's neighbor in the wheelchair had said that someone had been watching his house. Maybe the neighbor was in on the conspiracy. *That's right, Ruby, everybody is in on an elaborate scam to make you nuts.*

As I rumbled down the road, I leaned closer to the windshield and squinted. Except for the glow from distant farms, there was no artificial light out here. The night reminded me of when Wesley and I had spent the day feeding cattle in the far north field. Wesley had made reference to that same day in his letter.

No one passed me. Days-old, hardpack snow on the gravel road made the ride fairly smooth. The drive was giving me way too much time to mull over the contents of Wesley's letter and psychoanalyze him.

I wondered how much of Wesley's issues with women were related to losing his mother. Probably the most disturbing thing in the letter was that Wesley hadn't forgiven himself for his sexual sin and his partying because he'd been raised a Christian. What was this need he had to be perfect? Blah, blah, blah. This was giving me a headache. Why couldn't we just get over it and be together?

I turned onto the winding dirt road that led to Nathan's and snapped the headlights to off. A cloud-shrouded moon and stars provided very little light to navigate by. The Braille method of driving was a little scary. Scratch that. It was a lot scary. I stayed on the road by bumping into the bank on one side and listening for the sound of tires rolling from packed dirt to snowy grass on the other side.

By the time I drove up the final hill, my jaw was tight. Enough thinking about Wesley. Enough playing these silly spy games. Enough driving around in the dark. I wanted a *normal* relationship with him. I was enabling *unnormal* by helping him. He couldn't keep hiding in his work.

I pressed my brakes. Moonlight washed over the black rubble that used to be Nathan's trailer. Behind it stood the gray barn and the corral, now absent of cattle. The forest, dark and foreboding, marked the property line.

My Valiant made a sputtering, spitting sound right before I killed the engine. The Valiant has never run well. The chugging *ping* noises Wesley had fixed were back. If there were people watching in the woods, leaving the headlights off had been futile. The noise my car made would tell them I was here.

After grabbing the holstered Glock out of the jockey box and the magazines and ammo from the pockets of my down coat, I pushed the car door open. My nose wrinkled at the smell of burnt plastic that still hung in the air. I could feel a thousand eyes leering at me from the forest as I skirted around the remains of the trailer. Wesley knew I had an overactive imagination; he didn't need to feed into it with conspiratorial talk.

I treaded across the worn path that led to the barn. Starlight's glitzy coat was surprisingly warm. My footsteps seemed to echo. Not a single branch creaked.

Memories of that day in January we'd spent in the far north

field washed over me as I stared at the nearly dark sky. After feeding cows all day, we'd lumbered across the countryside in his dad's beat-up Chevy. Even though it was early evening, the sun had already set. Wesley stopped the truck in the middle of a field. "Ever see darkest darkness, Ruby?"

"What?"

He killed the engine. "You're used to the city. To always being close to an artificial light source."

We were so far out in the middle of nowhere I couldn't even see fence lines, let alone buildings.

He turned off the headlights. I had a brief, gasping moment of panic. We were in total blackness. No light anywhere.

"Come on," he'd said. Nylon made a slick rustling sound when his hand brushed my coat. His door creaked open.

My muscles were tired from lifting hay bales all day, but I opened the door and stepped outside. Keeping my hand on the truck to orient myself, I followed him to the open tailgate and hopped up beside him.

"This is darkest darkness," he had whispered.

Zac's Angus cows milled around the field, black animals against a dark background of sky and earth. Their hooves pawed and scraped the hardpack ground. A soft breeze carried the scent of manure and hay.

Wesley had slipped off my glove and laced his fingers into mine. I savored the melting sensation his touch had on me.

I leaned closer. It barely mattered if my eyes were opened or closed. Silence surrounded me, threaded around my rib cage. I rested my head on Wesley's shoulder. His proximity gave a sense of safety proportional to the fear created by the vast darkness.

He turned toward me. Warm fingers fluttered on my cheek. I tilted my head. The steadiness of his breathing surrounded me. . . .

"Ruby?" Wesley's voice came in a hoarse whisper. He stood silhouetted in the open doors of Nathan's barn.

"I'm here." My voice sounded faint, far away. The memory of that day and night in the far north field held a power over me that I did not care to admit. The rest of the world sucked back and fell away; his voice drew me as though there were some kind of golden cord connecting us. I cared about this guy. Messed-up mutant that he was, I cared about him.

"Come inside. I've been waiting."

This far from the trailer, the barn's smells—hay and grease—masked any postfire odor. The barn was decorated in early American busted farm equipment. In addition to the rusty Pontiac with the hood missing in the corner, there was a tractor without a seat. Several engines of varying sizes and shapes cluttered the dirt floor. I counted three tool boxes with the lids flung open. Wesley ushered me toward hay bales. A Coleman lantern turned down low rested on the floor beside the hay bales.

I handed him the gun, still cozy in its holster.

"Thanks." Before sitting down, he placed his weapon on the hay bale.

After setting the magazines and box of bullets beside the gun, I pulled his cell out of my purse and handed it to him. "Guess I don't need this anymore." Then I shoved my hands into the plush pockets of my new coat.

"Nice jacket." He gave my glitzy attire the once over and offered me a crooked-mouth grin.

"You look good, too." Shirttails of a Hawaiian shirt stuck out from underneath a winter coat that was two sizes too big for him. Pieces of duct tape accessorized the pea-green down coat. "Are the clothes from Calvin Klein's new bag-lady line?"

He chuckled and combed his fingers through his hair.

When I'd first met Wesley, he had longer, kinky curly hair that he tied back with a piece of leather. He'd cut it short after he sold his roofing business and joined the police force. Now his hair had grown out beyond crew-cut stage. The glittery highlights were more evident. He'd gone back to wearing the wire-rimmed glasses he'd had when I had first met him over a year ago.

He pointed at me. "Just for you, I swung by Zac's and got a shower. These were the only clothes Zac had that came close to fitting me."

"I appreciate that. You look nice in his shirt."

"I smell better, too."

His comment was an invitation for me to come closer, but I planted my feet. I could make all sorts of resolutions where Wesley was concerned; then when I got in his presence, his charm melted my resolve. Christian dating was all about setting standards, or so said all those books I read. What I wanted was a "normal" dating relationship, not sneaking around the forest with firearms. I didn't want to step over the line into the unhealthy zone.

I crossed my arms. "How are Zac and his tribe?"

"Good. Josie asked about you. I think she likes you."

"I like Josie. I'll give Julia a call." The small talk was irritating. A weighty subtext pushed against each casual word.

"They found a replacement trailer for Dad, but I don't want him moving back here just yet. I rooted through the rubble of the fire, and I found accelerant and a crude timing device."

"Cut the copspeak."

"Someone placed a candle underneath a taut string that was connected to a coffee can full of gasoline. Candle burns the string, coffee can falls down, gasoline hits the flame. The only drawback is that the area where the wax melts doesn't burn as fast."

"Why would someone want to harm your dad?"

"They didn't want to harm him. They wanted him to leave. Dad has a very precise schedule. He feeds the cows at a certain time of day, he spends the morning reading, and he goes to the library in Fontana every day after lunch. They waited until he was gone to the library to start the fire."

"So it was someone that knows your dad's routine."

"Everybody around here knows Dad's schedule. I've been watching that Lance guy. He goes to the library quite a bit—even he would know."

"I don't want to talk about this. I brought you your pistol. Please don't ask me to do anymore of this sneaking around in the middle of the night."

His jaw dropped. "I need your help."

"You need to go live at your house and work regular cop shifts. I want to go back to us spending time together and getting to know each other. That was so normal and so healthy."

"Regular hours is not what a police officer's job is. I'm supposed to stop being a cop?"

"Well, no. That's not what I meant. I—" This was such a pickle. His letter had said that when he was on patrol he felt like he was where God wanted him to be. Something here, though, felt a little out of control, like he was overworking a good thing.

"You don't get it, do you? I grew up with these people." He rose to his feet. "Those were Randal Spence's cattle stolen that night. Reslin couldn't follow the trail. We just don't have the manpower. All the evidence is gone." He shook his head. "It's gonna set Randal back financially." He touched his chest with a flat palm. "These crimes feel personal. I'm sure that Lance guy has something to do with it."

"I checked out Lance and met his wife. They're not criminal material."

Wesley kept chattering and pacing like he hadn't heard me at all. "I thought maybe he was storing stolen goods in the Campbells' barn. Campbells' farm and that building aren't really operational anymore. I just haven't been able to catch him." He lifted his head. "He has a wife?"

Someday Wesley and I will actually be on the same planet at the same time. "She doesn't leave the house much." I'd probably been looking at stolen goods the day Mom and I peered in the barn to find Wesley, and they must have been put there after Wesley had parked and taken off on a horse. Lance's proximity to stolen goods didn't make him guilty, though. "I don't think Lance and Starlight could talk locals into robbing for them. They really haven't connected into the community."

"Kinkaid is involved. I just know it. I don't suppose he explained where he got the money to build that house."

"You just want it to be him because he's an outsider." Wesley was acting like the bumbling sheriff in an episode of *Murder, She Wrote.* "Your xenophobia is getting in the way here." He was far from dumb. Did loyalty to his people make him fixate on Lance? "Maybe somebody you grew up with is responsible for all this. Did you ever think about that?"

Wesley's expression, a sort of explosion of his features, suggested that such a thought horrified him.

"I don't think this hiding-out stuff is helpful," I said. "Are you any closer to pinning all this on Lance or whoever is responsible?" I tried not to sound sarcastic. "Why don't you go home?"

His hands balled into fists. "I'm not hiding out. I stay at Zac's. I go back into town and stay with Cree. Someone is watching my house." He stepped toward me. "I need your help. I need your support."

The intensity of his emotion made me take a step back. "You're way too close to this, Wesley. Don't they tell you at cop school to keep your emotions out of your work? Get some other policemen out here, get Cree, turn it over to Reslin. You're losing perspective."

He studied me for a moment before turning and slipping off his coat. He stood with his back to me in that dorky Hawaiian shirt. The baggy, threadbare Levis were charming. "I just thought you could help me." After picking up the holster, he slipped it over his shoulder. "I'm protecting people. I'm doing a good thing here."

He was right; he was a good cop. I did want to be supportive of his work, but this whole thing echoed with tones from past relationships. The nice thing about not dating since I'd become a Christian was that I knew exactly who I was, separate from a guy. I didn't want to lose myself in some pathetic enabling role. I tilted my chin, took a deep breath, and planted my feet. "I have needs, too. I think you're working so much because where our relationship is going scares you." What we were going for here was a normal relationship. *Stick to your standards, girlfriend, stick to your standards.*

He turned and squared his shoulders, preparing for a defensive response. My mind had already begun to whir with brilliant comebacks when his rigid stance collapsed like a deflated balloon. He shook his head and stared at the ground. "People who fight this much shouldn't be together. You don't have to help me if you don't want to." His voice was barely above a whisper. "I just thought we worked well together. I thought you would give me your support."

I opened my mouth, but only a gurgling sound came out. My boots kicked up straw as I stepped toward him. His deep green eyes didn't waver.

He held up a hand, indicating there was nothing to be said. He took a step toward the door.

I knew I needed to say something about his guilt over the past, but I couldn't give away that I'd read his letter. "Wesley, God doesn't even remember all the things you did when you were a teenager. You don't have to earn back his favor by working so hard. I don't care if you aren't perfect."

His forehead wrinkled. My out-of-context comment had made no sense to him. Then he turned away from me. "I thought I was doing good with my work. I thought you would help me." He shook his head. "I've got my Jeep parked up the hill." He paused on the threshold but didn't look back at me. "None of this matters. I've been tromping around here for over a week. It's like they know my move before I make it. I'll stay at Zac's or Cree's until I'm sure they're off my house."

The darkness swallowed him up almost instantly. I stood at the door, listening to his fading footsteps and then the sound of his Jeep starting up.

Stunned, I slumped down on the hay bale, drawing my legs up to my chest and resting my head on my knees.

That was that. If our relationship was this explosive, maybe we shouldn't be together. He was doing exactly what I'd asked him to do. He wasn't going to sneak around the woods anymore. And yet he'd saved the news until after I'd refused to support him in his work. He'd run from my test, and I'd failed his. We were both such fraidy cats, so unable to trust. I had no idea where the line between supportive and enabler was.

Again, I could feel the Proverbs 31 woman breathing down my neck and shaking her head in disapproval. People at the city gate were bragging about her husband. I sat on that hay bale for close to an hour until I started to get cold.

I wandered back to my car in the dark, feeling my way along the dirt path with my feet. After I got into the Valiant and started the engine, I turned on the lights with a deliberate jab. So what if someone saw me. Crossing my arms, I stared at the skeletal remains of Nathan's trailer while my car warmed up. Snow, increasing in volume, drifted and swirled past the windshield. I clicked the push-button shift into reverse and backed out.

The winding road and the methodic turning of the wheel numbed my senses. *People who fight this much shouldn't be together.* I pulled out onto the main gravel road that led to the highway. Dark fields stretched beneath the moonlight. Pinching tightness invaded my neck and shoulders.

The problem was, Wesley was right. Who wanted a lifetime of butting heads with someone? If I put together a résumé applying for the job of wife, the page would be blank. Maybe we were both better for the kingdom as single people. Wesley could pour himself into his work, and I could pour myself into . . . what?

Snow twirled in my headlights, and I leaned forward to see better through the windshield. I had maybe ten or twenty feet of visibility. Windshield wipers swished back and forth, back and forth.

Like a bulb flashing on and off, I saw the deer momentarily. In and out of the headlights. Snow swirling around her. Racing across my field of vision.

A bubble of air caught in my throat.

My foot jerked off the gas. Then the *bang* of impact. Glass and metal crinkling. The car shaking, vibrating. Hands to face. Tires rolling, gravel to grass.

I lost the sense of where I was in space. Was I upside down, or did the car just spin around?

With a thump and a jerk, the car stopped moving. Metal still vibrating. I opened my eyes to a distorted picture of a dark land-scape. My windshield, still in place, was a thousand shattered diamonds. The car faced the road with the hind end in the ditch.

I took in a ragged breath, barely filling lungs that felt like they'd been scraped with fingernails. Long, red, vindictive fingernails.

It wasn't the car that was vibrating. It was me. My limbs spasmed. I had a sense of an uncontrolled trembling at my core, through my torso, and up into my brain. Like my spinal cord was being rattled. Still shaking, I groped for the seatbelt, pushed the door open, and fell out onto the snow.

I staggered to the front of the car. The hood on one side had folded like a fan. Oddly enough, one of the headlights was still working.

I heard noise at my back and turned to see the doe pushing herself to her feet. She straightened her back legs, took a few steps, then crumpled again.

I ran up to the road and stood four feet from her. The animal lifted her nose, struggled to get up. Her legs thrashed, running on air. Finally she stilled, laying her head on the gravel. Her breathing was loud and raspy.

I moved a little closer. She didn't react. I sat beside her on my knees.

"I'm sorry," I said. "I am so sorry."

Her ear twitched. The air was heady with the coppery stench of blood. I slipped my glove off and placed my hand on her middle by her neck. My fingers tangled with her warm fur. She didn't even stir, but I could feel a slight expanding and contracting.

Gusts of cold air hit me. My eyes watered.

The whitetail's chest moved up and down. My face and hand tingled from cold and falling snow. My toes went numb. I kept my hand on her while the expanding and contracting grew less distinct.

Her rib cage stilled.

I held my hand there until it went cold. I doubted I'd be strong enough to move her to the side of the road, but I tried anyway just to give her the dignity of not being run over again and again. My efforts were futile, and the exertion made me want to cry.

I trudged back to my car and felt along the point of impact. The driver's side of the car was crumpled. Metal bent into the wheel well. Even if I got the car started, that tire probably wouldn't turn. I tried anyway because I didn't have any other option. The car didn't even sputter when I turned the key in the ignition. That made me want to cry, too. Now I wished I hadn't given Wesley back his cell. What was I thinking? He already had a phone. Knowing Wesley and his spy games, his shoe was actually his cell.

I laughed at the thought, but it was laughter girded with unbearable desolation.

I got out of the car and did a 180. This was a main road. The drive from Lance and Starlight's place hadn't taken that long. They'd probably be glad to see me and offer me a bed with a blanket made entirely of soy products.

Temperature must have been a little above freezing. The snow had let up. I had hat and gloves and Starlight's warm coat. My ankle wasn't hurting that much.

I crossed my arms and trekked in the general direction of Starlight's place, leaving the lifeless deer behind me on the road.

Chapter Twelve

I don't know how far I walked. I stuck to the main road and with each turn kept thinking I would see something that looked familiar. No such luck. I didn't know the landscape as well as I thought I did, and it was hard to see much of anything in the dark. I'd only driven through this part of the country. Everything looks different when you have to hoof it.

After about two hours, my bum ankle started throbbing. Off to the west, a giant circle beamed like a Christmas tree, something I would never have noticed in daylight. In fact, it was the only light source in my immediate surroundings. I wasn't cold, but my legs were tight, heavy, and screaming for sleep.

Opting for the sure thing rather than the maybe of Starlight's house, I veered off the road and made my way toward the giant sparkling circle. Hopefully, it was a life-form other than cattle—someone with a driver's license or phone would be nice.

I kept my eyes on the beacon and trudged across the hardpack earth, dodging the occasional frozen mud puddle. Though I was able to put weight on it, my ankle hurt. After a couple of turns in the road, silhouettes of Ferris-wheel chairs materialized around the lights. An Airstream trailer rested beneath a yard light. Next to the Ferris wheel was an eight-foot-high wood fence. Old cars, appliances, and twisted pieces of metal bulged over the top of the fence. Shadows behind the Airstream suggested a shack or barn of some sort.

I stopped about a hundred yards from the trailer, wondering if the guy who lived here would be my deliverance, or if he was bald and played the banjo. Sunrise wasn't for at least three or four hours. No way could I be so lucky as to stumble onto the property of an insomniac.

I crossed my arms. What choice did I have? Try and find Starlight's? Trudge back to my car and wait for someone to stop? A light glowed in the trailer. I approached slowly, aware that people who own junkyards this size usually also have guard dogs.

A white, ghostlike cat sauntered out of the shadows and took up her post on a log. Like a gang positioning for a rumble, several more cats emerged from beneath the Airstream. Two cats, one black and one calico, crawled out of a doorless dryer resting by the trailer steps.

Yellow feline eyes assessed the prey in front of them, namely me. I've never been attacked by a herd of cats. But I guess there's a first time for everything.

"I just need a ride into town," I explained to the white cat who was the apparent leader. I pointed behind me. "My car broke down."

The felines, maybe eight of them total, flicked their tails. The white one lifted a paw and licked between its toes.

The door burst open. "Who's out there?" A man whose most prominent accessory was a rifle tromped down the aluminum steps. "What do you want?"

Automatically, my hands went up in the air. "Sir, my car broke down." The man narrowed his eyes. Maybe it was just my sequined jacket that made him squint. Fashion diva that I am. "I'd appreciate a ride into town . . . or if I could at least use your phone."

"Ain't got no phone." The man's defensive posture slackened.

He leaned the rifle against the trailer. I guess I was obviously not a threat to him and his attack cats.

"I know it's an inconvenience, but if you could give me a ride into Fontana where I could call somebody . . ."

The man had short white hair cut close to his head. He wore a new-looking flannel shirt in shades of red and black. His jeans were rolled up at the bottom, creating a seven-inch cuff. The leathery skin, ruddy cheeks, and fingers permanently darkened by grease suggested a life that had been long and hard and spent outside.

He lifted his chin. Again, his milky eyes gave my glitzy coat the once over. "Are you one of those new folks been moving in and building the fancy houses?"

"I'm from Eagleton." The stiffness in his posture did not ease. I glanced around, mentally scrambling for ice-breaker topics. "Nice Ferris wheel. Not everyone has one of those in their yard."

"Worked thirty years repairin' carny rides. Figured it was my due." His shoulders remained squared, eyes steeled, chin up.

"I know the Burgess family. That's why I'm in the Fontana area." My namedropping seemed to help. His jaw relaxed, and he blinked.

"Got no complaint with Nathan Burgess. That kid of his is a little wild. I got four kids myself."

The "kid" he was referring to must be thirty-something Wesley. I guess in an area this rural you sort of get frozen in time. To some people, Wesley would always be the rebellious son. The old man held a rough, callused hand out to me. "Emil Van Kriten." He paused like the name was supposed to cause some kind of reaction in me.

"Name's Ruby Taylor."

Emil squeezed my hand even tighter. "I just put the coffee on. I got a couple hours of work to do out in the yard."

The inflection in his words and the steadiness of his gaze made everything Emil said seem confrontational, even an offer of coffee. In the name of diplomacy and getting a ride into town, I chose to ignore the defensiveness of his tone. "I don't want to keep you from your breakfast."

"Won't be nothing open in town for another three hours, and I'm hungry. You'll have to wait while I get my work done. Might as well come in and have a cup of Joe."

I was at Emil's mercy. He was the one with the transportation. If he wanted to serve me a three-course meal made of sawdust, I had to accept. I followed him into the tiny trailer.

Emil took his place at a miniature stove. Behind him, an open door led to a bathroom. Cupboards rimmed the top of the ceiling. I sat on the bed-couch by the two-foot-wide table.

Emil placed a white coaster on the table. The coaster was made from the Styrofoam plates that meat comes on. "Got family around here?"

I'd hung out with farm people long enough to know that who your father and grandfather were was a way of assessing if you were okay. Fair or unfair, that's the way it was. "Just my mom and me. My grandmother lived in Eagleton for years. Mom and I got the house when she died. Her last name was Thomas."

"Thomas? Don't know any Thomases. Wife's been dead twenty years. All but one of my kids lives close." A moment later, he sat a steaming cup of very black coffee on the coaster. "My second oldest, Ethan, is down in California."

I took a sip of the dark liquid. The stuff was so strong my eyes popped open. I was sure a comment about it growing hair on my chest was forthcoming from Emil.

I sat the cup back down and had a gander at Emil's digs. Several antique photos were pinned to a cupboard. The first photo was of a man on a horse, holding a rifle. A dog perched beside the horse's back legs. A cowboy hat created a shadow across the man's face. The second photo was of the same man sitting in a throne-like chair, glaring at the camera lens. A woman in a Gibson-girl dress rested her arm on the chair. The expression on the woman's face suggested that she hadn't slept for days. Her shoulders drooped, and her gaze was downcast—a weary soul beaten down by life.

Emil broke an egg into a frying pan. "Hungry?"

"I'm good, thanks." I rose from my chair for a closer look at the photographs.

"My great-granddaddy Seb Van Kriten. He homesteaded this valley—one of the first." He stepped away from the stove to point at the photo of the man on the horse. "This one was taken about two weeks before he died." Emil rested his thumbs in his suspenders.

I stepped back and took a sip of the high-octane stuff Emil called coffee. "He doesn't look that old. How'd he die?"

Emil stared at me so long I wondered if I had mud on my face or food in my teeth.

"You don't know?"

I shrugged. The name sounded vaguely familiar.

The old man straightened up, cleared his throat, and then treated me to a history lesson peppered with profanity. Seb Van Kriten had homesteaded in the late 1800s and continued to buy up land for years until his property ran into the thousands of acres. Then one morning, neighbors got Seb out of bed and hung him.

Emil concluded the lesson by saying, "Great-granddaddy could have been a cattle king. I'm the oldest son of an oldest son. All this around here—" he swept his hand in a half circle "—would have been mine. All of it."

Nathan had said that Seb's kids had lost the land due to bad business decisions. Everyone had a different take on that piece of history. "Nobody went to jail for your great-grandfather's murder?"

Emil shook his head. "They could never figure out who done it. Thing about vigilante killing is that nobody talks." His face wrinkled as though he'd just smelled something rancid. "I betcha a dime to a dollar anyone got a chunk of granddaddy's land was involved." He whispered something about "no justice in the world" and returned to his sizzling breakfast.

I finished my coffee while Emil sat down to a plate of runny eggs and black bacon. Emil was one of those loud chewers who almost clanged his teeth together as he ate.

Strong coffee on an empty stomach is a good idea only if you plan on using your legs to leap to the moon. By the time Emil finished his breakfast, my extremities were all buzzy and tingling. I had to clasp my hands together to keep them from vibrating.

Emil tossed his napkin, which looked like it had once been a flannel shirt, on the table. He snapped his suspenders. "I suppose."

I twirled the empty coffee cup. "I do appreciate this."

The old man grunted and then rose to his feet and ambled toward the door. "You stay here. Help yourself to the coffee. Don't go anywhere. I'll get my work done."

Emil left the trailer without another word. From the window of the Airstream, I saw him amble into the junkyard. Emil was a little scary, and I didn't want to get on his bad side, so I resisted the urge to snoop around. I did the one thing I'd been given permission to do: I drank coffee—for two hours.

When Emil opened the door, I jumped. "Let's go."

Outside, a magnificent pink sky haloed the emerging sunrise. The black of evening grayed up. The air was crisp.

Emil grabbed the rifle he'd left leaning against the trailer. "Be just a minute." While he went to put his firearm away, I sat down on the log that had formerly been occupied by the white cat. Patches of snow surrounded the trailer. A muddy wet path led to the junkyard.

I heard a shrill meow and turned back toward the trailer, assuming I'd meet one of the members of the cat gang. A large Siamese raced up to the log. Meowing frantically, the animal rubbed against the log and then my leg. I gathered her into my arms.

As I ran my fingers through her fur, my heart rate increased. Siamese cats look a lot alike, but this one was wearing a hot pink collar, just like the one Georgia had bought Her Majesty. I checked her left ear for a distinctive nick. Her Majesty purred like she was glad to see me. I bent my face close to Georgia's baby. "Now how did you get all the way out here?"

The cat responded with a long meowing explanation that she just knew I'd understand. As I held her, I wondered two things: Did Emil have something to do with Georgia's robbery? And was Georgia's robbery somehow connected to Emil—his bitterness toward the people who killed his great-granddad and, according to Emil, took his land?

Emil slammed the trailer door loud enough to make me jump. The Queen leapt out of my arms but remained close to the log.

"Nice cat." Keeping my voice level, I chose my words carefully. "I have a friend who lost a Siamese cat." Chirpy, cheerful, and oh so casual. That was how I needed to sound.

Emil narrowed his eyes at me. "Truck should start right up." He pointed toward a battered green pickup.

"My friend really misses her cat. It would be neat if I could take her home a replacement, ease the pain of loss and all that."

Emil shifted his weight from foot to foot, then laced his hands together over his large stomach. I hadn't noticed the cold sore by his lips until now.

"You have so many cats," I said. "It would really help my friend." My heart thudded away, but I kept my voice calm.

Emil's stare peeled my skin off. "I like my cats. I like 'em all. Keep down the mice."

"Maybe the former owner has more Siamese like this . . . maybe you could have one of those instead." I needed to play this one close to my chest. This guy was my ride into town; I didn't want to let on that I suspected him of stealing one cat and maybe more. "Where did you say you got this one?"

"She just wandered onto my property." He averted his gaze. "Don't rightly know where she came from."

"She has a collar. She must have belonged to somebody."

"I bought that for her," he snapped.

The two other visible cats, one on the busted dryer and the other by steps, didn't have collars. Why buy a collar for one cat and not the others?

"She was mangy and half starved when she showed up here." Emil tromped toward his truck, leaving muddy boot prints in the crunchy snow.

That was a lie. Georgia fed Her Majesty like . . . well, like a queen. I suppose it was plausible that the thieves had dumped the cat and she'd wandered onto Emil's property. And maybe she would have been pretty starved by the time she'd shown up here, depending on how far she had to walk. But he'd lied about the collar, which made me suspect that the rest of the story wasn't true. At the very least, Emil was a cat thief. At most, he was somehow linked to Georgia's robbery, which maybe linked the robberies around Fontana to Georgia's.

All the cats looked well-fed. So I wasn't worried about the queen's health. It was Georgia's mental health that concerned me.

Her Majesty trailed behind me as I followed Emil through the mud and melting snow. I turned and scooped her up. For Georgia's sake, I had to get this cat back.

She wiggled free of my grasp, landed on the snow, and sat back on her haunches.

The cat was still staring at us when we pulled away from the property. I touched the truck window. *Hang on, Her Majesty, I'm coming back for you.*

Chapter Thirteen

On the drive to Fontana, I talked a mile a minute about absolutely nothing—partly because of all the strong coffee and partly because I was eighty percent sure I was sitting next to a thief. The idea made me more nervous than the strong coffee pumping through my veins.

By the time Emil pulled up to the Fontana Public Library, he had a full course description of every class I'd taken in college for both my grad and undergrad work. Since I didn't want to divulge too much personal information to the likes of him, I figured that topic was the safest.

Emil didn't turn off the truck engine. "Library or café should be open by now. If it ain't, I'm sure it will be shortly."

"Thank you. I really appreciate it." *You big, fat, cat-thievin' liar.* I gave him a smile that would have made Miss America hold onto her crown in fear of losing it to me. "You saved my life." I shut the door and waved demurely.

Emil had already pulled out and roared down the empty street before I even stepped up onto the sidewalk. My brain cooked with ideas of how I was going to get that cat back. I hadn't seen any other Siamese around Emil's property. So if I took her, I would have to arrange for a replacement cat. I hoped, though, it wouldn't come to that, and the law would help me get her back.

Behind me, the librarian flipped the sign on the door from "Closed" to "Open." All the other business establishments were still dark. I made my way up the concrete steps. It occurred to me that it would be nice to have some help from Wesley getting the cat back. Then it occurred to me that I didn't really want to talk to Wesley. Then as I opened the door to the library, I thought maybe I'd be better off just asking Reslin to help me.

Inside, I exchanged pleasantries with the fiftyish blond librarian, whose name was Daelynne. I found out it would be another hour before the café or the car tow place was open. Daelynne acknowledged that she'd seen me with Wesley. There are no secrets in a small town. I name-dropped Starlight and Lance because they were the only other two people I knew from the Fontana area, besides Julia and Zac. Daelynne said she knew Lance; he came into the library to do research. He must research what soy product to feed Starlight.

While I chatted, a hollow feeling threaded through my gut. I really missed Wesley. Honestly, a girl could get whiplash from these zigzagging emotions.

I phoned my mom, who very sleepily informed me she'd be out as soon as she woke up and got ready. Then I sat down and wrote dearest Wesley another letter I'd probably never send him. I had to expel all the emotion whirling inside me. I borrowed paper and pen from Daelynne and found a table back behind the shelves. Sunlight streamed through a dusty window as I started writing.

Dear Wesley,

You make me nuts. I miss you. I'm mad at you. I keep thinking of things I want to tell you. Some of it is about your work. After I whined and complained about your work. Isn't that funny? I found Georgia's cat at Emil's, which kind of links her robbery to the Fontana area. I don't know what

Emil's involvement in all this is. I have a hard time imagining him organizing anything more complicated than a Go Fish game. I know you and Cree think Georgia's robbery is separate, but I think not. The driving force in Emil's life seems to be that his great-grandfather was hung. I don't know what all this means. I just know I have to get that cat back before Georgia needs to be treated for depression.

The other things I want to tell you are about my heart. I know you don't want to talk to me anymore. I know you are tired of fighting. I'll respect that, and I have no intention of groveling, but it doesn't make my feelings go away. When I write these letters, it's almost like I can see you, hear your voice, smell that soapy-clean smell you exude when you don't live in the woods for days on end. Maybe this is my way of holding onto you, and maybe it's my way of letting go. Nothing is ever clear with you, is it?

What is it with us? We just start getting close, and one of us pushes away. You with your work; me with my arguing. Aren't people supposed to try to work through why they fight, anyway? My teeth are clenched right now. My life really is more peaceful without you, but it's also less full.

Honestly, you make me feel like I am sixteen again, totally unable to sort out or understand my own feelings. I just don't want to repeat the mistakes of the past. It's not just about jumping into bed; there is a whole pattern of behavior that needs to be avoided. That's what scares me. What scares you? Wesley, I—

I lifted the pen from the paper. I couldn't finish the letter. What was the point? When I had first become a Christian, I saw it as a second chance. I had allowed myself to become hopeful again that I'd find a good guy and we'd have a tribe of our own. That I could lay the woman in Proverbs 31 to rest. Now I might never be considering fields and buying them. No one was going to compare me to a merchant ship. Where did that leave me in the Christian equation for happiness?

I folded the unfinished letter and slipped it into my purse. I got up and wandered around, trying to shake my discontent.

The library was in a beautiful old brick building that had probably been built when the town was founded at the turn of the century. It had concrete sweeping stairs that rounded outward at the bottom. Inside the large single room, the wooden floor was stained dark, the walls had a fresh coat of bright yellow paint, and the whole place had that wonderful old-book smell. I counted eight rows of double-sided bookshelves. On the other side of the library, two closed doors took up most of the far wall. One of them had a sign on it that said "Future Home of the Fontana Heritage Room."

Incandescent bulbs covered with antique glass provided most of the lighting. Besides three dusty windows, the only other light source was two standing lamps positioned by worn leather chairs. Right next to the leather chairs, stood a table with a placard that said "Daelynne's Picks." Most of her picks were paperback romances where the guy had no shirt on and the woman was in danger of being arrested for indecent exposure. In addition to her novel picks, Daelynne displayed three non-fiction selections that all could have been subtitled "Why Ain't I Got Myself a Man Yet?"

I spent a little time browsing through the self-help books. The first one told me I was a good woman who just chose bad men. The blurb on the back of the second volume suggested that all men were entirely to blame for women not having lasting relationships, and what women needed to do was form support groups with other bitter, rejected women so they could gripe about the shortcomings of men. The third one told me medication might help.

Daelynne swept past me with an armload of books. "Those are for checkout now, honey. Be glad to set you up with a library card."

"Thanks, but I need to find Sheriff Reslin. He lives in Fontana, doesn't he?"

"Sheriff Reslin is my son. I'm so proud of him." Daelynne had a habit of bouncing while she talked. "He was in the military before he came back home to get elected sheriff for all of Colter County." She all but glowed. "I raised him by myself. I was a single mom before single moms were in style." She scrunched her brows together, which diminished even more space between her close-set eyes. "Why do you need to talk to Carl?"

Every time I tried to picture Daelynne sitting in a classroom at librarian college, I got a mental block. Maybe the city council, or whoever did the hiring, had waved the requirements for her. I opted not to burden her with the heady details surrounding my suspicions of Emil, cat thief aficionado. "Just a private matter that I need him to look into."

"He usually eats at the café with my grandson, Hayden, before he goes to his office in Eagleton."

"Thanks."

Daelynne blinked about forty times before hauling the books

to their respective shelves. Flipped-out blond hair bobbed against her neck as she bounced across the floor.

While Daelynne hummed and reshelved, I slipped outside. Fatigue made my muscles heavy. I collapsed for a moment on the library steps. I hadn't slept since my nap before getting Wesley's gun. I'd told Mom to meet me at the only café in Fontana. It took a good hour to drive from Eagleton.

The business part of Fontana was about seven blocks long. Most of the buildings were older brick structures, some with ornate facades. From where I sat, I could see a hardware store, a grocery store, a dry goods store, a second-hand store, and a drug store. On the corner was a bar called the Mint. I think there is some sort of federal law that every small town in Montana has to have a bar called the Mint or the Oasis.

Most of the businesses were still closed. The sign at the entrance of town said that the population was five thousand, ten times smaller than Eagleton. I wondered how much bigger the population got when the Potato Festival happened. The festival must draw in most of the surrounding agricultural community. And I knew a lot of sophisticated city people from Eagleton who thought the festival was a quaint little bit of Americana.

On a diagonal from me across the street was the used-car/farm-equipment dealership. The sign outside the office said "Vern's Used Cars." A man with reddish-blond bouffant hair, white shoes, and a white belt visible through his unbuttoned camel coat stepped outside. He placed pieces of poster board with the prices marked on them in the windshields of cars.

That was probably the guy who could tow my Valiant. I rose to my tired feet.

I was midway across the street when a gust of wind swirled through town. The man at the car dealership leaned over to pick up his bouffant hair, which had disconnected from his head and fallen to the ground. A second push of wind followed close on the heels of the first, and I got to watch the man chase his hairpiece across the entire used-car parking lot until it stopped underneath a SAAB with a dented door.

The man grabbed his hairpiece, shook the dust out, and placed it back on his head. At no time did he look around to see if anyone was watching. I stepped onto the sidewalk and strode past the dark windows of the dry goods store. The man, who I assumed was Vern, polished the hood of an older-model blue van. Vern had a corner lot with maybe ten or twelve cars parked outside along with two newer-model John Deere tractors. Vern's prices on cars looked pretty reasonable. Hopefully, my Valiant could be fixed, and I wouldn't be shopping at Vern's for a new used car.

Vern turned his head and grinned at me. His hairpiece was crooked, and sand particles dripped from it. The little bit of hair Vern had left was a perfect match for the reddish blond toupee. Even if Vern had been completely bald, I would've been able to tell he was an authentic redhead by the freckles that populated his face. He also had the red cheeks that often went with being sun sensitive. I have red hair—somewhere on the red scale between Irish setter and forest fire. We were members of the same club. He'd probably been called "carrot top" in school, too. Because we were in the same club and because Vern seemed oblivious to how silly his hairpiece looked, I decided to let him know before customers showed up and he started losing sales. A little embarrassment from me would save him the larger humiliation of being the butt of jokes and made-up songs in the Fontana schools and bars for years to come.

"Are you Vern?"

"That's right, Vern Mackafferty." After wiping his hands on his polishing rag, Vern strode over to me. He never stopped smiling. And it was a high-wattage smile, big wide mouth, lots of white, polished teeth. "Well, howdy there. Can I help you?"

"Actually, umm . . . your umm . . ." I pointed to my own head, then mimed straightening a toupee.

"Oh yes, yes." Vern nodded and chuckled. He used the side-view mirror of a Dodge truck that was close to him to straighten his artificial hair. He stood up straight and looked at me. "Better?"

I nodded my approval and gave him the thumbs up.

"Are you in the line for a vehicle, miss? I've gotten some really nice models in this week."

I couldn't believe it. Vern was going to try to sell me a car. He hadn't blushed at all when I informed him of his hair faux pas. Vern was one of those rare people who were incapable of embarrassment.

"Actually, do you tow cars? My car, a Valiant . . . I hit a deer out by Emil Van Kriten's place."

Vern just kept on grinning. "Sure, sure, we can go out and have a look at 'er." He readjusted his hair like most men would adjust a baseball hat.

I gave him my phone number. "I better get going. Nice to have met you."

"Nice to have met you, miss." Vern grabbed my hand and shook it. He had one of those contagious smiles. I couldn't help smiling back—even laughing. His salesman personality wasn't something he had to put on every morning; it was who he was. If we were at a potluck, he would probably try to sell me on eating someone else's potato salad. "If we can't get that Valiant up and running, I got some beauties. Reasonable prices."

"Thanks, Vern. I have to go find the sheriff."

Vern pointed toward the café. "He usually eats breakfast with his son, Hayden, before he leaves for work." Vern polished the hood of a Volkswagen bug. "Reslin's a good fella. He was real helpful when I had my break-in."

Vern probably had something nice to say about everyone. "Thanks, Vern. I'll give you a call about the Valiant."

"That's all right. We'll get 'er taken care of."

I left Vern to his polishing and headed up the sidewalk.

When I entered the café, Sheriff Reslin and the teenager whom I'd seen at Nathan's fire were the only patrons. The kid must be Hayden.

The place had polished wood floors, five tables pushed against two walls, and a counter with worn stools. The chandelier hanging from an ornate ceiling contrasted with the earth-tone curtains hung in dusty windows. The place had probably been quite elegant in its heyday.

Reslin leaned a shoulder against the wall, playing a handheld game while his son propped an elbow on the table and rested his chin in his palm. Two plates with only the orange peel garnish left on them rested on the table. The kid was built the exact opposite of his father. An oversized T-shirt and baggy pants made him look even more waiflike.

I walked over to them.

"Yep." Reslin didn't look up from the game.

"I don't know if you remember me. I met you at Nathan's fire." I spoke of it like it was a social event. I waited for him to react, to acknowledge that he remembered me. He didn't. "I want to report a theft."

He continued to push the buttons on the game, but his mustache twitched. "Theft?"

"Of a cat." Now that sounded stupid. "My boss—the owner of Benson's Pet and Feed—had some vaccine and muck boots and horse clippers stolen awhile ago. The thieves also took her cat. Emil Van Kriten now has the cat."

Finally, Reslin set the game down on the table. "So you think that old man took your vaccine and clippers?" He crossed his muscular arms. "Did you actually see the vaccine on the premises, and can you identify it as your vaccine?" He tightened his lips like he was trying to stifle a snigger.

Hayden, whose fuzzy brown hair stuck out at all angles, looked at me like I was from another planet.

"I didn't say he had the vaccine." Okay, so the whole thing sounded silly. "I just want to get my friend's cat back."

He held up his hand as if to calm me. "I'll go up and have a talk with Emil." He took a final gulp of coffee.

"Don't you want me to fill out a report or something?" I suddenly missed Wesley even more on a professional level. He would have sympathy for someone who'd lost a cat, even if it sounded silly.

Reslin rose to his feet, touched his waistband on his Levis, and adjusted his belt buckle. "You want to do paperwork on a stolen cat? Is this like a prize show cat or something?" Maybe it was just his brawniness, but Reslin had a way of seeming to tower over me even though I was taller.

Okay, so the whole thing seemed a little trivial to involve the police. Reslin didn't need to point that out—and take so much pleasure in it. "You know what? Never mind."

"I can go up and have a talk with Emil."

Reslin's son grabbed the handheld game and pushed buttons. I couldn't help but notice that Hayden was smirking, too. Beeping noises filled the empty café.

"Don't go taking the law into your own hands." Reslin twisted one end of his handlebar mustache. "I'll talk to Emil Van Kriten."

Somehow, I doubted he was going to do anything. "Never mind. It's just a cat." I stomped across the wood floor.

When I got outside, Mom had parked her Caddy and was shoving coins into the parking meter. The wind made her silky navy pantsuit ripple on her small frame. She tilted her head and smiled at me.

"Thanks for coming."

"No problem, dear. I dropped Nathan off at Georgia's store. They seem to be getting along quite well. Nathan is a sweet man. He's welcome to stay at the house as long as he needs to. But he talks incessantly about how the Mafia controls the cheese industry. You can only listen to that for so long without wanting to argue with him."

"Guess I should have warned you." I wrapped my arm across her back and squeezed her shoulder.

Mom adjusted her big purse. "Georgia said she'd work the day for you if you need time to get your car into town."

"I made arrangements to have it towed to Fontana. I think I'll be lucky to get it that far. I do need sleep, though." Since it was obvious that the law didn't care about Georgia's cat, I needed to come up with a plan of my own to get the Queen back, but I wasn't going to do that on an empty stomach. "Come on, Mom. Let's go have some breakfast."

We walked the twenty paces to the ornately carved wooden door of the café.

Reslin nodded at us as he and Hayden stepped through the doors of the café and headed down the street.

I thought I heard him say something about cats and then laugh. Mom and I stepped inside the café.

Chapter Fourteen

Which do you like better, russet or white?" Starlight held up our choice of potatoes, one in each hand. All around her, the metal and tile of her industrial-strength kitchen gleamed.

Brody, Julia's youngest, sat on the floor, eating food out of the dog dish while the well-groomed Pomeranian cowered in the corner. Brody had that effect on both man and beast.

Because I wasn't sure how this whole "women working together in the kitchen" was supposed to go down, I'd invited reinforcements in the form of Julia and her kids, making sure they showered and didn't put on deodorant when they came. Something about having Julia's tribe around seemed to take the tension out of any situation. I thought the extra company would be nice for Starlight, too. Because of her difficulty in leaving the house, she had a neediness about her that was easier to take if there were more people to absorb it.

Julia sat at the piano with Nellie playing "Peter, Peter, Pumpkin Eater." The two middle boys ran in circles around the living room, their faces and bodies wrapped in the gauzy drapes that descended from the high ceiling.

Josie sat on a hot pink stool, munching the apple pie Starlight had served her and reading the Flannery O'Connor short story collection I'd given her. The entire kitchen smelled faintly of rotting fruit, indicating that Starlight was still performing jam-making experiments.

Despite my best efforts, my mind was not on potatoes—russet

or white. I glanced out Starlight's kitchen window at the graying sky. It had taken me two days, but I'd found a look-alike cat for Her Majesty in a yuppie pet store. The similarity between the two felines ended at appearances. I called the decoy cat Sweetness. No way could I simply give the look-alike to Georgia and claim that it was Her Majesty. Georgia would figure out it wasn't her cat the minute Sweetness laid down for her first eighteen-hour nap. Besides, I kind of missed the Queen, too.

Theorizing that Emil probably went to bed early because he got up early, I'd made the decision to go back and get Her Majesty once it was dark. If I got lucky and caught the Queen in a good mood, she'd simply come when I called her. I could load her up in Mom's Caddy, set Sweetness free, and be out of there in no time. That was the theory.

I leaned on the counter and nibbled a corner of crust off of Josie's pie. "What do the Potato Festival rules say? Do we have to use the kind of potatoes grown around here? Why not something more colorful, like sweet potatoes?"

Josie scooted the pie a little closer to herself, but she smiled up at me. "I like the book," she whispered and then pressed the volume to her chest and closed her eyes. This girl was getting under my skin—in a good way. Anyone who regarded books as treasures could be in my club.

"Oh, that's a great idea." Starlight danced and twirled behind me.

She had a habit of fluttering her hands in front of her when she got excited. The mannerisms gave her a bird-like quality. She was a sparrow flitting from one place to another, never quite resting.

"At least sweet potatoes will make whatever we cook up look pretty," I said.

Starlight placed both hands on her cheeks. "Is a sweet potato really a potato?"

Is a sweet potato really a potato? Thank goodness I had all that education under my belt so I could ponder such deep, philosophical questions. Although my master's degree in literature had taught me how to find endless evidence of misogyny in classic literature, it hadn't taught me anything useful and connected with the real world. So there I was, thirty-one-years old, and I still didn't know if a sweet potato was really a potato. "We'll just mix it up with other potatoes so we won't be disqualified." I was shooting from the hip on this—I had no idea how to make up a recipe.

One of the boys, Alex, jettisoned across the room and landed on the stool beside Josie. He pulled the plate containing the apple pie toward him, wrinkled his nose, and pushed it away. "I want chips."

"We could make chips, Starlight." Inspiration in the form of a child is always helpful. "You know, potato chips."

Starlight made a perfect O with her collagen-enhanced lips. "Yes." She clasped her hands together and bounced. "Yes, yes, that will work. Everyone is going to be doing casseroles and stuff like that. That will make our entry stand out."

Alex furrowed his brow and placed his hand on his hips. "I want chips."

Julia stopped playing the piano and spoke across the large expanse of living room. "What is the magic word, Alex?" Had she actually heard him all the way across the room and above the noise of the piano? It must be a special gift you acquire when you have children—a sort of mommy radar.

The little boy sucked in his lips and hung his head. "Please, I want some chips. Pleeeeeeeeeze."

Starlight trotted across the floor, opened a cupboard, and pulled out a bag of chips. "Lance is such a health nut. I only have these chips when he's not around." She poured them into a crystal serving dish and placed them in front of the boy. "I hide them in my naughty food cupboard." The bowl of chips functioned as a vacuum, sucking all the children, including Brody, who had had his fill of dog food, toward the counter. Julia stopped playing the piano and traipsed across the tile floor.

"We can bake or fry chips out of different kinds of potatoes. Now all we have to do is come up with the spices." Starlight smiled. "I'm so glad you're helping me with this." Her voice was light and airy.

"No problem. It keeps my mom happy." In all my visions of a really good time, devising recipes with another woman had never come up. But if I was honest with myself for ten seconds, doing this wasn't unbearable, and it wasn't just about getting my mom off my back. I was almost having fun.

I've never seen a grown woman, let alone a senior citizen, skip around a room, but when I told my mother I was going to do the recipe contest, that's what she did. So this was a good idea all around.

"Maybe some garlic or other Italian spices." Starlight rooted through her cupboard.

"Spices, huh?" Julia walked up to the counter, brushed a hand over Nellie's blond head, and read the back of the bag of chips. "You sure don't want to put any of these ingredients in. You shouldn't put anything you can't pronounce into the food you make."

Out the window, the sky had turned from a light gray to a

charcoal. I needed to go get that cat. I took a chip and popped it in my mouth. "Where's Lance, anyway?"

"Paprika." Starlight pulled spices from cupboards and lined them up on the counter. "He said something about doing some more research."

"Is the library open at this hour?"

"No, it's not," said Josie without lifting her eyes from the book. "Daelynne opens early and closes early."

Starlight gathered the spices into her arms and carried them over to the counter. "It was open when he left four hours ago. He should be home any minute. If not, he always calls to let me know." She held up an industrial-size container. "How about onion salt?"

Julia picked up Josie's fork and helped herself to a bite of apple pie. "Wouldn't it be neat if you had some that were sweet and some that were spicy?"

"That's a great idea," Starlight almost squealed. "We could throw some apple chips in there. Make them really sugary and sweet—not the dry cardboard ones like Lance gets for me at the health-food store. Lance has me on this really strict diet that's supposed to help with some of my health problems, but honestly, sometimes I think a giant vat of chocolate would make me feel better."

"That could be arranged," I offered.

"Hey," said Julia, "chocolate is the only way I survived when all my kids were babies." She gathered Brody into her arms just before he did a face plant into the apple pie. She redirected his head and, while swiveling on the stool, rubbed her nose against his.

Starlight puckered her lips. "I do miss chocolate."

I appreciated Lance's effort to help his wife, but there were some things men just didn't get. I made a mental note to sneak Starlight some chocolate the next time I came. She could put it in her naughty cupboard right beside the chips.

We spent the next hour eating chips and apple pie and writing down different spice combinations and baking our first experimental batch of sweet and spicy chips. The sky grew even blacker.

I was left in charge of baking when Julia and Starlight went upstairs to see if there were any sequined jackets that fit Julia.

Brody had fallen asleep in the Pomeranian's bed. The little white dog slept outside the bed, lifting its head from time to time to lick Brody's chubby fingers. Nellie and the boys drew pictures with stuff they got out of the bag Julia always had with her. Josie kept reading.

After pulling the cookie sheet of chips out of the oven and placing them on the counter, I shouted up the stairs. "I need to run a quick errand."

"Can I go with you?" Josie asked as she slipped off the stool. The book I had given her lay opened on the counter.

"This is something I . . . kind of have to do by myself."

Her shoulders drooped slightly. "Okay."

Before I could console Josie, Julia leaned over the upstairs banister. "Come up and tell me what you think about these jackets. Help me pick one."

I bolted up the stairs and found the other two women in a room that had closets on three walls. Several sequined jackets and dresses were draped over a pink brocade fainting couch.

"Which one?" Julia held a blue sequined, denim-cut jacket in one hand and a bolero-style, white and pink one in the other.

"The blue one," I said.

"Take them both if you want." Starlight placed her hand on her slender hips. "I'm trying to dress more simply, to fit in with the locals." Her plan to blend in by getting rid of ritzy clothes would backfire if she clothed the whole county in sequins.

Starlight's beige, unfitted dress and chunky loafers did nothing to make her seem less glamorous. She wore no makeup or nail polish. Even with her attempt at drabness, she was bubbly and glowing. Like so many people who become performers, she had the ability to draw attention to herself even when she wasn't trying.

I turned toward the door. "I'll be back in about an hour." *Providing everything goes right with operation cat caper.*

As I stepped out into the hallway, I heard Starlight say, "Lance should have been home by now. Course he stops to visit with almost anyone. He's trying so hard to get to know people. I'm sure he just got busy talking. I hope he met someone nice."

Downstairs, the stool where Josie had been perched was empty. She must have availed herself of the facilities—that's fancy talk for "gone to the potty."

The air outside was below freezing, causing my skin to tingle instantly. With my breath gusting out in puffs, I slipped my gloves on and trudged toward Mom's Caddy.

I drove through silent countryside. The wide tires of the Caddy rolled over the hardpack dirt roads. Sweetness purred in the passenger seat.

Landmarks and hand-painted road signs popped up without warning in the headlights. I navigated almost by instinct, utilizing some odd, inner radar that became keener the more time I spent in this country.

Emil had the lights of his Ferris wheel turned on, so I could see his property from a long ways away. Black windows of the Airstream and an empty spot where the green truck should be came into view. This could be my lucky night. I clicked off the headlights of the Caddy about a hundred yards from his property. The Ferris wheel lights floated in space, a multicolored circle within a multicolored circle.

Several beams of light jumped across the property and through the junkyard. Probably someone riding around on an ATV. Emil had mentioned he had grown kids who still lived in the area. Maybe one had come looking for a car part or something.

I killed the motor and waited for the activity to die down. To pass the time, I stared at the ceiling, counted the grooves in the leather of the passenger seat. Sweetness kept right on purring, not even lifting her head.

Then I opened the jockey box. The two-week-old newspaper with the Potato Festival stories was still in there. I pulled it out to read the front-page story, which was about Vern Mackafferty's used-car dealership being robbed. I clicked on the overhead light. A black-and-white photo showed Vern standing outside the dealership. The thief or thieves had made off with twelve hundred dollars, a Charlie Russell sculpture, and a 1965 Mustang. In the article, Vern stated that he didn't care if the thieves kept the money, but that the sculpture and the car were his most prized possessions, and he didn't know if he would get over their loss. In the photo, Vern looked a little misty eyed.

That day I'd found Wesley's Jeep parked in the field, there had been a Mustang under a cover in the Campbells' storage shed. I wondered if the cars were one and the same.

Next, I flipped through the paper, scanning the feature article by the historian Martin Grant about the 1902 vigilante hanging.

Martin Grant . . . he was the author of a lot of Lance's books. The guy must live around here.

The article was a little different from the version Emil had told me. Emil had made his great-grandfather sound like some kind of put-upon saint. According to the article, Seb had acquired a lot of land through sneaky legal maneuverings and poker games. I flipped through the paper until a name in the letters to the editor caught my eye: Nathan Burgess.

Running the heater on the drive over had made the car hot. I slipped out of my glitzy coat, drew the paper close to my eyes, and read Nathan's letter. Nathan was upset about the increase in traffic on Old Gorman Road. He complained that it was upsetting his cattle and that the sheriff wasn't doing his job. But Nathan's homestead was in a valley. The only way he could observe the traffic on the road would be to climb to the top of the north-facing hill and watch it from there.

Nathan and I had been beside Gorman Bridge when we witnessed the cattle-rustling operation. I really needed to get hold of a map so I could understand why Nathan was bothering to hike up a hill to watch cars go by on Old Gorman Road.

I'd just turned to the information on the Potato Festival when I felt a cold hand on my shoulder.

Chapter Fifteen

A jolt of terror shot through me. My mouth opened to scream, but nothing came out. Then I saw a blond head in my rearview mirror.

"Josie!" I squawked. "What are you doing here?"

"I just wanted to come with you." She leaned forward so her head was very close to mine.

"Your mom will be worried." I pulled the cell I'd borrowed from Mom out of my purse. I wasn't about to be caught out here again without one. "I'll have to call and let her know where you are." I dialed Starlight's number and left a message on the machine. The two women were probably still upstairs.

Josie crawled over the back of the seat, moved the cat aside, and plopped down in the passenger seat. The nylon of her ski jacket made squeaky swishy noises as she got comfortable. The twelve-year-old crossed her arms and grinned at me. "So, what are we doing here? What's this cat for? Is this an adventure?"

"I'm going out to do a cat exchange, and you, young lady, are sitting in the car until I get back." Outside, two sets of bobbing lights emerged from the back of the junkyard and disappeared over the hill.

Josie tightened her arms over her chest, furrowed her forehead, and sucked in her lips. "I'm tired of always having to do little-kid stuff. I always have to take care of my brothers and sister. I never get to do grown-up stuff."

Always and *never.* Teenagers always say things in absolutes. There is never any gray area for them. They always exaggerate. "I'll do grown-up stuff with you. Just not right now. You stay in this car." Josie crossed her arms. "You know I'm good for it. I gave you a grown-up book, didn't I?"

She sucked her lips in and out before relenting. "Okay."

I lifted the sleeping cat off her lap. It looked like the activity had died down. I didn't see any more lights. Josie had uncrossed her arms, but her face was still bunched up in an adolescent scowl. I opened the door of the Caddy and slipped into the evening cold.

Sheriff Reslin's inertia about Emil had caused me to rethink my suspicions. Reslin had grown up around here. He knew what the townspeople were capable of better than I did. The more I thought about it, the harder it was to imagine a bitter, slow-witted man like Emil as part of the stealth team that had taken Her Majesty, let alone planned such thefts. Maybe he'd been telling the truth, and the cat had just wandered onto his land.

Her Majesty liked to sleep in high places so she could look down on everyone, and she liked to be as warm as possible. Sleeping outside was beneath her dignity even if Emil wouldn't let her in the trailer. I guessed that she was either in the shed or had found a place inside one of the cars that Emil stored in his junkyard. I opted to check the shed first.

With Sweetness resting in my arms, I slipped past the dark trailer. Ferris-wheel lights washed over most of Emil's small lot. The air was cold and quiet. The shed leaned to one side. When I pushed against it, the door scraped on the ground.

The inside of the dark shed was ten degrees warmer than outside. I felt along the wall and found a switch. An incandescent bulb hung from the slanted ceiling. Despite the rundown appearance of the shed on the outside, Emil had insulated and laid down straw bales and old coats for the cats. All Emil's cats looked well fed, so I wasn't worried about Sweetness being taken care of. Yellow eyes stared at me from everywhere. Several of the cats lifted themselves lazily off their beds and stretched. In addition to the cat condos, the shed contained an old Willis Jeep.

Faded wooden merry-go-round horses with chipped paint cluttered the dirt floor. There was also a giant teacup and a large metal clown head. How homey.

I walked around the room. One of the cats meowed at me. I looked over at the loft. Sure enough, a set of blue eyes set in a field of black fur glared at me. I put Sweetness down. The mellow feline made herself comfortable in a straw bed beside a one-eared calico. She lifted her chin as if to say, "This looks real cozy, thanks."

"Hello, there," I said.

Her Majesty yowled indignantly. She rose to her feet, stretched, and curled her tail into a tense question mark.

The ladder to the loft wobbled as I climbed. Some of the slats bent to a dangerous degree when I placed my weight on them. I held out a hand to the Queen. "Come here, kitty kitty." Her Majesty swished her question-mark tail side to side. "Boy, is Georgia going to be glad to see you."

The feline strutted over in my direction and rubbed against my hand. She let out that ear-splitting meow characteristic of Siamese. The cat did not stiffen when I gathered her close to my chest. She was purring by the time I glanced down at the dirt-and-straw floor. I needed to use both hands to assure I'd make it down the rickety ladder without breaking bones. "Sorry about this, Your Majesty." I leaned as far as I dared and dropped the cat to the floor. She shook off my dropping her like it was no big deal. The cat sat on her hind legs and watched me climb down the ladder. I wondered for a moment if I had the right cat. Normally when you dropped Her Majesty from any height, she punished you for days. My fears were allayed when she hissed at a tabby cat that came within three feet of her.

I was on the last rung of the ladder when the door scraped open. Josie slipped inside. "There's a bunch of people coming this way toward the property."

"Didn't I tell you to wait in the car?"

She pointed toward the west wall of the shed. "They're coming from there. I can see headlights. Lots of them."

I gathered Her Majesty into my arms. "Guess we better get out of here." I yanked on the door, and the buzz of motors swelled through the open door. The sound was maybe a hundred yards away and growing louder by the second. No way did Emil have that many children coming to look for car parts at this time of night. I closed the door and clicked off the light. "Maybe we'll wait." Her Majesty nuzzled and purred against my turtleneck sweater. I wrapped my free arm around Josie and tried to sound calm. "Let's wait over here." In the corner of the room, beneath the loft, and by the giant tea cup were several hay bales we could hide behind. We only had to roust two cats out of their beds.

Outside, the ATVs whirred and buzzed. The shouts and cursing of men permeated the insulated shed. Headlights flashed across two dirty windows on either side of the door.

Josie leaned against my shoulder. "Who are they?"

"I don't know." I had deja vu of the cattle-rustling operation that Nathan and I had witnessed, and I wondered if this was the same thing. All my suspicions of Emil returned tenfold. What if Emil was the engineer behind all the thefts? Reslin hadn't been reluctant because he knew Emil's character but because he was afraid of Emil.

The Siamese purred in my lap. "You said you wanted to do grown-up things, Josie. It doesn't get much more grown-up than this."

"My fingers are getting cold." She rubbed her hands together. "I left my gloves in the car. I don't have pockets in this coat."

"Find a cat to keep them warm."

"A cat muff." Josie giggled, and I listened to her move straw around. A moment later, I heard a cat purring.

We huddled for a while in the darkness, listening to the symphony of cat-purring and the noise outside. Over and over the sound of the engines faded and increased. Each time I thought they were leaving, a vehicle buzzed by the shed. The Ferris-wheel lights were visible in one half of the window to the right of the door.

"How much longer?" Josie's voice was a thin wisp of sound.

"I don't know, sweetie." I'd left my purse in the car, with mom's cell phone. I had no way to reach Julia and Starlight. I couldn't call Wesley or Sheriff Reslin and have them shut down this whole thing immediately. Judging from the sound of the machines and voices, there had to be at least a dozen men outside. I couldn't overpower them. I couldn't hope to sneak to the car without being caught. I was helpless—not a state I liked to be in.

"My legs are cold." Josie's whisper drifted through darkness. "And they're starting to fall asleep."

I felt for Josie's legs and piled straw around them. "Does that help?"

"A little."

I laughed, a sort of half-winded chortle. "You can always pile another cat on you."

Josie said, "I hope we get to leave soon."

"Me, too." I shivered and fastened the top button on my coat.

"Thanks for being nice and not getting mad at me because I hid in your car," she said.

"No problem." I just hoped I could get her home in one piece before she froze to death . . . or worse.

"You're nice. You'd be a good mom."

"Thanks, I'd like to be a mom someday." Men and machines buzzed by outside. Straw rustled as we readjusted our positions. We sat in silence for a moment. My throat constricted. "I was a mom for about twenty minutes when I was nineteen years old." I swallowed hard, laced and unlaced my fingers. "I had a little girl—I gave her to a mom and dad who really loved her and could take care of her." I hadn't told anyone about my little girl—not even my mom. When I was nineteen, I'd been wild, freed from the foster-care system, angry at my parents, and living from boyfriend to boyfriend. For some reason, Josie seemed like a safe person to talk to.

Josie scooted a little closer to me. "Mom says adoption is cool."

"For my little girl, I think it was the best thing. In some ways, it's hard. I miss her . . . wonder how she's doing. She'd be about your age. Do you suppose she's like you . . . helps take care of her little brothers and sisters, likes to read?"

"Do you want her to be like me?"

"Yes, Josie, I'd like to think she's just like you."

"Maybe you'll see her someday." Josie's shoulder pressed against mine.

"If she wants to find me, she'll find me."

It was odd to be sitting in piles of straw with the cold seeping through our clothing—it was odd that in the freezing cold, warmth and understanding washed over and through me. I might never know my own little girl—and probably, she'd be better off and happier if that were the case. I didn't need to disrupt her happy life for my "closure."

"Does anyone know about your baby?"

"Nobody in the life I have now." I decided then that I needed to keep it that way. Telling Mom would only further break her fractured heart. She didn't need to know she'd been denied a grandchild because of my bad choices. Maybe someday, if I ever found a husband, I'd have to tell him. Some secrets, though, need to remain secrets. "It'll be our secret, okay? Nobody else will know."

"Okay." The idea seemed to delight the preteen. "Our secret." In the dim light, Josie held up her hand. All the fingers but the smallest one folded down. "Pinky promise."

"Pinky promise." Our little fingers laced together.

The door swung open. My heart revved up to four-four time. Someone flicked on the light. Josie and I crouched a little lower and pressed against the back wall. Part of my view was blocked by the Willis Jeep, but I could hear voices.

"Put 'em over there. We'll get them later." The voice belonged to a man of middle age.

Someone brought in boxes of stuff I couldn't identify. An expensive-looking saw, and muck boots just like the ones stolen from Georgia's place were brought in and placed in a corner by the door. The boots and saw still had the price tags on them. The other man had his back to me. His full-length leather coat nearly touched the dirt floor. Long brown hair fell past his shoulders.

When he turned around, his belt buckle was visible through the open coat. My chest tightened as all the air left my lungs. What are the chances of two guys around here owning the same flashing-neon belt buckle? Whoever the guy was in the leather coat, he had Lance Kinkaid's buckle.

All sorts of scary scenarios raced through my overactive imagination. *Put the brakes on, Ruby.* Lance was probably back home mixing up cardboard tofu shakes for Starlight. The thieves had probably stolen from Lance just like they had robbed everyone else around here.

Josie's petite, cold hand found mine in the dark. Both cats had stopped purring.

The two men were in the shed for maybe two minutes. The light went out, and the door scraped shut.

"I want to go home," Josie whispered in my ear. Her fingers dug into my shoulder.

The racket continued outside. I heard cars starting up and an engine noise that probably belonged to a truck.

We waited for another twenty minutes, Josie resting her head against my shoulder. I scooted more straw around us, and Her Majesty dug her claws into my thigh every time I moved.

Outside, men shouted at each other. More motorized vehicles raced past the shed. At last the mechanical buzz of the vehicles dimmed. The voices stopped.

The lack of cat purring augmented the silence. Josie breathed deeply, and her head warmed my shoulder. Her hand clamped around my upper arm.

Another twenty minutes—time for my legs to go numb—must have passed.

"Josie, I think they are gone," I whispered.

She stirred, lifting her head off my shoulder and releasing her grip.

I scooted away from her. When I stood up on my knees, Her Majesty yowled. I crawled out from behind the hay bale and stumbled toward the light switch.

"Let's get out of here, kid."

Josie was already on her feet. I scooped up Her Majesty, who stiffened beneath my touch. Lovey dovey time was over for the Queen; she was back to her old crabby self. I sure hoped Georgia appreciated what I'd gone through to get her cat back.

The tags on the stolen stuff said they were from Fontana Ranch Supply. Among the piles of stuff were a football trophy and a framed, black-and-white photo of a man standing with Frank Sinatra. A mixture of stuff with obvious monetary value and personal stuff, just like with Georgia, just like with Vern.

The sky was still dark when we stepped outside. Emil's Ferris wheel glowed like a Christmas tree. Holding the cat in both hands, I treaded down the hard-pack dirt path. Josie held onto my coat. Emil's trailer was still dark, and his truck was still gone. His yard light must come on automatically. I stared across the field to where I'd parked the Caddy. A big blank space stared back at me. The Caddy, Mom's Caddy, was gone. I'd just become a statistical anomaly. I'd lost two cars in less than a week.

Her Majesty squirmed in my arms.

"Where did the car go?"

"Think they stole it, Josie." My breath was visible in the chilly air. "These guys would steal the proceeds from Girl Scout cookies if they had a chance."

Far as I could tell, Emil hadn't been here. Emil was bitter and ill mannered, and it took people skills to manipulate folks to steal for you. Maybe the thieves knew Emil was gone tonight. They'd used the Campbells' shed to store Vern's car; maybe that's how they remained undetected—by storing the stolen stuff in different places. Was Emil involved or not? I just didn't know what to think.

"My hands are cold. I don't have pockets in this coat."

"I know, Josie. You told me that. I'm thinking." Still holding the squirming cat, I turned 180 degrees to the junkyard. We didn't have time or enough heat energy to walk out to the road and hope to catch a ride. I needed to get in touch with some form of law enforcement before the thieves came back and hauled all the evidence away. Julia was probably tearing her hair with worry over Josie. "Come on, maybe there's something in there that runs." *And has keys,* came the afterthought.

Once inside the high fence, we found two Volkswagen Beetles stacked on top of each other and a 1965 Mustang in mint condition—the same Mustang I'd seen in the Campbells' equipment storage shed and in the newspaper article. This had to be Vern's baby.

While Her Majesty made herself comfortable on the leather interior of the backseat, I rooted around for a key. I found it under the driver-side floor mat.

Because the car belonged to Vern, I didn't feel so bad about taking it. Things were not looking good for the home team. Emil sure had lots of stolen stuff on his property, from Georgia's place, Vern's car dealership, and now Fontana Ranch supply. The thieves weren't limiting themselves to stealing stuff off of farms.

I slid the key into the slot, and the Mustang hummed to life. I'd gotten so used to the roaring sputter of my Valiant that such a smooth start was a welcome change. It was nice to drive a healthy car instead of one that sounded like an old man with smoker's cough. I pulled the Mustang out of its hiding place and veered toward the open gate of the junkyard.

On the road and out of earshot of Emil's, I gunned the engine. The Mustang clicked through the gears with unbelievable ease. Even on a dirt road with hardpack snow, the car handled well. My heart pounded from the exhilaration of driving such a beautiful machine.

"Ruby, aren't we going awful fast?"

"This car is fantastic." Gearing down, I eased off the curving dirt road that led away from Emil's house and turned onto the straighter gravel road. I had it into fourth gear within seconds. I glanced over at Josie, who had a white-knuckle grip on the door handle. I let up on the accelerator. "Sorry, kiddo. It's just such a pleasure to drive a car that handles so well."

The sky was still pitch black when we hit the paved roads that led into Fontana. My watch said it was midnight.

"I'm never going to sneak off again. I don't care how much my mom makes me watch the babies and change everybody's diapers." Josie put her hand on her cheeks and shook her head. "Never."

"At least being with me isn't boring, huh?"

Josie nodded.

I had no idea where Vern or Sheriff Reslin lived. I stopped on the empty streets of Fontana beside the town's only phone booth. "I'm going to get you home as quick as I can." I reached over and touched her blond head. "Hang in there, kid."

The only address listed under Reslin was Daelynne's. Vern,

however, lived in a house behind the dealership two blocks away. When I got back to the car, both kid and kitty cat were sleeping soundly. Josie had crawled into the cramped backseat, and Her Majesty curled against the little girl's neck.

I turned the car around in the middle of Main Street and zoomed up to the used-car lot. It was lighted in two corners with street lamps. What a pleasure it was to drive such a sweet running car. I regretted having to return the Mustang.

Vern lived in a large, ranch-style house behind the dealership. Metal lawn furniture with the chairs stacked on the table populated the yard. Three inches of snow blanketed most of the lawn.

When I peeked in the window of the door, I saw a glowing television and a bald head. Vern must me a night person. I rapped gently on the door, and about a minute later, Vern, complete with crooked hairpiece, opened the door and grinned at me. He wore a plaid bathrobe and slippers.

"Well, hello there. Busted Valiant, right?"

"That's me."

"Dad, who is it?" Just over Vern's shoulder, two redheaded children wandered into the living room. They were maybe junior high age, a boy and a girl.

"Honey, did I hear the door?" From the other side of the hallway, a woman with the same carrot-colored hair appeared.

There was a whole tribe of them. My clan of lost people. I was in Redheaded Land.

"Vern, I have something for you." I turned slightly so I wasn't blocking Vern's view of the street.

Vern's eyes grew round. "You found it. You found the Stang." He drew his fingers to his lips.

The girl slipped in beside her father. Her red hair fell in soft waves around a freckled face with petite features. "You found Daddy's car!"

"Listen, I need your help. I have a little girl I need to get home, and I have to get hold of the sheriff."

"Sheriff lives about ten miles east of town. His home phone is unlisted." Vern rooted through a pile of papers on the desk. "I might have it from when I was robbed."

He handed me an old envelope. "He doesn't like to be bothered at home unless it's an absolute emergency."

"Trust me, this is an absolute emergency."

I dialed the number. It rang about twelve times, and then a very shrill female answered. "What do you want? People are sleeping." Guess I couldn't get lucky enough to find a whole town of insomniacs.

"Sorry to get you out of bed. I need to talk to your husband, Sheriff Reslin."

"Deputy Farsnel is on call tonight."

I didn't know Deputy Farsnel. "Please, I need to talk to Sheriff Reslin."

There was a long pause.

"Please, it's an emergency."

A heavy sigh vibrated across the line. The phone crackled as it was set down.

I waited with my ear pressed hard against the receiver.

Mrs. Mackafferty put a cup of hot tea in my hand. Vern and his children had slipped into their boots and coats and gone outside to weep over the Mustang. The Mackafferty living room was done in rich shades of green and purple.

Someone picked up the phone.

"Carl and Hayden are gone. I think he said something about ice fishing. I really need to get to bed. I have to open up the taxidermy shop early tomorrow."

"Sorry to have bothered you, Mrs. Reslin." I pressed the hang-up button but held onto the phone.

I wasn't nuts about calling Deputy Farsnel. That left only one other person to call.

Vern and his kids returned, Vern carrying Josie in his arms. "Can't leave this pixie out there. She'll catch her death." He laid Josie on the forest green couch.

Vern's son held a bloody scratched hand up to my face. "Your cat is mean."

"She's not my cat." I made a deal with myself. I would call Zac's. If Wesley was there, fine. If not, I'd get hold of Deputy Farsnel. When I dialed Zac's number, he picked up on the first ring.

"We've been worried sick. Ruby, where have you been? Is Josie okay?"

"She's fine. She's here at the Mackaffertys." I watched as Mrs. Mackafferty put a quilt over Josie. "Listen, is Wesley there crashing on your couch?"

"Yeah."

"Roust him out of bed. He needs to meet me at Emil's, pronto. I got a line on a robbery that just took place." I wrapped the phone cord around my wrist. "Did Julia make it home?"

"No, she and the kids stayed with Starlight. Lance hasn't come home, and Starlight had some kind of an anxiety attack."

My throat constricted. It took a substantial amount of effort not to let my mind wander through worst-case scenarios for Lance.

I didn't know if Lance had been wearing the belt buckle when he left for the library. The thieves could have taken it out of Starlight's house or his car.

"Just have Wesley meet me there. Can you phone Julia and come get Josie?"

"Sure."

"Tell Wesley to park a ways from the junkyard and not to wake Emil if he's there."

"Okay, sure."

"Tell him to wait for me. And tell him I want him to come because it's official police business."

"Got it. Listen, when are you two going to work things out? I'm getting awful tired of his whining."

So Wesley was whining about me. That was somewhat flattering. "That's his problem. Just have Wesley meet me. He'll be glad to have this case over with."

"I'll tell him. I'm halfway out the door to get Josie. I'll let Julia know."

"Do you want me to wait here with Josie?"

"Not if this is an emergency. The Mackaffertys are good folks. She'll be okay until I can get there."

"Thanks." I placed the phone in the cradle. The entire Mackafferty family was fussing over a very listless Josie, bringing her cups of hot cocoa and offering to make her microwave s'mores.

"Josie's dad is going to be by in a little bit to pick her up." I took a step closer to the couch. "Vern, it would take too long to explain why, but I'm without wheels, and I really need them." *Please, please let me drive the Mustang one more time.*

Vern swaggered over to the door and pulled a key off a rack

that contained at least a hundred keys. "There's a Suburban over in the lot you can borrow until I get your Valiant running. No charge. I appreciate you finding my baby."

Bummer, I wouldn't get to drive the Mustang. Beggars can't be complainers. I'd take the Burban.

"Real nice vehicle. Top-notch interior, 1997, only a hundred thousand miles, brand new tires." Vern couldn't resist throwing in a sales pitch.

I took the key from him. "Thanks, Vern. I like things I can find a parking space for."

Josie sat up on the couch with a steaming mug. Her cheeks were rosy, and the tip of her nose was red. I told her the Mackaffertys would take care of her until her dad got there. She took a sip of her cocoa and thanked me for letting her do grown-up stuff.

"We'll do it again. Only next time not quite so grown-up."

She smiled over the steaming mug.

"We'll stay up with her until her dad gets here," Mrs. Mackafferty reassured me.

I said goodbye to my people of Redheaded Land and eased the door open.

The last thing I heard was Mrs. Mackafferty suggesting to Vern that they invite me over for dinner sometime. I closed the door behind me.

Chapter Sixteen

I nabbed Her Majesty out of the Mustang before cutting over to the used-car lot. The Suburban was parked in the front lot next to a cute little Accord. I unlocked the door just as Her Majesty slipped from my grasp and jumped onto the car seat. Her fur fluffed enough to make her look three pounds heavier.

"You ungrateful critter. I rescued you. The least you could do is say thank you."

The feline lifted her chin and turned three circles on the passenger seat before settling down to knead the upholstery with her front claws. I crawled up into the seat and positioned myself behind the steering wheel. The vantage point gave me a feeling of super power, the ability to look down on the whole world. When I was driving my Valiant, I could feel every rock in the road. Being this high up disconnected me from the environment and created the sensation of floating.

My Mickey Mouse watch told me it was one fifteen. I turned the key in the ignition and pushed the heater buttons to hurricane force. While the car warmed up, I made plans.

Mom usually didn't get up until six. I needed to call her before she had a chance to worry. I'd already gotten her out of bed once this week; I didn't need to do it again. I wasn't sure how I'd break the news to her about the Caddy.

Fontana was dark and still as I pulled out onto the two-lane highway. The headlights of the Suburban illuminated fields blanketed in snow, black cows against white backgrounds. Sparse patches of bare trees huddled in the open fields, their branches made crystalline from the snow.

The Suburban handled like a large barrel with wheels, not at all able to take the turns like the Mustang. I tried to keep my eyes from tearing up. I'd driven the Mustang for less than half an hour, but it had been time enough to fall in love. But alas, the Stang belonged to another. Woe is me.

I turned off the main highway and onto the curving dirt road that led to Emil's land. My mind was buzzing—partly because I was fighting exhaustion and partly because so much had happened in such a short time.

Lance was missing, and one of the thieves had his belt buckle. It didn't make a lot of sense that Lance would be in any jeopardy just going to the library to do research. Something else must have happened. Because of the presence of so many stolen goods on his property, Emil was looking more guilty than ever.

I blinked hard three times and shook off the fatigue. When I clicked on the radio, it was playing a country-western song lamenting the loss of both a woman and a pickup truck. "Come on, play some Johnny Cash," I said to the radio. Her Majesty lifted her head. I knew she secretly liked the man in black, even if she wouldn't admit it.

Keeping my eyes on the road, I twisted the dial. I had a choice of static or really bad static. I turned it back to the country-western station. At least the noise would keep me awake.

Emil's lighted Ferris wheel was the first thing to come into sight, and I rolled up and down the hills that led to his property. I had one more hill between me and the junkyard, and still I hadn't spotted Wesley. Zac's place was about the same distance from Emil's as Fontana. *Wesley should be here by now.*

I pulled the car over and killed the headlights. Emil's truck was still gone. My watch said it was almost two o'clock. The sky was a rich charcoal. This time of year, it didn't get light until almost seven and it was dark by five.

To kill time and to keep myself awake, I turned the Suburban around on the narrow road. That way the car faced the direction that Wesley would be coming from. I could flash my headlights at him to let him know I was there. A few minutes later, I turned it back around, thinking it would be better if I watched Emil's in case something happened.

The singer on the radio crooned about true love accompanied by a slick electronic background of violins and horns. Yeah, I had to agree with Georgia, the older country-western stuff was better.

"I really liked driving that Mustang," I said to the cat, not because she cared, but because she was the only one in the car.

She yowled at me, disgusted that I had polluted the air, her air, with my voice. I stared into her blue eyes. In the newspaper about Vern's place being robbed, he'd said that the sculpture and the car were his most prized possessions. They mattered more to him than the money. Anyone who spent ten minutes in the feed store watching Georgia coo and fuss over Her Majesty would know how much that cat mattered to her. Nathan, too, had described Persistence the bull in an affectionate way. A trophy and a photo, surely prized personal mementos, had been with the stuff stolen from Fontana Ranch Supply. Had the thieves hit Benson's Pet and Feed three times because they were trying to get the cat? But whoever robbed our store must have cased it first; they knew exactly where the expensive stuff was. Maybe the expensive stuff was just a cover for what they really wanted. Maybe these crimes were not about profit.

Maybe they were personal—like whoever did the stealing wanted to hurt his victims emotionally. That was the only way taking stuff like cats and trophies made sense. It was possible, too, that the crimes were both personal and for money.

What if the crimes weren't linked by region or just perpetrated against farmers? Vern, Nathan, Georgia, Fontana Ranch Supply—all of them had lost something precious to them, and I suspected the other farmers had as well. I glanced down at the purring queen. No matter how I rearranged the puzzle pieces, stealing Georgia's cat was personal because the thieves sure weren't going to get any money for her. The sculpture and the Mustang and the bull had some resale value, but how much could anyone get for a trophy and a photo of Frank Sinatra?

I zipped my glitzy coat up and shoved my hands in my pockets as the car grew colder. Where was Wesley anyway? I'd have to run my theory by him when he got here. If I thought about it for two seconds, I liked helping him with his work. Why then, had I been such a chucklehead and not been supportive of him when he asked for it?

My eyelids felt really heavy. I leaned against the cold glass of the window and closed my eyes. The woman on the radio sang about the man who'd wronged her and something about getting even. . . .

I jerked awake. My head had been resting against the window. I squinted. The sun shone through the windshield, and the car was freezing. Her Majesty had crawled up into my lap not because she loved me but because it was warmer.

A man who was not Wesley walked toward the Burban. Reslin's baseball cap was pulled down over his eyes, but I recognized his handlebar mustache, plus he swaggered like a guy whose thigh muscles were a little too buff. His car was parked where Emil's truck should have been.

I rolled down the window.

He waved a gloved hand at me. "Sorry it took so long. Feed store in Fontana was robbed last night."

Duh. And I know where all the stuff is that they took. Reslin probably hadn't gone ice fishing; he might have already been out on the call for the ranch supply when I phoned his house. "I guess you didn't get the whole message. Where's Wesley?"

"I called him to help me with the robbery." Reslin rested his forearm on my rolled-down window. Reslin had dark circles under his eyes. His face sagged. Like he'd aged overnight. Not being able to put an end to these robberies must be frustrating. "He asked me to deal with you." The sheriff scratched his neck, never making eye contact.

Deal with me? Lovely. Reslin was the ambassador to the relationship challenged. I swallowed hard, balled my hand into a fist, and chose to get over my hurt about Wesley. "They took more besides my mom's Caddy. I know where your feed-store inventory is." I pushed open the car door, forcing Reslin to step back. "And I found Vern's Mustang on this property."

The sheriff looked only mildly irritated at having to step out of the way. He was Zac's age, but intense concentric lines around his mouth and eyes made him look older than forty-something.

He stared at the cat lounging on my car seat but said nothing. Guess he figured the great cat war between Emil and me wasn't worth his valuable law-enforcement time.

Reslin slipped off his gloves and slapped them against his hand.

"You think Van Kriten has something to do with the robbery of Hickman's store?"

"I don't know. I just know the stuff is here. I'll show you." I trudged toward the shed where Josie and I had spent a few fright-filled hours. As we passed the sheriff's car, I noticed a person sitting in the passenger-side seat.

"My son," said Reslin. "My own father wasn't very involved in my life. I'm trying to be different. Hayden comes with me on calls sometimes."

Reslin had some serious problems with the way he talked to women, but I had to give him credit for being a good dad.

I trudged through mud and crunchy snow toward the shed. "Where is Emil, anyway?"

"Thursday night is his poker night. He probably stayed in town and slept off his drinking."

Weird. Georgia's store had always been robbed on a Thursday, too.

So Emil played poker every Thursday. My boot sank into the mud. Everybody in Fontana knew everyone else's schedule. This entire country was a glass house. You couldn't burp without someone making note of it.

By the time I passed the dark Airstream and headed up the trail to the shed, a herd of cats was following me. Reslin stomped behind. I pushed the shed open and flicked on the light. Hope sank like a lead balloon. None of the boxes were there.

The sheriff leaned into the shed, shaking his head. Then he stared at me for a long, uncomfortable moment. "Ms. Taylor, are you taking any kind of medication?"

Great, now Reslin thinks I'm nuts. "A kid was with me. Zac's daughter." I stepped inside and kicked straw around, searching for any sign of the stolen inventory. They must have come for it in the short time I'd gone into town. I certainly would have heard them if they'd done it while I was sleeping. "She saw it." Several cats trotted to the edge of the loft and peered down at us.

"A kid?" Reslin took off his hat and rubbed his hair. "Why don't you just file a report for your missing car."

My teeth clenched. "What about the Mustang? That links Emil to Vern's robbery."

Reslin furrowed his brow and scratched his cheek with his knuckles. "The Mustang is still here?"

A heaviness pressed on my shoulders. "No, I drove it off the property. But Vern can verify."

"Vern saw the Mustang on Emil's property?"

"Well no, but—"

"Do you have something against Emil?"

"No, it's not that. I know what I saw." Reslin's questioning wasn't out of line. Other than what Josie could tell him, which it seems Reslin would not hold in high regard, it sounded like I was hallucinating. "Certainly there are tests you can do. You can match the tracks in the junkyard to the Mustang tires."

"We don't have that kind of funding or manpower. Ms. Taylor, I appreciate what you're trying to do here. Trying to get Wesley to pay attention to you." He was using that condescending tone again.

I planted my hands on my hips. "Excuse me? I know what I saw."

"We'll talk to the kid when my stronger leads die out. I got a robbery in town to deal with."

"And I'm trying to help you. I can tell you what was taken in addition to the inventory. There was an autographed photo of Frank Sinatra and a trophy." I punctuated my information by lifting my chin.

Reslin did that staring thing he used as a sort of intimidation technique. Like I was going to back down now. Score one for me. I had him. Hickman must have reported the trophy and the photo as stolen. He took a piece of gum from his pocket, unwrapped it, and stuck it in his mouth. I had the privilege of a front-row seat at the two-minute Juicy Fruit show. He took the gum out of his mouth and flicked it on the straw beside my boot. "I can find ten people in town who saw Emil last night." He steeled his eyes, not blinking, then turned and headed back down the hill.

I slipped out of the shed and trotted behind him. "He gets his minions to steal for him while he creates an alibi every Thursday night."

"Emil Van Kriten is an old man." Reslin was momentarily distracted by his son getting out of the car and slamming the door. Hayden's shoulders drooped, and he hung his head. Had the kid been up all night with his father?

Reslin looked away from his son and leaned close enough to violate social space rules. "Emil's lived here all his life and never had any problem with the law."

Since when did residency make you exempt from suspicion? "He's not doing the heavy lifting." Reslin's need to defend Emil seemed inflated, even if they were from the same town.

Reslin took out another piece of gum and chewed some more.

"Maybe I'm wrong; maybe they're just using Emil's to store the stolen stuff. What would it hurt to at least question him?" I softened my tone. I'm the first to admit that I'm not the queen of diplomacy. But I was smart enough to realize continuing in this antagonistic vein would gain me nothing.

"We're anxious to get to the bottom of these robberies." Again, he took off his hat and rubbed his thick curly hair before rolling his eyes. "We'll look into it."

At least he was listening to me. "Lance Kinkaid is missing, too. You might want to look into that."

"I know. His wife has been calling the station all night." Reslin checked his watch, then he closed his eyes and pinched the top part of his nose. "I got my deputy on that."

"I think Lance is linked to the robbery somehow. One of the thieves we saw had on his belt buckle."

"Missing people usually show up within twenty-four hours." He turned back toward the sheriff's car, where his son leaned against the driver-side door. "This robbery is my priority," he shouted back at me.

I stood with my hands shoved in my pockets as he trekked across the muddy snow. The sheriff may have listened to what I told him about the robbery, but he had totally disregarded anything I said about Lance. I wondered if the same suggestions came from Wesley or another male he would take them more seriously.

Reslin slapped his son's back. They opened the doors of the sheriff's car and climbed inside, then he turned the vehicle around and disappeared over the hill.

Guess I might as well do the same. A still, small voice told me I'd better get over to Starlight's.

I passed Emil in his battered truck close to the turnout onto the main road. I was already on the gravel road so it wasn't obvious

I'd come from his place. He zipped by me, concentrating on the turn. He didn't know me from Adam in my Suburban getup. We passed without acknowledgment, and I waited for a moment on the road until his truck slipped out of sight.

Chapter Seventeen

I sat behind the steering wheel of the Suburban and stared at Starlight's huge front door. Snow drifted out of the sky in lazy swirls. I'm not good at dealing with my own pain, let alone other people's. But I knew I needed to act like a grown-up and stay with Starlight until we heard news about Lance. Her Majesty rested against my leg, purring with the intensity of a small-engine plane—her version of offering moral support.

Julia's car was still parked outside. Mom and Georgia were driving in from Eagleton after I'd called them from a pay phone in Fontana. That way I could surprise Georgia with Her Majesty. Even with all this backup, the primary job of comforting Star was mine. I opened the car door, gathered the cat into my arms, and walked toward the mansion.

Julia answered. She wrapped her arms around me and ushered me inside. Her Majesty leapt from my grasp and headed into the kitchen. Her stiff, upright tail swung back and forth like a metronome. The downstairs was quiet. No kids anywhere.

Julia must have read my mind. "Zac dropped Josie off and took the older boys with him. She and Nellie are sleeping in Starlight's guest room."

Julia made no mention of Brody, but my guess was he'd found a corner to collapse in. For a two-year-old, he had pretty good survival skills.

"You look tired," I said.

"It's been a long night." She sighed, unclipped her claw-like hairpiece, untwisted her long hair, and then let it fall down her back. While she spoke, she opened and closed the clip. "She fell apart a little after you left." Julia gazed up toward the banister. "At first it was just pacing and worrying, but then she hyperventilated."

"Where is she now?"

"I think she ran into the bathroom just a minute ago. I hope Lance comes home soon."

"Me, too." So Lance hadn't tried to get ahold of Star. Not a good sign. It took some effort to make the corners of my mouth curve upward in what I hoped looked like a supportive smile.

"I can stay as long as you need me." Julia touched my arm. "I can come up with you."

"Get some sleep. My mom and my boss are on their way."

After a deep breath, I sprinted the distance to the stairs and raced up. By the time I knocked on the bathroom door, I could barely breathe because of the tightness in my rib cage and throat. I rapped gently on the door. "Starlight, it's me, Ruby." Visions of all the sharp objects available in a bathroom danced through my head. "What are you doing in there?"

"What do most people do in the bathroom?" Her voice sounded clear and strong. "I'm fixing my hair." Footsteps strode on tile, and the door swung open. "I'm chemically sensitive—not suicidal. Get your medical conditions straight." Her eyes were red from crying. But the sarcasm in her voice told me she had unexpected fight in her.

So what if she was slinging hostility at me? At least she wasn't still falling apart. I peered around at the huge bathroom behind her. "Claustrophobia wouldn't be an issue in there, either, would it?"

She laughed. "I think I have enough to deal with without adding any phobias, thank you."

Her expression darkened. She lifted her chin and closed her eyes. Then she fell forward into my arms.

I held her. "Starlight, is there someone I can call?" I patted her back. "Do you have any family?"

"My mother is dead, and I lost contact with my only sister years ago. Lance is all I have." Her voice quavered.

"How about the people who came here for church service?"

"They were Lance's friends really . . . if you want to call them that. Mostly they were businesses we used. I think they just came because they wanted us to keep spending our money with them."

Her crunchy immobile hair grazed my cheek. I stepped out of the hug and touched her semi-bouffant, which collapsed and sprang right back into place.

The corners of Starlight's mouth turned up. "I have a thing about hair control."

"I have to ask." Maybe if we talked about something trivial, it would get her mind off Lance. "You can't wear anything with perfume in it, but you use astonishing amounts of hair products."

"When I was first diagnosed, we met a guy who'd invented all-natural hair products without perfumes. Lance helped him market it. That's where some of our income comes from."

That was an income source I never would have guessed. "It's so bouncy." After touching her hair and watching it spring back into place one more time, I tilted my head toward the stairs. "Why don't I make you a hot cup of tea? Then maybe you can get some sleep."

"I'm not—" She shook her head. "I'm not tired." She massaged her temples.

"But you haven't slept all night." Her eyes glazed. Just like that, she had slipped back into falling-apart mode.

She gazed at me for a long moment. "I just . . . um . . . I just . . . um." She laced and unlaced her fingers, and then her hands fluttered up to her forehead. "I . . . I . . . I just don't know what I'm supposed to do next." She shifted from side to side. "What . . . what am I supposed to do?"

I grabbed her trembling hand. She was unstable, alternating between being strong and falling apart. "Come downstairs with me, and I'll make you a cup of tea." I held her hand at the wrist.

She closed her eyes. Her whole body was shaking.

"Just come downstairs and have a cup of tea. I have some friends coming; we're going to stay with you until we get word of Lance . . . until you feel comfortable being alone."

She took in a deep breath. Her huge chest moved up and down. "I can do that."

"You'll have to open your eyes, or you'll fall down the stairs, Starlight."

Starlight kept her eyes closed, but she smiled. "That's not a problem. With these breasts, I'd just bounce right back up." Then she laughed at her own joke—a frantic, high-pitched laugh. "Wouldn't I?"

"Open your eyes, Starlight. That's the first step."

She was still shaking terribly. "I'm working on it." Her lips moved like she was praying, and then her eyes opened, misting instantly. "Here I am."

"There you are." I swung my arm behind her back, squeezed her shoulder, and escorted her down the stairs.

Julia was waiting in the kitchen with the kettle already whistling. Nellie spooned something out of a bowl. Her blond curls were flat on one side of her head, and her cheek was still red from pressing it into a pillow. Starlight sat on the stool beside Nellie.

"I hope you don't mind. I found some cereal for Nels." Julia placed a steaming cup beside Starlight.

"I'se hungry." Bits of half-chewed cereal accented Nellie's pearl teeth.

Starlight held the mug in shaking hands. Tea splattered on the countertop. Nellie placed a small hand on Starlight's wrist.

Star got that faraway look in her eyes as she trailed a finger through the tea puddle. "Where could he be?" she whispered.

I poured myself a cup of tea. "He just said he was going to the library, right?" I hated this feeling of helplessness. I had to fight the impulse to bolt and start combing the countryside for Lance. Reslin's deputy was handling that. My job was to be here with Star.

Starlight took a sip of her tea and wrapped her hands around the mug. "He said he was going to the library. Lance is fascinated by local history. He did articles whenever we moved to a new town. He was working on a follow-up article about the vigilante killing."

"A follow-up article?" I sat my mug down on the counter. "That article was written by Martin Grant."

"Lance is Martin Grant. It's a pseudonym. His real name sounds like a soap opera star, don't you think?"

I nodded. Glad I wasn't the only one who thought so.

"Lance didn't think anyone would take him seriously if he used his real name." Starlight touched Nellie's soft curls.

All this time, I'd assumed he was researching ways to help Star with her health problems. Bits and pieces of a theory started to come together in my head. But it was a theory I kept to myself.

What if Lance had finished at the library and then gone up to interview Seb Van Kriten's closest living relative, Emil? But Emil was gone because it was poker night, and instead Lance had stumbled onto the ring of thieves. Or Emil was involved, and Lance had caught him before he left for his game. But why would Emil want to harm Lance? If anything, the old man would appreciate Lance's interest in his great-grandfather.

I checked my watch. It was not quite 8:00 A.M. I wanted to get to the library and see if Daelynne knew what Lance had been re-searching and where he'd gone afterward, but I didn't want to leave until Star was a little more stable emotionally. I sat down on the stool beside her. Her Majesty had made herself comfortable in the dog bed. And besides, I had a cat to return.

"I need to get a table and chairs for this place." Star squeezed her eyes shut, and her voice trembled. "Lance was going to do that next week."

"Don't think about it, Star. We don't know anything for sure yet." I touched her shoulder. "Just drink your tea."

Julia poured a cup of tea for herself. For a long time, we lis-tened to the *crunch, crunch* of Nellie eating her cereal. Starlight stopped shaking enough to sip her tea. When her cup was almost empty, Julia poured her more.

"Are you sure you don't want to try sleeping for a little bit?"

"No, I can't." Star peered over her steaming cup at the piles of produce in her kitchen. "I need to do something with that fruit Lance got for me. I tried making jam, but I've ruined every batch. One batch was like syrup, and another was like rubber."

If focusing on things like jam disasters was going to help Star-light, that was what we'd do.

"That's an art form that I never mastered." Julia craned her neck to look at the heaping baskets of apricots and strawberries and apples. "A lot of the older women in the church know how. I wish they'd teach me."

I shrugged. "I do peanut butter and jelly."

Julia sputtered, cupping her hand over her mouth to keep from laughing. "Don't feel bad. When I was in college, before I married Zac, I thought I was going to be Susie career woman, living on the maid's cooking and takeout."

"What changed your mind?"

"Two things. My oldest, Jason, was born. I looked down into his face and knew I didn't want strangers raising him. Took me awhile to get the hang of farm life, but I liked being with Zac."

Julia seemed so natural in her role as mother and wife. Dummy me, I'd assumed she was one of those Christian women who'd always aspired to be a wife and mother, like it was in her DNA. Maybe it was a role you grew into gradually. Proverbs 31 didn't mention how many batches of jam that woman ruined before she got it right.

I sat awhile longer, sipping tea. Nellie finished her cereal and disappeared into one of the bedrooms. While Her Majesty had made herself comfortable in the dog's bed, the persecuted Pomeranian lay on the cold tile floor a safe distance from the cat.

The doorbell rang. The dog lifted its head and let out a single sharp bark. Feeling he had done his duty, the little dog rested his chin on his paws and closed his eyes.

I slipped off the stool and padded across the sunburst-patterned tile. Two women came through the open door like a whirlwind. Mom had ridden with Georgia because she was without a car. Both of them held bags of groceries and bulging totes. Mom's huge purse was brimming with stuff. Judging from all the items they brought with them, they must have cooked up plans on the long drive from Eagleton.

"I'm here. The party can start," Georgia roared as she swept into the room. It seemed like a really strange thing to say considering they'd been called to comfort a woman whose husband was missing. I'd leave the care plan up to the two women who had more wisdom than me. If a party was what would help Starlight, then a party is what we'd have.

Starlight lifted her head and managed a wan smile.

"Since you and Starlight are doing a recipe together for the potato festival," Mom said, placing the bag of groceries on the counter, "I thought we'd work together to come up with some ideas." Mom pulled out a whole ham.

My gut clenched. I knew Mom was only trying to help, but that big ham sitting on the counter made me a little defensive. Just because she put ham in her recipe didn't mean I had to have it in mine. "We already have an idea. We're doing chips and dip." Star and I hadn't discussed dip, but I wanted it to sound more elaborate.

"Chips and dip." My mother touched her slender fingers to her cheek. "How interesting."

Insecurity over my cooking skills crept into my solar plexus. "You don't think it's a good idea?"

"It's your recipe." Mom patted my hand. "You do whatever you want."

She was trying hard not to interfere—to be supportive. But I could tell she thought our chip idea was amateur.

Georgia placed her hands on her ample hips and furrowed her brow. "Where's all the furniture?"

Starlight rose to her feet. "I haven't had time to buy much."

Georgia's comment distracted me from sinking into deep despair over my cooking skills.

"This place is big enough to run a small herd," Georgia said. "Scooch that couch on over here." She pointed to the sofa in the far corner by the piano. "I'll need to spell myself now and then, and I ain't sittin' on one of these skinny things." She slapped the pink bar stools.

Starlight, Julia, and I pushed the couch closer to the kitchen area.

"Now," said Georgia, the party planner. She pulled CDs out of her heaping tote. "We can listen to Lynn or Donna or Tammy. Where's your player?"

God bless that old woman. Knowing that most people didn't own a turntable, she must have stopped at a truck stop or something and gotten those CDs. However rough Georgia was around the edges, I really appreciated her heart.

Starlight retrieved a CD player from a side room, and the party got into full swing.

Georgia wandered into the kitchen and laid eyes on Her Majesty. Her hand flew on her chest. "Oh my . . . Oh my . . . Oh my. My baby . . . My baby." She gathered the cat into her arms. The Queen did not turn into all bones like she did so often when you picked her up. Georgia danced around the kitchen. "I was so worried about you." She swayed back and forth to Loretta Lynn. Finally, she looked at me. "How on earth?"

"It's a long story." Getting to watch Georgia dancing with a cat made all the trouble I'd gone through worthwhile.

"What's with all the fruit?" Georgia asked as she wandered around the kitchen, bouncing the Queen like a baby.

Starlight blushed and hung her head. "I wanted to learn how to make jam, but it's not turning out. I followed the recipe."

"Oh, sweetie," my mother swirled into the kitchen. "You don't learn jam-making from a book. You learn it from another woman. I love making jam." She wrapped her arms around Starlight and led her toward the counter. She picked up an apricot. "With fruit this ripe, you want to cut the sugar a little."

"You do, huh?" Georgia held Her Majesty up so they were nose to nose. "I always do what the recipe says. What you got to dabble with is the cooking time." She lifted her chin in the air matter-of-factly.

"Oh." Mom found an apron hanging on a hook and put it on. "We all have our different ways. That's not how I do it."

Though it never came to blows, Mom and Georgia argued through two batches of jam about the right way to do things while Tammy Wynette lamented in song. Steam and sweet smells rose from the kitchen. Georgia's party idea seemed to be helping. I saw only flashes of worry in Starlight's expression.

I found myself less anxious to leave, enjoying the laughter and the music . . . and the cooking. Julia crawled onto the couch and fell asleep. Once she woke up, Josie entertained Nellie by playing the piano. Without trepidation, Brody picked Her Majesty up and carried her around the living room. The Pomeranian followed subserviently at the back of the procession.

"Ruby, get over here and stir this fruit." Mom pulled me from the couch with her eyes. She placed her hand over mine when I grabbed the wooden spoon. "Just gentle stirring; keep it from burning to the bottom."

"So do you think chips are not a good idea?"

Mom wiped sweat from her brow. "It's your recipe."

"But you think chips and dip are dumb?"

"It is your recipe, honey. I never should have brought the ham."

"I like our chips, Ruby," Starlight piped up.

Georgia hummed along to Tammy's song and danced while she poured rich red jam into jars. "When we had the ranch, Glen used to say that I canned or turned into jam anything that wasn't nailed down. Now with all the kids grown, it just doesn't make sense to do it. I do miss it."

Mom put her palm on her chest and shook her head. "Oh, I just love canning." Her face was flushed from all the moisture in the air. I'd never heard two women speak of cooking processes with such affection. They were the two most content women I'd ever met, so maybe they were onto something.

Georgia placed a hand on her hip and stared at the ceiling. "I remember after I pickled a bunch of cucumbers. I put the jars along the windowsill." She shook her head. "The light shone through them. It was the prettiest thing."

I stayed almost two hours and reluctantly said goodbye. Georgia caught me at the door. "Thanks for getting my cat back."

I shrugged. "No problem." It had been a huge problem, but somehow it didn't matter. A picture flashed through my head of a much younger Georgia staring at the early morning light passing through her pickle jars.

Georgia glanced back at Starlight, who sat next to my mother on the couch. Mom was showing her how to do cross-stitch, an item she must have pulled out of that purse of hers. Josie sat on the other side of Mom, leaning into her.

Star was in good hands.

I stepped outside, crossing my arms against the mid-morning chill. Wind blew, and cloud cover was dark enough to suggest snow later in the day. I swung open the colossal door on the Suburban and crawled up. The cold didn't bother me as I sat staring at Star's house. That still, small voice whispered that even if nothing ever got resolved with Wesley, even if I never met a guy who was marriage material, I'd be okay. I wouldn't die of loneliness. Sometimes making jam was about more than making jam.

I turned the Suburban around and headed toward the last place we knew Lance had gone: the Fontana library.

Chapter Eighteen

The drive into town was a blur. I had the faint impression of a distant clock ticking. When Wesley and I were on speaking terms, he'd said the most significant time after a person goes missing is the first twenty-four hours. Hope of finding the person alive kind of got cut in half after that. I gripped the steering wheel tighter and prayed for Lance's safe return.

I parked outside the library and bounded up the stone steps. Daelynne stood behind the counter with her face buried in a risqué romance novel.

"Hi, Daelynne. Remember me?"

"Oh, sure. You're Wes Burgess's girl from Eagleton."

Not quite, but I wasn't in the mood to quibble over semantics. I've never been anybody's "girl." I have an identity and a name all my own. "Something like that. Was Lance Kinkaid here last night?"

"Yes, right before I closed and went over to the café for dinner. I stayed open an extra twenty minutes for him. Real nice fella. Kind of flashy. Carl told me he's gone missing." She leaned close to me with all kinds of exaggerated intrigue in her voice. "Do you think I was the last person to see him alive?"

"We don't know that he's dead, Daelynne." I moderated my voice so that Daelynne wouldn't pick up on my irritation over her turning Lance's disappearance into a pulp mystery. "Do you remember what he was looking at?"

"He's been looking at our collection in what is going to be our

Heritage Room." She pointed at one of the closed doors to the side of the counter. "It's not technically open to the public. I need to get Roger O'Connell over here to build me some shelves and display units. All the artifacts chronicling the county's history are in there."

"I don't suppose you remember what he was looking at?"

Daelynne sucked in and released her lips. "I could tell you where he was standing when I peeked in. I haven't had time to put the stuff away that he was reading." She pulled a gigantic key ring from beneath the counter. "No one but me is authorized to go through the artifacts, but I just thought since Mr. Grant, I mean Lance, had written so many articles about local history, it would be okay. I suggested he quit writing about the vigilante hanging and research something more pleasant."

Daelynne had a tendency to walk toe first like a ballet dancer, which made her hair bounce even more. She opened the door. The moldy aroma of the past filtered into the main room. "He was standing in that corner when I looked in and asked him if he wanted anything. I remember because I was supposed to go meet my son and grandson at the café for an early dinner, and Lance was making me run late. I got over to the café, and they weren't there. I couldn't get ahold of them all night."

The room was narrow, maybe ten by twenty feet. Papers, boxes, rusting tools, and even a saddle cluttered makeshift shelves made of plywood and brick. Floorboards creaked as I made my way toward the corner.

Daelynne leaned on the door frame and chattered. "We're hoping to have the remodel done by Potato Festival time."

This town sets its clock by the Potato Festival. I stared down at a pile of blue weathered papers that said "Caption" at the top. Below that, it read "Abstract of the title to the following described land situated in the County of Colter, State of Montana." The document then went on to give a bunch of directions: n.e. quarter of this and s.w. half section of that. I pointed to the pile of papers and raised questioning eyebrows toward Daelynne.

"Those are abstracts. They show the record of exchange of a piece of land."

I unrolled a huge map on metal rods. The heading at the top read, "County of Colter, Montana, 1905, prepared by Colter Ranch and Land Investments, Eagleton, Montana, K. L. Smythe, draftsman." The map was divided into numbered squares that were subdivided into four squares. Each of the little squares had the number 160 and a name on it. Much of the land was owned by the Northern Pacific Railroad Company. A name caught my eye. *Mackafferty* was written on lots of the squares.

The whole map was huge, maybe five feet by eight. I rolled it down a few more inches. The name Hickman came into view, the guy who owned the ranch supply, and Spence, the guy whose cattle had been stolen.

I glanced back at the abstract. Beneath the description of the land there was a *no. 1* and beside that is said, "shows patent, Van Kriten." The numbers went down to thirteen with Spence, Mackafferty, and Hickman listed beside words like *Release, W. Deed,* and *Mortgage.*

Daelynne took a step across the worn wooden floorboards.

A theory crystallized in my brain. I pulled a pen out of my pocket and found a piece of scrap paper, then wrote down all the other names. What if Lance had figured out something about the

221

robberies—that all of the people being robbed connected back to this map? None of the landowners were called Benson, but I had a theory about that, too. There were other names I didn't recognize. I suspected Georgia's maiden name was on the map as were some others who'd been robbed.

When I turned toward Daelynne, she was biting a fingernail. My touching this stuff made her nervous. "Do you have other maps—like from 1901?" That would have been a year before the hanging.

"They'd be down underneath. Be careful. They're very fragile."

"I know." Kneeling, I lifted the maps to read the years written in the corner. Daelynne was probably going to watch me until I was done. Did she think I was going to smash her artifacts? "Here we go." I pulled a map from 1900 and placed it carefully on the makeshift table. I looked back and forth between the two maps. Sure enough, most of the land that belonged to Hickman, Olsen, Spence, and Mackafferty had belonged to Van Kriten in 1900.

"You can just leave those out. I'll put them back." Daelynne ran a finger over her eyebrow.

"Lance didn't say where he was going?"

She touched her poofy hair and shrugged. "I was in a hurry."

I noticed a stack of letters and envelopes next to the map. A ribbon, obviously not old, lay beside the stack like someone had undone it to read the letters. A phrase in the letter caught my eye, "taking my baby into your home." I lifted the letter by a corner. The date at the top said 1933. The letter floated to the floor, and I was left holding a torn corner of yellow paper.

Daelynne gasped, loudly and repeatedly. Her hands spasmed in front of her face. "Those are historical documents."

"I'm sorry. I didn't realize how fragile—"

"I told you," she whined. She swooped down to the floor and carefully picked up the letter, holding her hand underneath it. All the color drained from her face. "I think you'd better go. I never should have allowed you in this room. Only I am authorized."

That was pretty much the end of my museum tour. Daelynne walked me to the library door. Just to drive her point home and make sure the guilt went in good and deep, she slapped a palm against her chest and raised her eyes heavenward. "I shouldn't have let you touch historical documents. But I just had to be nice."

I hadn't meant to break the letter, but I wasn't about to feed into her guilt fest. "Lance wasn't by any chance going up to interview Emil?"

Daelynne blinked rapidly. "He already did that with the first article. Emil is the only one who wants to talk about that hanging anyway." She wasn't going to cooperate with me about anything since I'd ruined her historical document. "If you want my opinion, Lance never should have done that article." Her agitation about the ruined letter seemed to be causing other feelings to rise to the surface. "It might be interesting to him, but it's just a shameful part of our history that we'd rather forget. Colter County has so many interesting events to be proud of. Why not write about those? Why make Emil Van Kriten the center of attention?" She all but spat his name out.

"I'm sorry about the letter." When I touched her shoulder, she stiffened. Something told me I wouldn't be issued a library card any time soon. Nothing was going to get resolved here. I said my goodbyes.

I burst through the heavy library doors and breathed another prayer for Lance's safe return. A whirlwind of snow whipped down Main Street past Fontana's single stoplight. Across the street, in the car dealer's showroom, a redheaded person, no doubt Vern, polished his Mustang. My aorta clenched up. *Forgive me, Lord, for coveting, but I would give anything to drive that car again.*

I needed to ask Vern a question about land ownership. Besides, as much fun as the Suburban was to drive, I was a little worried about the status of my Valiant. Sharp snowflakes stabbed my face as I crossed the street. Vern's "Open" sign was on the door. The entire front wall of the store was glass. I had a clear view of Vern leaning over to polish a headlight. His fake hair separated from his head.

Vern smiled when he saw me tapping on the window. He sauntered the short distance to the door and opened it up. "Hello there, Miss Ruby."

"Vern, I need to ask you a quick question."

"Sure, sure. Come on inside. Just got the coffee put on." He ambled toward the coffeemaker, which was on a table next to a desk piled high with papers.

Before I had a chance to tell Vern I didn't have time for coffee, he put a steaming paper cup in my hand.

Vern wandered back to the Mustang. "How does she look?" His face beamed. "Can't thank you enough for getting her back for me."

"Vern, do you own any land around here?" I took a small sip of the coffee.

"Family used to. Grandpappy sold it all off after the war. We've been three generations in the used-car business. I have fond memories of being a boy on the ranch, but a good year is when you break even."

"Where was the land?"

"Some of it was river-bottom land, real nice rich soil."

"Who owns it now?"

Vern shrugged. "It's been divided and subdivided. Lot of little millionaire gentlemen-farmers' ranches out there. The only way you can hope to stay in business as a rancher is to already have a source of income. Sad, isn't it?"

"Yes, it is." I shoved my hands in my jeans pockets. Now for the important question. "Were any of your relatives involved in that hanging that took place a little after the turn of the century?"

Vern stopped polishing the Mustang. He stood up straight, and all the color drained from his face. On a light-skinned redhead like Vern that meant his skin turned pasty white. "Nobody knows for sure what happened." He twisted the polishing rag in his hands. "If Emil wouldn't keep bringing it up, this town could forget about it. Nobody knows why Van Kriten was taken out there that day, and nobody knows who it was took him out there."

"That's probably what the history books say. But everybody around this town knows who did it, right?"

"Is your coffee hot enough?"

"Vern, you didn't hang that guy. You don't need to be ashamed."

Vern tossed the polishing rag on the hood of the Mustang and stepped a little closer to me. "You don't understand about bloodlines in a small town. What my daddy did defines who I am and his daddy before him."

"You're a good, decent person, Vern. That's what should matter."

"Bottom line, Ruby. The day they drug Van Kriten out to that tree was a shameful day for this whole valley. The history books don't record who did the killing or why, so we don't know."

"So you're saying I should just drop it."

Vern nodded. "I like you, Ruby."

I had a feeling Vern had told me more than anybody else would in this town. Suddenly, the whole town had motive for harming Lance because he was digging up stuff nobody wanted to be reminded of. Emil was the only one talking, and his version of history was a little distorted. In Emil's mind, anybody who got the land was guilty. I didn't understand why no one wanted to talk about something that happened a hundred years ago, but I'd never been connected to a community for any length of time. Because of my father's habit of embezzling, we'd moved every two or three years.

"Thanks for answering my questions." I sauntered toward the door.

"Is that Suburban working out okay for you? Could give you a real good deal on it."

"I miss my Valiant. You are going to have it done soon?"

"Got my son hammering out dents right now." He patted my back. "I'll have it ready for ya in no time."

I allowed myself one more loving glance at Vern's Mustang. "That's good to hear, Vern. Good to hear."

"Can't thank you enough for bringing the Stang back to me." His hand touched a headlight. "Now I'll be able to drive it in the Potato Festival parade—just like I do every year."

Did I mention that this whole town sets it clock by the Potato Festival? "It was my pleasure, Vern." And that was no lie. I turned slightly to gaze out Vern's floor-to-ceiling window. Wesley and Reslin were across the street. Both men had on winter coats. Wesley's arms were crossed, and their heads were close together.

I barely registered Vern saying that he was going to find a way to pay me back. A tow truck pulling Mom's Caddy crossed my field of vision.

I bolted toward the door. "Gotta go. I'll check back with you about the car." The winter chill hit me hard when I stepped outside.

Across the street, the two men had grown to a huddle of eight or nine. I watched people step out of the hardware store, the café, and the other businesses. People came to second-story windows and gazed out as the tow truck made its way to the end of the street, turned around in an empty lot, and drove back toward Vern's.

Like a living creature, the town had a heartbeat and instinct all its own. Everyone knew Mom's Caddy and Lance were missing. The two were linked even if it wasn't logical. A voice that only the citizens could hear whispered to them that the parading of the Caddy indicated a far greater doom. And so they came to their windows, stepped out on the sidewalk, stopped their daily work to watch and wait.

A dozen trucks and SUVs covered in mud took the parking spaces on either side of the street. The huddle of men continued to grow. The tow truck pulled behind Vern's used-car lot. As I crossed the street, I combated the sensation of being in a vice, of not being able to get a full deep breath. *Breathe deeply, Ruby, breathe deeply.*

When another pick-up, spattered with mud, bloodhounds baying and yipping in its bed, rolled down Main Street, I stopped on the yellow, dashed line. The huddle dispersed, leaving Wesley alone on the sidewalk. The driver of the truck containing the bloodhounds found a parking space. I knew that within twenty minutes whatever news the men brought into town would flow through the creature's veins. Everyone would know.

People from the stores stepped back inside. They still stood close to the windows—murky, distorted images that were more impression than picture—ghost people standing behind glass, arms crossed, waiting . . . waiting.

Wesley turned slightly. He lifted his head, made eye contact. His stance was crumpled like he wore chain mail that weighed him down, made his shoulders droop and his head heavy. I knew the look on his face. I knew what it meant. For a moment, it swept through my mind that I could turn and run and not have to hear the news, that I could pretend like I wasn't deeply enmeshed in this tragic unfolding.

I steeled myself and swallowed hard. Both my hands curled into fists. Leaning forward, I willed my feet to move and crossed the remainder of the street.

I stepped up on to the sidewalk and waited for Wesley to speak.

Chapter Nineteen

News of death travels through a filter. A muffling or numbing invaded my body. As Wesley chronicled the details, I had the sensation of rocking in a hammock. I could hear God saying, "I know this will all be too much for you to bear. I will hold you like a baby through each moment. Slip inside this cocoon. I will whisper reassurances and prompt you to keep living by saying, 'Breathe now, child, breathe.'"

Wesley placed a hand on my shoulder.

"They found him down by the riverbed. Blunt force trauma to the head. We haven't located the murder weapon. It looked like someone was getting ready to toss him into the river but ran out of time or was interrupted. The body is on the way to Eagleton for autopsy."

Wesley was hiding behind his official police script. We all have our coping mechanisms.

"I'll tell Starlight. She's become a friend."

"The police have already been sent to her place. She'll have to come in to identify the body."

I squeezed my eyes shut. Why hadn't they let me go to break the news to her—not some anonymous police officer? I let out a gust of air. What was done was done. At least Julia and the others would be there. I had to deal with the here and now. "She has some health problems that have to be considered. I can bring her in."

Wesley placed his hands on his hips. "My guess is that something went wrong with the thefts and Lance's men turned on him."

"Excuse me?" A feeling of reeling backwards, of the blood rushing to my feet invaded my senses. I braced myself on a parking meter. "No, Wesley, it wasn't him. What about Emil?"

"Ruby, the body wasn't found anywhere near Emil's. Neither was your car."

"Lance made his money marketing scentless hairspray. He didn't need to make it stealing."

Wesley tapped his foot on the concrete. He was probably trying to process the phrase "scentless hairspray." The watchers at windows and most of the crowd had gone back to what they were doing. The front end of the tow truck stuck out from behind Vern's. Down the street, Reslin stood leaning against a window. It was the first time I'd seen him without his son.

Wesley scratched the day-old growth of beard on his cheek. "Ruby, they found the stolen goods from the ranch-supply place on Lance's property. Those bricks he has stacked around his house are hollow in the middle. That's where he was hiding the small stuff."

"I saw those stolen goods at Emil's house."

"The robberies always took place on Thursday. Emil has an alibi for every Thursday of his life. His place and Campbells' place were used to move the goods around. That's how they kept from being detected or caught."

"Why can't you put Lance in that same category?" I knew why. Everyone was content with the mastermind being an outsider. Xenophobia rules. "What if Lance was set up, framed?"

"*Now* who's believing in conspiracies." To his credit, Wesley's tone was extremely gentle. Nothing was said in a "see, I told you so" way. "His fingerprints were all over the goods, Ruby. I'm sorry."

"Really?" Forensic evidence trumped any theory I had about character. My argument slipped from my hands in increments. Was it possible that someone could be a really great husband and a criminal? Had his proclamation of faith been a big charade? I didn't believe it. But I didn't have a lot of ammunition to refute Wesley's assumptions. "I just thought that Emil was getting his revenge on the descendants who hung his great-granddad. There's a map in the library." When I spoke the theory out loud, it sounded stupid. Who could hold a grudge for a hundred years? A person would have to inherit the bitterness like some men pass on rifles and tools, father to son, father to son.

Wesley cupped his hand over my elbow. "Do you need to sit down?"

I nodded. He led me to his truck bed with the tailgate open. "Your mom can probably get her car back in a week or so." He lifted me up into the truck bed. "There's no reason to believe it was part of the murder. We just need to make sure."

"Where did they find it?"

"Abandoned on Old Gorman Road."

My brain felt like it had miniature bats fluttering inside. Maybe Lance was guilty. No. No. I refused to believe it. "Is there any reason to believe Starlight is involved?"

Wesley shook his head.

That settled it. My job was to help Starlight through this time. I couldn't control the accusations or the evidence. Right now, I couldn't prove Lance's innocence, but I could be a support to Star.

Wesley leaned against the tailgate.

I turned slightly. "This is your dad's truck. The one we took out to the north field that day."

"Yep." His gloved hand brushed my cheek.

I swung my feet back and forth, and we both silently relived the good memory of a day spent working as a team—and our one-and-only kiss. Even if we couldn't handle parts of our lives, we did work together well. "Wesley, I—"

"Please." He lifted his hand. "We'll just fight again, Ruby. I got a lot of work stuff to deal with today . . . alone."

I pulled my glove off and trailed my fingers over the ridges of the tailgate. There was so much to admire about Wesley, so much that I loved. But he was right. We'd probably just end up fighting again. I swallowed. "Okay."

"I need to talk to Reslin."

I nodded. He slipped past me. His hand rested momentarily on the corner of the tailgate. My fingers inched toward his hand but did not touch him.

He walked away down the street, his boots pounding on the concrete and growing dim.

⌢

In the month that followed, there were no more robberies, which only confirmed Wesley's theory. A few days after they found Lance, Nathan's bull, Persistence, appeared in a field not far from Zac and Julia's house. The animal was a lot skinnier than the photographs Nathan had of him in his wallet, but he was alive and just as sweet as ever. Vern's Charlie Russell sculpture didn't surface.

Nathan moved back to his property in a new trailer, and I put my energy into hanging out with Starlight and perfecting our chip recipe for the Potato Festival.

Starlight was able to get out when I previewed places for the possibility of toxins. Any place with new carpet was out of the question. She told me the smells from that made her feel like she was breathing through a straw. The restaurant at the community food co-op proved fairly safe if we went during slow times and sat far away from people. Most of the people who worked there didn't wear perfume or shave. Some of them didn't even bathe. I thought it was ironic that the place Lance would have loved, the land of soy smoothies and organic lettuce, proved to be the safest place for Starlight.

Starlight insisted on coming to the Potato Festival with me. If the toxins got to be too much for her, she could retreat to her car and go home. But we would try.

For both of us, unfinished business hung in the air. We knew that Lance was innocent. But I was at an impasse as to how to prove it. Everybody else in Fontana seemed content to think an outsider had been the cause of their trouble. And now with the thefts stopped, they weren't willing to revisit the crimes.

Starlight put all her energy into just remembering to breathe everyday. She was mostly okay . . . considering. She took meds for depression and anxiety, and both of us prayed that there'd come a time when she'd no longer need them.

On the day of the Potato Festival, I stayed over at Star's. We'd worked all night, perfecting our chips. Turns out we didn't do dip with them, but we had some sweet potatoes that were sugar coated and some that were dipped in chocolate. The regular white potatoes had spices on them, some of them Italian and some of them taco-type spices. They were luscious, especially the chocolate-dunked ones. Though my original reason for doing the contest was to be company for Star, I found myself praying against a competitive spirit that rose up in me. We'd put a lot of work into these chips, and so help me, Lord, I wanted to see the grand prize on our recipe card.

The plan was to leave my Suburban at Star's and take her Lexus. After over a month, I was still driving the tank Vern had loaned me. Every time I asked him about my Valiant, he assured me with a wide grin that he was working on it. He would always follow up his reassurances by saying, "How that's Suburban working out for you? I could give you a sweet deal on it."

We each wore one of Star's glitzy coats. I got a cute pair of ballet flats with a leather flower on them. I'm five eleven. If I wear heels, small children run from me, screaming, "Mommy, the redheaded giant is scaring me."

It was late April, and most of the snow had melted. A chill still hung in the air, but the sun shone more, and the ground softened. We started to get more hours of daylight.

Star had hired people to finish the construction on the yard. She had a huge rock driveway with a sculpture in the middle. The ground was still bare dirt. In another month or two, she'd be able to plant. Mom and Georgia agreed to help her with a flower garden.

Starlight carefully placed the completed chips into a plastic container while I polished the crystal display plate. "Got the recipe card?"

She held up a pink card with a gold border done with glitter pen. We had been quite artsy-craftsy in putting together the recipe card. I was pleased as peaches with what we'd been able to pull together.

Timing was everything in assuring that Star got to stand by our chips while the judges made their choice. We needed to avoid deodorant- and perfume-slathered crowds and get to town as close to the time of the recipe contest as possible.

Star's Lexus rolled smoothly down the country roads into town. I'd made arrangements with Daelynne for us to wait in the library, which was technically closed, after we set up our stuff for judging. That way, Star wouldn't have to be around smells until absolutely necessary.

Daelynne was still bent out of shape about the historical document I'd ruined, but she agreed to let us in.

When we got to town, Main Street was closed off. We parked in a designated empty lot and pulled the stuff for the recipe contest out of the backseat.

The town buzzed with activity. Two hot-air balloons floated overhead. A marching band led the parade down Main Street and turned a corner headed toward the fairgrounds. My lower lip quivered as Vern and his family drove by in the Mustang. Balloons and streamers flowed out of the windows. Two more classic cars followed.

After that came a group of men on lawnmowers. The list of events published in the *Fontana Ledger* said that later men would race those wild, angry machines on a special track beside the fairgrounds.

Nathan, along with some teenagers, came next, each of them pulling their prize bull. Shined up and fat, Persistence ambled down the street, displaying his huge muscles and straight back. Kids pulling lambs on leashes came next, followed by another marching band.

We had only been in town ten minutes, and already Star was

cupping her hand over her nose. This wasn't going like I'd planned. I thought we'd be able to park closer to the fairgrounds. The crowd was so thick there was no way to avoid them and their smells. I screamed in her ear, "Let's get you over to the library. I'll set up, and then you can come right when the judging starts."

Star nodded. Her eyes were watery, and she coughed. I hoped this hadn't been a mistake.

Crowds lined the streets. Children jerked balloons and bounced up and down. I spotted Zac with Brody on his shoulders. The two-year-old rubbed cotton candy on his dad's bald spot. Julia and the other children stood close by. Josie waved at me. At the end of the street, Wesley and Cree sat on horses—Wesley on a black mare with a black mane and Cree on a bay. Cree had said something to me about them volunteering to work security for the festival. Probably wasn't too hard a job, and they got to ride cool-lookin' horses.

A cacophony of engine noises, band instruments, cheering people, and hooves pounding on concrete assaulted our ears. The smell of manure and exhaust hung in the air.

I waited for a break in the parade action and crossed the street. Grasping Star at the elbow, I pushed us through the crowd by the hardware store. A loud roar went up as the centerpiece of the parade rolled by, a battered truck filled with potatoes, symbolic of the ones that would soon be put in the ground. The final float was the Potato Queen with her court. This year they'd chosen a busty blond with big teeth as the winner. What a surprise.

I dragged Star to the back side of Main Street. We turned the corner, and the noise dropped by half. Star took her hand off her nose. Her breathing was wheezy.

"Are you okay?"

She touched her throat. "Just a little swelling. And a small head-ache. I'm okay."

I was pretty sure she was lying, but it was her call.

The back side of Main Street consisted of a gravel parking lot filled with cars and beyond that small houses surrounded by old-growth trees. If I'd been a Potato Festival veteran, I would have known I could park here, closer to the fairgrounds. Oh well. Next year.

A newer-model Subaru pulled into a parking space along the narrow street where we were walking. A man with a vague famil-iarity to him stepped out of the car.

He had a long slender nose that blossomed into a ball at the base and smooth silver hair. "Are you ladies here for the Potato Festival?"

We nodded in unison.

"My wife and I come up every year. I grew up around here." He held out a hand. "I'm Ethan Van Kriten."

Now I knew why he looked familiar. "You're Emil's kid?" The man smiled and blinked his long eyelashes.

"One of them. My brothers and sister all live around here. I settled in California."

"How nice of you to come back for the festival." I never would have pegged Ethan as being related to Emil. Although he had the same steely eyes, the man possessed none of his father's gruff unfriendliness.

"We enjoy it. I miss the open country."

I leaned on the Subaru. A sculpture resting on the backseat caught my eye. It was of a cowboy on a bucking horse.

Ethan must have noticed my face pressed against the glass. "It's a Charlie Russell. Do you like it? Dad gave it to me. He won it in a poker game."

I couldn't take my eyes off the bronze. On the other side of the building, the second marching band had stopped in the street, pounding out an incessant rhythm that matched my increasing heart rate. "That's what he told you?" The words *blunt object* kept circling through my head. What a convenient way to spirit a murder weapon out of town—give it to your kid.

Ethan's jaw dropped slightly. "Yes, that's what he said."

My tone had been too cutting, too accusatory. My guess was that Ethan was an innocent in this whole thing. I steered toward the back entrance of the library. "You enjoy the festival, Ethan. Nice to have met you."

My heart was racing by the time we knocked on the back door. Daelynne, dressed in a flowing beige pantsuit, opened the door. Her hair was piled on top of her head, and she wore dangling earrings. "Daelynne, could you do something for me?"

"I *am* doing something for you." She crossed her arms. "I'm letting you stay in the library. I'm only doing this for your friend."

"Please, it will only take a minute." She really needed to get past that historical document issue.

Daelynne's mouth tightened so her lips almost disappeared.

"I need you to look up the February edition of the *Ledger* that talked about Vern's robbery."

Star sniffled. She pulled a tissue from her pocket and massaged her forehead. Daelynne turned toward Star and the harshness in her expression softened. "Why don't you come in, dear? I got rid of all the air fresheners and everything." She ushered Star in.

What was I? Chopped liver with a parsley garnish? Or at the very least, suddenly invisible. We made our way through a room filled with piles of books and magazines. "Daelynne, it's really important. It might help us figure out who killed Star's husband."

Star planted her feet and cocked her head at me. She fingered the handle of the tote that held our crystal serving dish.

We stepped into the main part of the library. Daelynne scolded me the whole time she stomped across the wooden floorboards. "You are a troublemaker, Ruby Taylor." Her high heels pounded on the painted wood floor. "Honestly, I need to get over to the fairgrounds." She disappeared behind a bookshelf. "I'm one of the judges in the recipe contest." Our chances of even placing fell through the floor. I contemplated scratching my name off the recipe card. Daelynne liked Star. Drawers opened and slammed shut. She came out from behind the bookshelf, holding a newspaper.

Whatever pettiness she had about me and her prejudice toward outsiders was overcome by her sense of justice or maybe it was sympathy for Star. It didn't matter; I had my newspaper.

"Thank you. Thank you." I gushed.

Star set her tote on the table that held Daelynne's Picks. She touched her lacy collar and smoothed over the sequins on her bolero jacket. "We're entered in the recipe contest."

After shoving the paper in my direction, Daelynne turned to face Star. "My son, Carl, is a judge, too. Do you know Carl? He's the sheriff for all of Colter County."

Reslin was also one of the lawmen who'd decided that Lance had been responsible for the thefts.

I don't know if it was because Star wanted to win the contest as bad as I did or because she figured Daelynne had nothing to do with her son's professional judgment, but Starlight was extremely cordial in her response. "I haven't met him directly, but I have heard of him."

Daelynne went into her I-was-a-single-mom-before-it-was-in-style speech, and recited the litany of her son's accomplishments. Their voices faded to the background as I wandered the library, trying to find a place to lay out the newspaper. There was no picture of the sculpture on the front page. I scanned the print to see if there was a description of it.

Daelynne had her counter stacked with books and knickknacks. I peeked into the room that contained the stuff chronicling the history of the county. Whoever Daelynne had hired had done quite a bit of work. Some of the artifacts and documents were arranged in display counters. The place had been painted, and a new window had been put in. I found a flat spot on the counter and spread open the newspaper to page five, where the story about Vern's robbery was continued. In the second-to-the-last paragraph, the reporter mentioned that the sculpture was a Charlie Russell bronze called "Bronc Twister." The sculpture was valued at around four hundred dollars and was a cowboy on a bucking horse.

I swallowed and tapped my finger on the glass display case. Well, well, well. Emil had had Vern's Charlie Russell all this time. My driving the Mustang off Emil's property and Emil being a long-time Fontana resident had freed him of suspicion. I didn't want to make the same mistake again. I couldn't just pull the sculpture out of the car and take it to Reslin or Wesley or Cree. There were all kinds of rules about evidence tampering. This time, I wanted to make sure something stuck to Emil.

"Don't touch anything in there."

Daelynne's sharp remarks seized up my heart and made me jump. Her wrinkled forehead and clasping and unclasping of her hands communicated genuine fear.

My being in here made her nervous. "Daelynne, I know how much this stuff means to you. It looks real nice."

Her stance softened a bit. "We had hoped to have it open by now, but there's still work to be done." She nodded, but her hands kept opening and closing. "I need to get over to the fairgrounds." She was trying really hard to be polite. "You better get over there, too. There's a deadline for having your entry in."

"I know."

"I'm real sorry for Starlight and all she's been through."

"Thank you."

She checked her watch. "You really need to get out of that room." Her feet pounded across the floor, and the front door creaked open. Right before she left, she shouted, "Please get out of that room."

"I will," I said more to myself than to her. I had fully intended to exit the room right away. While I folded the newspaper, my gaze traveled to the display case. The letter I'd torn over a month ago was sitting on top of a pile of yellowed paper. The phrase *little Emil* caught my attention. I pressed my nose against the glass.

Star came to the door of the museum room. "We need to get over there if we're going to make the deadline, Ruby."

"I know." The greeting of the letter said, "Dear Mrs. Van Kriten."

Chapter Twenty

Carefully, I recovered the letter and held it to the light. The date in the corner said 1933. The letter was written in big chunky letters, similar to a third-grader's handwriting. It was faded, so I had to tilt it sideways to see the script.

Dear Mrs. Van Kriten,

I cannot thank you enough for takin in little Emil. What with times bein so tuff and all.

I think God was looking out for both of us. You with no babies to call your own and me and Harry with three mouths to feed already. I warn you, Emil loves to eat. If he gets to squalling too much, put him on the sheepskin to calm him down. Harry has a brother up in Canada who may have some work for him fellin trees. I am hoping our luck will improve and we will be able to come back to Montana in a few years. I hope I will be able to come back for Emil. I know I am leavin him in good hands. Taking my baby into your home was a tru act of love.

Jess

I placed the letter back in the display case underneath the other letters; no need for anyone else to find it until I established its significance. I guess Jess never came back for her kid. The letter had been next to the maps that Lance had been examining, and the ribbon that held it had been undone, so maybe Lance had read it. I didn't know how this information played into everything. What if the news Lance had given to Emil wasn't about the pattern of the robberies but about Emil's true bloodlines? Would having your identity ripped from you make you angry enough to kill?

My guess was that Daelynne hadn't even read the historical documents she had so carefully arranged. Maybe nobody in this town knew—the thing that was Emil's whole identity, that he was the oldest son of an oldest son, a Van Kriten, wasn't even true.

"Ruby." Star touched her watch. "We have ten minutes to get over to the fairgrounds and set up."

I filled Star in on the letter and my theory about the Charlie Russell sculpture. "Star, I think I can get Emil arrested for killing Lance, but time is of the essence right now. Can you set up by yourself?"

"If it means justice for Lance. You'll be there for the judging, won't you?"

"Sure, sure. This will only take a minute." I ushered her toward the table where I'd set the Tupperware container of chips. "I've just got to find Wesley or Reslin and have them officially remove that sculpture from the car." I handed her the container. "Carry them flat so they don't break."

Star shrugged and giggled. "We wouldn't want that. We'd have chip bits instead of chips."

I assessed the situation out the front door. The crowd had thinned a bit. With the end of the parade, most people were making their way to the fairgrounds. Enough people milled around and moved in and out of the shops to make it hazardous for Star.

"Probably best if you go around the back. I arranged to have our table far away from the others. If it gets to be too much, maybe Mom was able to park a little closer. You can go sit in her car."

She nodded. "Sometimes if I can just get fresh air away from people I'm okay."

Outside, I saw Wesley on his black horse. He slipped around a corner and up an alley. "There's a policeman. I'll see if I can catch him."

As I pushed open the door and bolted down the stairs, she called out to me that she'd be all right. People chatting on the streets and going in and out of the stores slowed my crossing the street. I got bumped several times and had a few close calls with manure the farm animals had left.

A strong hand wrapped around my forearm. "Hey, there."

I looked up into Emil Van Kriten's face. He applied pressure to my arm.

"Hey, there," I gasped. My heart raced.

He grinned at me, revealing a brand new set of dentures. Wonder where he got the money for those? He leaned close, shouting in my ear above the mumbling of the crowd. "Enjoying the festival?"

The sickening sweet stench of beer assaulted me. I wanted to blast him with everything I knew and had found out. But now was not the time for that. I twisted slightly, and he tightened his hold on me. The lustful look in his eye frightened and repelled me.

"It's been great fun so far." Lance had left the library a little after closing. I wondered what time Emil took off for his poker game. I wanted to ask him, but the last thing I needed to do was set off any alarms. If he was Lance's murderer, Emil was real good about covering his tracks and remaining above suspicion. He wasn't going to get away this time.

I jerked free of him.

Emil's eyes were glazed. He swayed. "Hey . . . hey . . . don't go . . . getting so . . . upset." His words dragged out like he had to think about each syllable for a long time before saying it.

My stomach turned. I glanced at the crowds in the street. His whole attitude creeped me out. My heart pounded incessantly.

"I gotta go, Emil." The noise of the crowd masked the quaver in my voice.

I darted down the alley. When I looked back, Emil was swaggering back out into the street. Rotten-food smells swirled through the air. No sign of Wesley. I ran farther up the alley. Smells of cooking meat drifted out of a window. This was the alley next to the café. I could hear the faint clomping of horses' hooves but couldn't discern where they were coming from. There had been horses in the parade. No guarantee that even if I tracked down the sound it would be Wesley.

I wandered the streets for another ten minutes, looking for Wesley. Star must have gotten to the fairgrounds by now.

Maybe my chances of finding police assistance would be better there. I ran down the remainder of the alley. Houses, a beauty shop, and a funeral home occupied the street behind Main Street. Both the businesses had "Closed" signs in the window. Ten or fifteen people walked around, peering into the windows.

The noise of the festival grew louder as I made my way up the street. Venders selling popcorn, hot dogs, balloons, necklaces, and festival trinkets lined the dirt road that led up to the fairgrounds. I passed several floats that had pulled off the parade route and parked. The Potato Queen kneeled on the ground in her spar-kling gown, helping a little girl bandage the leg on her lamb. One of the members of the queen's court dabbed at tears on the little girl's face. Oblivious to the dirt on her gown, the queen pulled a pin out of her hair to fasten the bandage while making comfort-ing sounds to the little girl and the animal. I made my way up the road, thinking about how often my assumptions about people got me into trouble.

The fairgrounds consisted of three metal buildings: one large one, with two smaller ones on either side. One of the smaller build-ings also had a series of corrals and pens around it, which were now full of sheep and cows. The two smaller buildings were la-beled Building A and Building C while the center building was called the Lonnie James Memorial Building. Don't ask me.

Daelynne had said that Reslin was also judging the recipe con-test, so he'd probably be the easiest lawman to find. I figured the building without the corrals must be the one where the recipe contest was taking place. The lawnmower races drew a good-size crowd. NASCAR eat your heart out. There was so much spillover from the people cheering for the riders that they blocked the en-trance to Building C.

Fighting claustrophobia and the inability to breathe that comes with sardine-like conditions, I pushed past people. Bodies, elbows, and shoulders smashed into me. Twice I saw the golden glint of Wesley's hair, and twice I lost him in the crowd.

In shuffling toward the wide entrance of Building C, I didn't so much as make my way there—rather I got propelled by the crowd. I stepped inside and took a deep breath. The building was huge and airy, and the crowd a great deal thinner. Thirty-foot ceilings revealed exposed beams. Lights had been mounted on the walls about ten feet off the ground. Displays of quilts and sewing projects and jams and cookies cluttered shelves.

In the far corner, a platform had been assembled and painted for the potato recipe contest. Several people were moving from table to table, pulling plastic spoons from their pockets and tasting. Daelynne stood beside a table where a little four-foot sprite of a woman held her creation in a casserole dish. The small woman had gray blue hair and a contagious smile. Mom and Georgia stood beside their table. They'd decided to join forces with their recipe ideas. Dressed in matching pink suits and white pumps, they looked downright cute. No sign of Reslin.

People milled around the displays, creating a sort of hushed mumbling background noise. I moved closer to the contest platform. The table on the end was set up with the chips and our recipe card.

Starlight was not there.

Mom waved at me when I was maybe twenty feet from the platform. I pointed toward the end table. Mom shrugged. Star had made it to the contest but left for some reason.

I didn't know what the full effect of too much toxic smell exposure would be. But because I've been blessed with both the ability to worry and a great imagination, I pictured her passed out on the bathroom floor, slowly drifting into a coma. The restrooms were on the other end of the building opposite the recipe contest. I walked through an exhibit of home-sewn aprons with matching scarves, probably 4-H projects. Some of the sewing projects had blue or red or white ribbons on them.

A sign that said "Sponsored by Reslin Taxidermy" caught my

eye. I recognized Carl Reslin's son, Hayden, standing beneath the sign, along with a table that displayed a stuffed bobcat with teeth bared, and an antelope. The skinny kid's stoic expression looked like it had been carved out of stone. Since that first time I'd seen him at Nathan's fire, something about him had changed. He looked older, tired. The smirk was gone from his face.

A brunette in a denim shirt that said "Reslin Taxidermy" on it stood beside the stuffed and mounted wildlife. She was pretty in an Amazon sort of way. I assumed she was Reslin's wife. She and Reslin were both built the same, squarish and muscular. If they made a movie together, they could call it *Attack of the Brawny People.*

A roar erupted outside, signaling the end of the lawnmower races.

I walked over to the brunette woman and leaned close to her. "I'm looking for your husband." Hayden stepped away from the table and didn't make eye contact with me.

Reslin's wife shrugged. "He's supposed to be up judging the contest."

Great. The two people I desperately needed to find, Starlight and Reslin, were MIA. Hayden turned his back to me, indicating he didn't want to talk to me. I felt a tap on my shoulder, turned, and was assaulted by a wash of pink. Georgia and Mom stood together like conjoined twins.

"Ruby, you need to get up there. The judging has started."

Right now, the recipe contest was the last thing on my mind. "I know. I need to find Sheriff Reslin and Star."

"Well, hurry." They actually walked in unison back up to the platform. The voices outside grew louder. I spotted Reslin just as a huge wave of people flowed into the building. I do mean a wave of people. It was as if someone had cut the corner on a plastic sack and water gushed out. All the people who'd been watching the races suddenly became fascinated by quilts and homemade jam.

I rushed over to Reslin and grabbed his elbow.

The noises of the crowd swelled to a roar.

I shouted into Reslin's ear, "I need to talk to you."

"About?" Reslin glanced in the direction of the recipe-contest platform.

"It's about Lance's murder." People bumped against me. "I think I found the murder weapon in Ethan Van Kriten's car. It's the sculpture that Vern Mackafferty had stolen. The car is over in the lot behind the library."

Reslin raised one corner of his mouth. His handlebar mustache twitched.

"I'm serious. I don't know what this means." Because of the increase in noise level, I had to yell into Reslin's ear. "But there's a letter in your future museum that shows Emil is not really a Van Kriten. He was taken in by the Van Kritens during the Depression."

People pushed through the crowd, and I was slammed against Reslin's chest. His strong hands wrapped around my wrists. He put his lips very close to my ears. "None of this is important, Ruby. You need to let it go."

I knew that Reslin had issues with believing women were capable of intelligent thought, but I hadn't counted on being summarily dismissed. He still hadn't let go of my wrists. Out of the corner of my eye, I caught site of Ethan Van Kriten. "There he is. Emil's kid. At least look in the car."

Reslin increased the pressure of his hold on my wrist. I glanced at Ethan, standing beside a petite, silver-haired woman who touched a nine-patch quilt done in reds and purples. Ethan smiled and waved at me.

My gaze traveled back to Reslin. I felt suddenly lightheaded. Blood rushed past my ears. The men were built differently, but resemblance in the face was uncanny. The first time I'd seen Ethan by his car on the back side of Main Street, I thought he looked familiar, but now I realized it wasn't because he resembled Emil. It was because he had the same long lashes and a nose that blossomed into a ball at the end—just like Carl Reslin.

My throat constricted. The memory of Emil coming onto me in the alley filled my brain. While Daelynne had proudly touted the badge of single motherhood, she had never said who Reslin's father was. Emil had to have been thirty and Daelynne still a teenager when her son was born. My gut twisted. Now I understood Reslin's resistance to investigating Emil.

Reslin's grasp on my wrist was cutting off the circulation. "Emil is your father, isn't he?" The crowd roared and pushed around us.

Reslin's face purpled up, and he bared his teeth just like the bobcat his wife had stuffed.

"Let go of me," I demanded. My only thought was that I needed to find Wesley. Wesley equaled safety. I turned slightly. Reslin dragged me toward the restrooms. My hands were not free. I couldn't grab anyone and let them know that Reslin and I were not buddies on our way to the powder room. I leaned close to a middle-aged woman with dark glasses.

"Help me. Please, help me," I shouted to be heard.

The woman got pushed away by the crowd before she could respond. I tried a second time, shouting into the ear of a bald man with a Band-Aid on his forehead. He stared at me, not comprehending my plea. We were packed so tightly there was no room to twist and break free. I tried anyway, which caused Reslin to wrap his arm around my waist, locking my arm against my hip in a steel trap. He pulled me to his side with such force that the wind got knocked out of me. My cheek grazed the abrasive fabric of his shirt.

Reslin's mustache brushed my ear. His voice cut through muscle and bone. "I think you'd better come with me."

Chapter Twenty-one

Reslin's arm was like an anaconda around my waist. Steel bands of muscle pressed into my rib cage, growing tighter and tighter. He was all but carrying me. I looked back at the crowd, searching for help. For one moment, I saw Wesley. Towering above people, he looked right at me. Wesley was safety. I hoped my expression conveyed the level of panic I felt. Maybe too much emotional distance had been put between us. He couldn't pick up on my signals anymore. *Oh please, God, don't let that be the case.*

An instant after our eyes met, Wesley was sucked back into the sea of people.

I managed to grab at two more people with the fingers of my pinned arm, but they returned only an angry glance, as if they thought my tugging their shirt was just plain rude. Reslin dragged me across the floor, pushed a door open, walked a few feet, and then pushed another door open. My guess was that we'd gone through one of the restrooms and then through another door. The whole thing happened quickly; I had no time to absorb any of my surroundings. Plus, he squeezed me so tight around my waist I couldn't breathe. White and black dots populated my field of vision.

We were suddenly in darkness as the door eased shut behind us. A moldy odor hung in the air. Maybe it was just the lack of warm bodies, but the temperature dropped. I had the sensation of being carried down stairs and of concrete surrounding me. Were we underground? In a basement?

Reslin kicked open a door and dropped me to the floor. I fell backwards, sucking in air and gasping. I heard a faint click, and a bare, incandescent light jumped to life. It took me a minute to focus. We were in some kind of storage room. Floor-to-ceiling shelves were stuffed with boxes, bags of ribbons, loose papers, and books.

He slipped inside, pressing the door shut and leaning against it. "You just had to keep nosing around, didn't you? This thing has been put to rest." He wasn't shouting, but an undercurrent of rage invaded his words.

"It's not put to rest. Lance didn't steal that stuff. His widow is suffering. Doesn't that matter to you? Or don't you care because her family hasn't lived in this valley for a hundred years?"

"What am I going to do with you?" He reached into a pocket in his jacket. My breath caught in my throat, fearing he was about to pull a gun and answer his own question. Instead, he pulled out a cell phone. He looked at me one more time, shaking his head before he pressed buttons on the cell.

While he dialed, I scrambled to my feet. Reslin moved closer to the door. The walls were solid concrete, no windows.

He spoke into the phone. "Hey." Whoever was on the other side of the phone recognized Reslin's voice with one word. "Listen, I need you to do a favor for me. Go on over to the library in that stupid museum Mom's been setting up."

He was getting rid of evidence. "No. No," I shouted. I couldn't help but notice the tone of bitterness when he said *Mom*.

Reslin raised his hand. I dove toward him, screaming my objections. He stepped to one side. I grabbed the door handle. He kicked the door shut with his boot. He spoke into the phone, "Just a second. I have to deal with a problem." I felt his hot breath on my face as he spoke. "What am I going to do with you, woman?" The way he said the word woman dripped with disdain.

He pushed me back against the far wall. I slammed into the shelves; several empty boxes fell to the floor. Reslin opened the door and slipped outside, still talking on the phone.

My back hurt from where I'd hit the shelves. When I tried to twist the doorknob, it didn't budge. It was either locked or being held shut. I pressed my ear against the door. Silence. One Mississippi. Two Mississippi. Reslin talking again . . . loud. He wanted me to know what he was doing. He said something about Ethan and the Subaru.

My gaze traveled upward; even the ceiling looked impossibly solid. The only route of escape was the door. Right now, a large, strong man stood in the way.

The door opened, and Reslin stepped back inside. "I've taken care of things."

"You mean you destroyed evidence."

"Evidence of what? No one is going to believe your story now."

"I know what I saw." I'd told Star about the letter, but I hadn't shown it to her.

"You've cried wolf too many times with the Mustang and the cat. People around here already think you're a little crazy. Without evidence, no one will believe you. Just let it rest."

"I can't let it rest." Even as I objected, I had the awful feeling that Reslin was right. Even good people like Vern didn't want to dredge up ancient history and the town's dark secrets. It was like the entire town felt guilty for what happened to Emil's alleged great-grandfather, so everyone gave him a pass on behavior.

Everyone in Fontana over fifty probably knew that Emil was Reslin's father. I wondered if the town had taken care of Daelynne by giving her the librarian job. I felt sorry for her and even a little bit for Reslin. Why hadn't Daelynne left town when she found out she was pregnant? Why torment your kid for the whole of his childhood? "My friend is hurting, and her dead husband's reputation has been smeared. I can't let it go."

Reslin shook his head. "Why doesn't she just leave town? She's got the money."

So that was his solution. It was all on Star's shoulders. I still wasn't sure what Reslin's level of involvement was. "Emil is your father, isn't he? What—were you robbing all those places to win favor with Daddy?"

Reslin flinched.

"You weren't going to get the land back." I paced. My beautiful ballet flats tapped the concrete. Since I was pretty sure I was going to be dead before the day was out, I wanted some answers. "Why did you do it? Why take that stupid cat? You wanted to hurt the people who hurt Daddy's ancestors, is that it? Don't you see how twisted that is?"

Reslin crossed his muscular arms, leaned against the wall. Every time I said *Daddy,* he flinched or twitched.

"'Cept it turns out Emil isn't a true Van Kriten. It's all a lie, isn't it? You broke the law for a lie. That's what Lance found out, isn't it? To him, it was just an interesting historical tidbit. He didn't understand how the information would affect you guys. He didn't understand about bloodlines. Which one of you killed him?"

"Shut up." Reslin's face pinked up.

"You only stole on nights when Emil had an alibi, and you, of course, were above reproach." If he was getting this upset, I must be on the right trail. "Did you involve your own kid, too? Hayden was always with you, wasn't he?"

"Shut up. I'm a good father—I am." Sneering, he slammed a fist into his palm.

The jab about his kid really got him riled. A thought occurred to me. If I got Reslin mad enough, he'd lunge toward me to make me stop talking, meaning I'd have a millisecond when he wasn't guarding the door. I wasn't stronger than him, but maybe I was quicker.

"Do good fathers teach their sons to steal?"

Reslin scrunched up his nose and narrowed his eyes at me. He bared his teeth when he spoke. "I . . . said . . . shut . . . up."

"He's your dad, but you had to pretend like he wasn't. Emil is your father." This whole thing was starting to feel like a twisted episode of *Star Wars. Use the force, Ruby, use the force.*

"Shut up. Shut up." He took an eensy-weensy step away from the door.

"Which one of you killed Lance? Was it you? You defended Daddy's honor with murder, and Emil still doesn't acknowledge you?"

"Shut up. Shut up. Shut up." Reslin's face turned beet red.

"Why didn't your mom just leave town? You must hate her for tormenting you all those years." No response. "You killed Lance, didn't you?"

"No! That's not what happened!"

"Then who, the old man?"

"No! You don't understand!" He dove toward me. I zigged when he zagged, but the room was too small. He grabbed me by my sequined jacket and pulled me back, swinging me in a half circle. He pushed me into a corner and came toward me.

I kicked him hard in the shin. He winced but held his ground. He shook his head once and bolted toward the door. In the moment it took for me to get my bearings, he opened the door, stepped outside, and slammed it shut. A bolt or a lock slid into place.

I ran toward the door and beat on it. I yelled and pounded until I was exhausted. My throat was raw. A concrete room is pretty soundproof. I fingered the hinges on the door. It was an ordinary door, quite old. *If I had a tool to pry the hinges off . . .*

I pulled boxes off of shelves. I found trophies and ribbons, a recipe book from the 1950s, a jar of jam with a 1984 date on it, a whip, and an electric bull prod that still worked. Judging from the level of dust and cobwebs, it had been awhile since this room had been used. Reslin probably knew about it from his childhood 4-H shows. Most of the boxes held books, and paperwork on judging criteria for everything from embroidery to the qualities of a prize lamb. The closest I got to a tool was a pair of rusty scissors.

Out of desperation, I used it on the hinges. My hand slipped as I tried to push the rod out of the round things. I sliced across my palm. Stinging pain ran up my arm. I collapsed on the cold floor. The cut was shallow and not bleeding much, but staring at it made me want to cry.

Mom and Georgia would probably start looking for me. But they'd never think to look here. I'd die in here, and they'd find my skeleton in a hundred years when they excavated to put a subdivision over the old fairgrounds. My bones would be the topic of great gossip and maybe DNA testing. Who was this mysterious woman? Had she been murdered? Locked in the room by accident?

I rubbed my eyes and sighed deeply. Musing about being the star of a Discovery Channel documentary did nothing to cheer me up. Everything I knew about the robberies and Reslin would die in this room. I grabbed the dusty package of blue ribbons sitting on a lower shelf. I didn't know if Starlight was okay or dead or on her way to the emergency room. By now, one of Reslin's thugs had disposed of the sculpture and the letter.

Tiny beads of blood created a line across my palm. I had sore fists from beating on the door. On top of everything, I'd probably been disqualified from that stupid recipe contest. Those chips were good, too.

Using the bag of ribbons as a pillow, I lay on the cold floor. The incandescent light glowed above me. If I turned it off, this place would be pitch black. Not something I wanted to experience. Darkest darkness. The last time I was in darkest darkness I wasn't alone.

Had Wesley understood the look of fear on my face when Reslin was dragging me into darkest darkness? Or had he simply dismissed it? I felt an unbearable longing to be in his arms . . . safe. I was always safe with him. That winter evening in the north field when he'd kissed me, I was safe in darkest darkness. His hand had fluttered over my cheek. Warmth had surged through me as he leaned close and touched his lips to mine.

"I'd never do anything to hurt you, Ruby," he had whispered.

The incandescent light burned above me like an unforgiving sun. Wesley had kept his word. He hadn't done anything to hurt me. Not emotionally, not physically. When he became afraid of failing because I was hinting at marriage and kids, he hadn't lashed out at me. He'd retreated into his job. Whatever his struggles, he'd shown he was not like the other men I'd known. I could trust him.

That night in Nathan's barn, he wasn't retreating. He was asking me for the one thing he needed from me—my support. The one thing every man needs from a wife. Not three-course meals and a house decorated entirely with recycled string and magazines. Wesley just needed to know I was backing him. And I wouldn't give him even that because I was still into the protecting-my-heart mode. That was my test, and I had failed. How is it that two people can like each other so much and not be able to risk pushing past their fear of being hurt?

I bit my lip hard and stared at the light bulb until my eyes watered. I turned my head, and the plastic bag of ribbons made a squeaky noise. None of this epiphany mattered because I probably wasn't going to get out of here anyway. If I had a pen and paper, I'd write Wesley one more letter.

Dear Wesley,

I know now that you are good and that I can trust you. I am so sorry I wouldn't support you in your work. I see now how important that is to a man. We do work well together. Life with you would be an adventure. I'd run into burning buildings with you, jump off of high mountains, because your motives are pure and I know you would never do anything to hurt me.

Love, Ruby

I prayed for a miracle, knowing it was the only thing that would save me at this point.

Chapter Twenty-two

The bolt on the door suddenly clicked and the knob turned. I wondered how long I'd been in this room. Had I fallen asleep? I jolted to a sitting position. The light bulb burned above me. *There's no dust on the bulb. If they keep a fresh light bulb in here, maybe this room is still in use.* I hadn't thought of that before. Hope budded inside me.

"Hey . . . I'm in here. I'm here." My watch said two o'clock—A.M. or P.M.? I'd no way of knowing. "Somebody's in here." I rose to my feet. "I'm here."

The door eased open.

My stomach clenched.

"Yes, you're here."

It was Reslin.

Hope disappeared like morning mist. But I fought off that sense of weariness and defeat. I would not acquiesce to the part of me that just wanted to give up. This was not the end. Reslin had come back. This was an opportunity for escape.

He grinned. "Were you planning on going somewhere?"

Already my mind was spinning, planning. I could not overpower him physically. Once he had hold of me, I probably wouldn't be able to get away.

"Why did you come back?" I stepped toward a side shelf that contained the bull prod. "I thought you left me here to die."

"Not here. You might be found."

So that was how he'd been spending his time—setting up a way to get rid of my body.

Out of the corner of my eye, I could see the bull prod. The door was still open. If he'd just take a couple of steps inside. He needed to be close enough so he wouldn't have time to get out of the way from the electrical charge of the prod.

"Come on, Ms. Taylor, let's go." Reslin didn't step any closer.

I put a trembling hand to my forehead. "I haven't eaten in hours. I'm . . . I'm feeling a little lightheaded."

He still wasn't moving.

"If I don't get food every three hours, I get really . . ." I rolled my eyes and kind of swayed foreword.

"Oh, man," he groaned.

I let out a little helpless moan. It was a great acting job. Even I was convinced I'd be doing a face plant at any moment.

With my head bowed, I saw Reslin's boots move toward me. Heels pounded concrete. One step, two, three.

I patted my forehead with my hand and watched out of the corner of my eye. "I just feel so dizzy." My voice was a thin wisp of sound. *Nice touch, girlfriend. Come on, Reslin, get a little closer . . . just . . . a little . . . closer.*

I leaned toward the prod on the shelf. My fingers quivered. *Come on in. Just one more step.*

His boot moved.

I grabbed the prod, pivoted, and pressed the button in a single motion. I got him in the upper arm. He yelled and took a step back. I touched the prod to his shoulder and dove through the open door. The hallway ran both ways. It must be an underground tunnel that connected the buildings. The hall behind me, the one that led to the recipe contest and quilts, was dark.

It took me only a nano second to decide to follow the lights in the other direction. My pretty flats sounded *tap, tap, tap* on concrete. I gripped the cattle prod and ran hard. Reslin wasn't behind me. I stopped at a door along the hallway. The handle didn't budge. The hallway behind me was empty. No Reslin. There wasn't enough current in a bull prod to knock someone out. Certainly, there wasn't enough to kill him, was there?

I kept on running, following the lights as they turned a corner. A doorway loomed in front of me. My heart beat hard and fast. *Please be open. Please be open.* I glanced behind me. Still no sign of Reslin. My hand touched the doorknob. I held my breath. Blood drummed past my ears.

The knob turned. I exhaled.

I pulled the door open and ran up steps. Dark sky stretched over me.

The aroma of straw and manure filled the air. Hooves clodded on dirt. Lambs brayed. I'd come out into the corrals where the prize farm animals were being kept. Some of the owners had hooked lights onto the wood fences, but my vision was limited.

A whole afternoon and an evening had passed. Cows and sheep stomped, their hooves, making a hollow clicking sound on hardpack earth. Straw rustled.

I slipped through several corrals, disturbing all the little critters' sleep. Some of the sheep gazed at me, mildly entertained by the woman in the sequined jacket who raced through their pen. Others rose on wobbly feet and lifted their chins as if to say, "Oh, a surprise feeding. How nice of you."

I slipped past a metal sign that said "Cow/Calf Pairs." A Holstein and her baby along with several others were just beyond the sign. The maze of fencing was huge, but I could make out silhouettes of several trucks and stacks of hay bales, indicating where the corrals ended.

Still gripping the cattle prod, I climbed over and through the fences, using a gate when I could find it, making my way toward the edge of the corrals. I passed a sign that said "Bulls" and chose the pens I crawled through with more caution. Not all bulls are nice. I had to zigzag a little to avoid an Angus who snorted and moved toward me in a way that suggested he hadn't completed his bovine anger-management classes.

I stopped to catch my breath and survey the area around me. Near as I could tell, I was within two or three pens of getting out of the maze. A frosty chill hung in the air. Potential for overnight freezes lasted until late May.

Something nudged my lower back. I spun around, half expecting to see Reslin. Instead I got a face full of cold nose.

"Well, hello there, Persistence." The white of the bull's eyeballs was the only thing I could see clearly. "Did you win a big prize?" He stepped closer, blowing moist breath on me. I scratched behind his ears like Nathan had said he liked. After setting the cattle prod on the ground, I petted down the length of his back. He leaned against my hand, all one and a half tons of him.

The cacophony of barnyard noises continued, hooves against earth, straw rustling, and cattle mooing, but a decidedly human noise entered the mix. A whispered curse word drifted over the top of the corrals.

My back muscles contracted. I exhaled a stream of air. Peering over Persistence's straight strong back, I tilted my head, turned slightly one way and then the other. With such limited lighting, most of the area was shadow and dark corners. I knew Reslin wouldn't give up easily. For some reason, he'd gone a different route than chasing me down the hall.

With my heart leaping and somersaulting, I stepped away from Persistence and crawled through two more corrals. I climbed over the last corral, which was empty, and bolted toward one of the trucks.

Even if there weren't keys in there, downtown Fontana was only a few blocks away. I was pretty sure Vern would help me get to Eagleton. On the chance that any of the other good citizens felt a loyalty to the sheriff, I knew I needed to get my information to the Eagleton police.

The door handle of the truck was cold to the touch when I squeezed it open. I shoved my head inside and felt for the keys in the ignition. Nada. Under the mat? Nothing.

I straightened up and was about to check the passenger-side mat for a key when I sensed that the livestock and I were not alone. It's not that I saw or heard anything. But the hairs on the back of my neck came to attention. Eyes pressed on me. I was in his crosshairs. He had a lock on me. And now he was staring, watching, waiting.

That primitive hunter-gatherer instinct that signals something threatening kicked in. My heart pounded. Adrenaline coursed through my muscles, at the ready for an impending attack.

I backed away from the truck, turned slowly, and waited for clearer sensory information about my pursuer.

Chapter Twenty-three

Sweat snaked down my tensed back muscles. Visions of other Discovery Channel documentaries flashed through my head. You know, the ones where the pathetic baby antelope gets surrounded by a pack of wolves as they slowly close in for the kill.

Indistinct and far apart, boots padded on dirt.

I wheezed a breath. Strange how not being able to see clearly affected my sense of hearing. It sounded as though the footsteps were coming from all directions. Had Reslin rustled up his band of thugs? Was that why he hadn't followed me down the hall?

I swallowed hard and licked my lips while my heart went *kuthud, kuthud, kuthud.* Footsteps in the direction of the corrals grew distinctive, closer together. My hands curled into fists. I inhaled halfway, a quick jabbing breath. I bolted in the opposite direction of the footsteps.

I hadn't gotten a hundred yards when I slammed into a body. A male voice cursed as we fell into the dirt. Still on all fours, I scrambled away from my assailant. Like a band of hot steel, his hand wrapped around my ankle.

I flipped over and kicked him in the chest with my free leg.

He called me a name I can't repeat because I am lady. My kick was enough to get me free and to my feet. Totally disoriented, I just ran. I'd come up with a plan and figure out where I was as soon as I was safe.

Almost immediately, something suctioned around my waist and arms. I had never been lassoed in my life. I had no frame of reference for how it might feel. But I was pretty sure the tightening around my arms and waist was rope. I dug in my heels but was pulled backward anyway.

The same strong arms that jerked the rope, flipped me to the ground and tied me up like a calf. This was humiliating. I felt really sorry for those poor calves that endured this. There was not even time to fight back or protest. The motion was done quickly and expertly. Abrasive rope dug into my wrists and ankles.

"Got 'er, Dad." It was Hayden, Reslin's skinny son. The kid had some strength underneath those baggy clothes—and a few cowboy skills.

I was unceremoniously loaded into the backseat of a car. Reslin and his son climbed into the front seat, and we drove out of town. I could not begin to imagine what their exact plan was, but I was sure my death was on the agenda.

Even though my wrists and ankles were tied, I wiggled around and managed to sit up. Hayden glanced back at me but said nothing. We passed landmarks and road signs including one for Old Gorman Road.

Two questions flashed through my head: First, was there a Young Gorman Road? And second, I wondered if the hill we'd just passed was the one Nathan Burgess had climbed to watch the increasing traffic. It had bothered him enough to write a letter to the editor about it, and then his trailer had been set on fire. Maybe when Nathan said he had evidence in his saddlebag, it wasn't about grassy knolls and shadow governments. What if Nathan had been writing down license plates or taking pictures of the cars that passed on this road?

"Dad, maybe we should put something on her eyes."

Reslin's beefy hand rested on the steering wheel. "Doesn't matter. She'll be dead in an hour."

Oh good, it was nice to know the timeline for my demise.

Hayden made a gurgling sound.

I couldn't physically fight my way free, but maybe I could talk my way out. "Was your son helping you steal all that stuff, Carl?"

"You leave my boy out of this. I'm a good father."

Again, Hayden glanced back at me and then stared at his hands.

Reslin's response seemed strange. I wasn't questioning his parenting skills—although having your son be part of a ring of thieves wouldn't rack up points for the Father of the Year award.

We drove past a lighted sign that said "Reslin Taxidermy." I could see the outline of a house and surrounding buildings up the road. Old Gorman Road narrowed. The river where they had found Lance's body and Mom's Caddy was in the opposite direction, but it all connected with Old Gorman Road.

The vehicle bounced more. I doubted the Montana Highway Department even knew about this route. At best, it was a two-lane path probably created by people driving it over and over.

Hayden kept glancing back at me. His hand tensed on the back of the front seat.

"This is for you, Hayden. This is all for you." Reslin barely spoke above a whisper. Hayden turned his head toward the dark window.

The road grew rougher, jiggling the body of the car as we moved forward.

Reslin gripped the steering wheel. "Do you know what it was like playing basketball, seeing him cheering for his sons? I was the better player. Why didn't he cheer for me?" Reslin slammed his palm against the steering wheel. "I went into the Marines for him. Not like that pansy Ethan, Mr. Architect."

I wasn't sure if he was talking to me or his son or himself. Was he trying to justify what he was about to do or what he'd already done?

"I invited him to the ceremony when I got elected sheriff." Reslin shook his head. "He didn't even show."

We traversed several more hills. The lights of Emil's Ferris wheel came into view.

"Dad, can't we please stop all this?"

"He owes me," said Reslin.

With exercised skill, the sheriff drove the car down the hill and parked it beside the Airstream. He must drive this way a lot. Reslin had built his own home within shouting distance of Emil's. There was something poignant about that. Reslin was a thief and maybe a killer. But I couldn't get the picture out of my mind—a boy playing a basketball game, searching the stands for the dad he didn't really have.

The sheriff continued to rant. "Gave him enough money to build a house out here. You think he would have at least gotten a new trailer."

Before father and son were out of the car, Emil burst through the door of the trailer in his usual fashion, wearing a scowl and holding a rifle. I angled my torso slightly so I could reach the window handle. So far, I didn't need to hear the conversation. Both Emil and Reslin were shouting at each other, complete with matching big-arm movements. Hayden stood to one side, shoulders hunched, hands shoved into his pockets.

I managed to get the window rolled down a couple of inches.

Reslin shouted, "You owe me. I did all this for you. You owe me."

Emil grumbled and growled, "I never asked you to put me in danger by keeping the stuff here."

Reslin continued. "She knows too much. She saw the letter."

"There ain't no letter. There never was. That rich feller was lying." So that was Emil's tactic, denial.

"This is for my boy. This is for Hayden. I'm a good father."

Emil swayed from side to side. "You're a waste of space. You always have been, and you always will be. You and that dumb mother of yours."

A long moment passed, the two men staring at each other.

Reslin tugged at his mustache. "I know where the letter is now." He crossed his arms. "I can show it to anyone I please."

Reslin had resorted to blackmail to get his father to act like a father.

Emil made a growling kind of noise. "This is the last time. The absolute last time."

Then the two men stalked off toward the junkyard. Were they going to kill me and hide my body in there? No, Emil wouldn't allow the possibility of any part of the crime being connected to him. That was probably why they'd tried to put Lance in the river.

Hayden lifted his head and watched as the two older men disappeared behind the fence. Then he scrambled toward the car. He opened the back door and crawled in beside me. The boy pulled a pocket knife from his coat and sawed at the ropes.

"I can't do this anymore. It was me. Dad is protecting me. I killed that Lance guy with the sculpture."

"You don't need to cover for your dad."

Hayden shook his head and untwisted the rope around my leg.

"We were sitting in Emil's trailer waiting for the other guys to get there. Emil had already left. That was the night we were going to hit the ranch supply in Fontana. That Lance guy shows, and he tells us about the letter, but he doesn't tell us where he saw it. Lance didn't get it. He just thought it was interesting. He didn't know about Emil and Dad.

"All I could think was all of this had been for nothing. Dad broke the law for nothing 'cause Emil isn't even really a Van Kriten. I just kept getting madder and madder inside, and that sculpture was sitting right there. Lance just kept talking like it was all so funny."

The kid loosened the rope that bound my wrists. "I hit him twice. Both times I was thinking I was hitting Emil, getting him out of our lives forever. He won't go away. You can't hurt him. You can't get rid of him." Tears streamed down his face. "Dad didn't want anyone to get hurt. We were always real careful about that. You know what he wanted?" He swiped at his cheek.

"What, Hayden? What did your father want?"

"He just wants Emil to acknowledge that he's his son. That's all Dad wants." He touched his hand to his forehead. "I just want Dad to stop. It keeps getting worse and worse, the things he does. Now he's going to kill you, for me. To prove he's a good father. It's all messed up in his head. We have a good life. Why can't he just let this go? Emil is never going to treat Dad like his kid. Why can't Dad see that? Why can't he see it?"

He yanked the rope away from me. "I'll go to jail. I don't care anymore. I just want it to end. I just want it to be over."

"How did Lance's fingerprints get on the stolen stuff?"

"Dad knows how to transfer prints. He thought it would end any further investigation, making Lance look guilty."

He glanced at the front seat. "Dad took the keys. You can't use this car." He craned his neck toward the Ferris wheel, where Emil's truck was parked. "Emil never takes his keys out."

"Thank you, Hayden. You're doing the right thing."

"I just want it to be over. I don't want anybody else to die."

I slipped out from one side of the car, Hayden from the other. I peered around the front bumper. Emil and Reslin came out of the junkyard, carrying a metal box. My coffin, no doubt.

My heart rate accelerated. A hundred feet of open ground stood between Reslin's car and Emil's truck. It was dark, but unless they turned their backs, they'd see me. Hayden trotted across the field toward the two older men. Was the kid going to distract them for me?

If I got out of this alive, I needed to make sure the authorities knew what he'd done for me. He was just a kid. Far as I knew, Emil had never stolen anything or committed the murder, but it was his bitterness over what he thought was his birthright and his sin with Daelynne that had fueled all the trouble. Hayden was right. It was like you couldn't touch Emil.

Hayden reached the other two men. I don't know what he said to them, but they put down the metal box and turned slightly. I darted forty feet and slammed into the ground. I lifted my head. They were still looking toward the junkyard.

I stood up just at the moment when Emil turned around. While the expression *sitting duck* looped through my brain, I watched Emil dart back toward the junkyard fence to grab his rifle.

I ran the remaining distance toward the truck. The first gunshot zinged through the air and hit the dirt with a muffled poof. The second one hit close to the heel of my shoe. I zigzagged and dove into one of the seats on the Ferris wheel. A shot tinged off the metal seat. It was only a matter of time before Emil's aim got a little better.

Pulling my knees up to my chest, I made myself small inside the metal bucket. Seconds passed. No more shots were fired. I heard footsteps.

The Ferris wheel jolted. My seat moved upward, creaking and swaying the whole time. This thing was old and rusty. The squeaking and clanging of metal was like something out of a cartoon. The seat moved not only back and forth but side to side, screeching like a dying animal.

The grinding motor and gears stopped. Metal continued to creak. My seat swung back and forth, creaking, squeaking, creaking.

Was Emil lining me up to get a clean shot?

My heart felt like it had squeezed down to the size of a walnut. Did I even have a pulse? Every inhale and exhale took tremendous effort.

I waited. The conversation between Hayden and his dad gradually grew louder. I heard Hayden say something about not caring if he went to jail. Reslin went on and on about wanting better things for his son than he had.

I had a hard time not feeling sorry for Carl Reslin. He'd tried to be a better father than the one he'd had, which wasn't that hard. Just breathing and being in the same room made you a better father than Emil had been to Reslin. Reslin's obsession with fixing the past had ruined Hayden's future. Emil wasn't ever going to change, but he'd milk Reslin's need for a father for all he could get. *Sometimes you just got to let go, Carl.* I peered over the side of the Ferris wheel and got an instant dose of nausea. From the ground, this contraption didn't look that big, but when you were up at the tippy top—Mount Everest, baby, Mount Everest. They had put me up here to keep me from running. If I tried to climbed down Emil would take pots shots at me.

Hayden continued trying to talk Reslin and Emil out of what they had planned. Reslin kept repeating that they were all in too deep.

Something pinged against the side of the seat that ran parallel to the junkyard. It wasn't loud enough to be a gun shot. I was real familiar with that sound by now. I hooked my hand on the side of the seat and lifted my head just above the rim.

Down below was the most welcome sight I'd ever seen in my life.

Chapter Twenty-four

Wesley, hidden below in a circle of appliances, waved at me. Relief doesn't begin to describe the emotion that rushed through me. I thought I'd never see his face again, that face that I so dearly loved.

How on earth had he known to come out here? He mouthed something I couldn't understand. Then he leaned back and threw something up into the air. The something was attached to a rope. The something hit me in the forehead and bounced back toward the ground.

I groaned and rubbed the spot. When I peered back over the side, Wesley was leaning across a stove with no burners, his face lit with laughter. Of all the Prince Charmings in the world, I fell for one who thinks it's funny when I get beaned in the head.

He stopped laughing long enough to say something, but I still couldn't understand. His lips were moving, but I had no idea what he was saying. I leaned out of the bucket and put my hand by my ear.

He repeated in a shout-whisper.

I still couldn't hear. At the risk of being noticed by the fearsome threesome, I leaned even farther.

He got louder this time. "I don't think those cross bars will hold. I'm sending a rope up. You need to catch it, hook it, and slide down."

I nodded. I couldn't see Emil and the others. They must have moved to the other side of the trailer. My guess, though, was that even if I couldn't see them, they were keeping an eye on me.

Wesley again tossed his beaning device. I reached for it but missed. From the looks of it, Wesley had attached some sort of metal hook to rope that looked a lot like the stuff I'd been tied up with. If you searched long enough, you could find almost anything in Emil's junkyard.

He tossed the hook again. I leaned way out of the seat. The hook arced through the air. I stood up in the seat. *Come on, Ruby, make your arm longer, stretch, stretch, stretch.*

The hook whirred as it circled through space. I saw the glint of metal. I felt the seat sway and my feet disconnect from the seat. I felt myself falling. I screamed. My hand wrapped around something. After a second, I opened my eyes. I was hanging from one of the main metal bars. I kicked. One of my beautiful ballet flats fell off. What a time for a wardrobe malfunction.

Wesley continued to toss the hook. It clanged against metal two or three times.

I found footing. But my reprieve was short-lived. In a sizzling display of sparks and busted glass, the footing broke beneath me. I'd stepped on a light.

I turned and ducked my head to avoid the flying shards. From underneath my arm, I saw Emil running across the field, rifle in hand.

"Ruby, I'm right below you." Wesley had managed to hook onto something and climb up. He hung from the rope to the right of me. "This isn't going to hold long," he said. "You need to drop down here. I'll catch you."

"Catch me!" My hands slipped on the metal bar. I wasn't going to be able to hold on much longer. Six feet of terrifying space hung between us and below that another thirty feet to the ground. "You'll catch me?"

"Jump this way." He must have felt my resistance. Here I was arguing with him again after I promised myself I wouldn't do that. "Do you trust me?"

Emil stopped about a hundred yards from the Ferris wheel. He lifted and leveled his rifle.

Very funny, God. Earlier in the concrete room when I thought I was going to die, I'd said I trusted Wesley. But I had meant emotionally.

"Come on. Jump, Ruby. I'll catch you. Do you trust me?"

Emil tilted his head to look through his scope.

Oh, yes, Wesley. I trust you. I trust you in every way.

I let go of the bar.

Emil's first shot hit the metal above me where I'd been holding on.

I slammed against Wesley's chest. He grunted from the force but wrapped an arm around my waist and held me tight.

My face was inches from his.

"Hey," I said.

"Hey," he said back.

Emil fired two more shots. He hit the lights, causing more fireworks.

With the sparks flying around us, Wesley kissed me. Tingling warmth flooded over my skin. His arm held me, pressing firmly against the middle of my back. He pulled free of the kiss. "This isn't going to hold long."

I was still caught up in the dizzy hot energy of his kiss and wasn't processing what he was saying. The bar the hook was attached to bent, and we slipped down three feet. Metal creaked everywhere. Now I understood.

"Hold on."

I wrapped my arms around his neck, and we slid down the rope. Our feet touched the ground outside the fence of the junkyard.

Wesley grabbed my hand. "Let's get you to a safe place."

I am in a safe place, silly man. I'm with you. "What about those guys?"

"Cree and a bunch of brass should be on their way. I phoned them when I saw those guys pull up with you."

I wondered how he knew to come here, but there was no time. We pushed through the tall grass. Rifle shot ricocheted off the fence and the ground—two, three, four times.

I suspected that Emil's tenacity had little to do with his wanting to protect Hayden and a lot to do with my knowing he wasn't really a Van Kriten.

We slipped around the side of the fence. Wesley ran toward an ATV standing in the field.

I stopped.

"Something wrong?" He swung his leg over the four-wheeler.

I stepped closer and gazed down at him. "I was just kind of hoping my rescue would include a ride on that beautiful horse you were on earlier."

"Sorry. This is the best I could do." He grabbed me, pulled me close, and kissed me. His lips pressed hard against mine. His hand fluttered over my cheek. "When I thought something had happened to you, I realized . . ."

I traced the line of his eyebrow with my finger.

Another shot zinged past my head. I cupped my hands over my ringing ears.

No time for mushy stuff.

I hopped on the back while Wesley started the motor, then we sped up and over the hill. I wrapped my arms around his waist and rested my head against the solidness of his back.

We rode for about forty-five minutes before he stopped at the top of a hill. He killed the motor, and I glanced behind us. No sign of anyone.

"They're not going to be able to get Emil on anything," I said. "His bitterness and manipulation is what caused this whole thing, but he's kept his hands clean."

"Attempted murder." Wesley placed his huge hand over mine where it rested on his stomach.

"Attempted murder?"

"Of you. I was a witness."

At least that was something. "How did you know to find me?"

"Starlight told me about the letter in the library and the sculpture. Someone got to the letter, but Ethan turned over the cowboy statue. So I guessed that Emil was trying to hurt you. I came here. Reslin and his kid were kind of a surprise."

There would be time enough to explain everything to him. "Is Starlight okay?"

"Yeah. She had some sort of breathing problem, but she's okay. She asked me to give this to you when I found you." He pulled free of my grasp and got off the ATV. He shoved his hands in his jeans pocket and pulled out a very wrinkled red ribbon. "For your chips. I had some. They were good."

I took the ribbon from his hand. "Red? What does that mean?"

"Second place. Purple is grand prize. Blue is first."

"That's pretty good for the first time, huh?" The prize was nice. But Wesley's saying he liked my chips made me feel warm all over.

He nodded and turned slightly. "Sun's coming up."

To the east across the rolling prairie, light rimmed the mountains. I crawled off the ATV. Wesley grabbed my hand and pulled me toward him.

"So you were right," I admitted. "There was a kingpin behind it all. Sometimes there is truth to conspiracies. At least the Mafia doesn't control the cheese industry."

"Actually, that's true." He rubbed the back of my neck. "I remember reading about it in a class. The Badger State Cheese Company in Wisconsin was run by some mob guys."

"Uh-oh, does that mean there was a second shooter?"

"Let's not talk about that." He kissed my forehead. "Ruby, when I realized you were in danger I . . . I don't want to live another day without you. I'll quit my job if you think I need to."

"Is that what you want?"

He shrugged. Obviously, it was not what he wanted, but he was willing to do it for me.

"How about this?" I said. "You keep doing what you've been doing 'cause you are good at it, and I'll let you know when I think you are running from emotions you don't want to deal with. We can work through things, and you don't have to pay for your past."

He touched his head. "I know that up here." He placed a flat hand on his chest. "But this part of me doesn't always get the message."

I slipped my hand beneath his so I could feel the pounding of his heart. "And I promise not to argue with you."

Wesley turned his face toward me, eyebrows arched in disbelief.

"Well . . . I'll *try* not to argue with you."

"You don't have to quit totally. You're right. We should try to work through things not run from them. Old habits, you know. Besides, I don't want to be married to a shrinking violet. I like that you have a mind of your own."

I leaned closer to him. "Wesley?"

"Yes."

"Did you say, 'married'?"

"No, you must have heard wrong." He smiled his crooked-mouth smile, then winked at me.

"Yeah, I must have heard wrong." His heart beat beneath my fingertips, and his hand warmed mine.

We watched the sunrise together, and I thought I could stand to watch about a hundred thousand more sunrises with Officer Wesley Burgess. And if need be, I could live through a hundred thousand darkest darknesses with him.

Chapter Twenty-five

Two days after they arrested Reslin, Hayden, and Emil, Vern called me and told me he finally had my car repaired. I wasn't there for the arrest, but Cree told me that Reslin repeated over and over, "I love my boy. I love my boy."

Turns out Nathan really did have all kinds of evidence in his saddlebag. None of it related to the Oklahoma bombing or Waco, but he had license plate numbers and photographs of the cars and people who traveled Old Gorman Road. Even Nathan, though, hadn't pegged Reslin. Nathan had just assumed that Reslin was on his way home since his house was just off of Old Gorman Road.

Among the gang of thieves arrested was the long-haired man in the leather coat. He still had Lance's belt buckle. He confirmed what Hayden had said about Reslin placing Lance's fingerprints on the stolen goods.

It bothered me that bitterness wasn't a punishable crime. Emil's inability to let go of something that happened a hundred years ago was in a way more destructive than the thefts because it infected everyone around him.

Wesley and I drove into Fontana in the loaner Suburban. The day was warm enough for me to wear my new pink sandals with sequins that Star had given me. I was grateful that this would be the last time I had to be a tank commander.

Through the floor-to-ceiling glass windows, I saw Vern and his entire family on the showroom floor, standing beside a vehicle with a car cover on it. Junky old clinker that it was, I'd missed that old Valiant.

Vern shook my hand when we came in. "Ruby, I cannot thank you enough for getting my Mustang back, and they tell me that once the trials are over I can have my Charlie Russell as well."

"Shame about Hayden," said Vern's redheaded son. "I feel sorry for him in a way."

I nodded while that Bible verse about the sins of the fathers and the third and fourth generation whirled through my head. All Reslin had to do was accept that Emil would never act like a father, and he could have saved the one thing he loved—his own son.

Vern rubbed his hands together. "Anyway, for all you've done for me, I thought I at least owed you fixing up your Valiant at no charge."

"Thanks, Vern!" This was good news. The damage to the Valiant was severe, and they'd worked on it for a long time.

Vern trotted over to the covered car. He craned his neck at me and grinned.

Wesley rested his hand on my lower back and leaned close. "Can I get a drum roll, please?"

It felt good to have him so close. "Do you know something I don't know?"

Vern's son stepped forward, spreading his arms as though he were on a stage. "Unfortunately, the metal was so bent and the engine so damaged it would have cost more to repair the car than it was worth."

My heart sank. What had they done to my Valiant?

Vern's freckle-faced daughter moved over to the covered car.

Now she and her brother were on either side of the front bumper. "However," she said, "we still felt we owed you a debt of gratitude for all you've done for us and for this town."

Vern's wife added, "I don't know why we put up with Emil for so long. It was like the whole town felt guilt for the hanging, so we gave Emil a pass on his bad behavior. We believe you, Ruby, that he's not even a Van Kriten. No matter what happened to that letter."

This whole shebang sounded rehearsed. Vern and his family had put together a show on my behalf.

Vern's wife walked to the side of the covered car. "We noticed how much you liked Vern's red Mustang."

My heart danced. They were going to give me the Mustang. They were going to give me the red Mustang. They liked me. They really liked me. *I'd like to thank the Academy for this award.*

"It took us quite awhile, but I think we found a suitable replacement for the Valiant."

Vern, you joker, it didn't take you anytime at all.

"So without further ado, we give you, Ruby's new car."

The kids rolled back the cover. My little heart went pitter-pat when I saw the silver bucking horse on the grill. Then I saw blue-green.

The kids pulled back the final section of cover.

"It's a 1965 Fastback, same year as mine. Runs like a dream." Vern was all smiles.

My eyes misted and a huge lump stuck in my throat. "You found me my own Mustang," I croaked. The car was a beautiful shade of turquoise.

"All leather interior," Vern's son added. "Dual exhaust, front disk brakes, 289 V8."

Wesley leaned close to my ear. "You deserve a car that runs good."

"Why don't you take her out for a spin?" Vern adjusted his hairpiece.

"I can't believe this." My voice was hardly above a whisper. "This . . . this is so much better than I ever hoped for . . . than I ever even dreamed."

After hugging all the members of Vern's family, Wesley and I jumped into the Stang with me in the driver's seat. It took every ounce of control I had to obey the speed limit through town. Once we hit the highway, though, I gunned it, pressing my pink sequined foot against the accelerator. The engine surged, and I laughed. My heart rate increased. The needle eased toward seventy.

We sped past fields full of heifers with calves gamboling around them. Leaves on the trees were greening up. The roads were clear and free of ice.

I slipped into a curve, barely slowing down. "This baby handles."

Wesley leaned toward me, our shoulders touching. "Aren't you going a little fast?"

"Aren't you up for an adventure that goes by at eighty?"

"You're on." Wesley smiled and crossed his arms. "Put it to the floor."

Fields of spring clicked by at high speed. The engine revved. Wesley and I raced toward Eagleton and life filled with promise and possibility.

Romance Rustlers and Thunderbird Thieves
A Ruby Taylor Mystery
By Sharon Dunn

0-8254-2496-8

In the first Ruby Taylor Mystery, Ruby enters a harrowing, yet hilarious, quest for truth as she sets out to right the many wrongs of love, with helicopters, flying buffalo, and a heart-pounding chase scene put in for good measure. Before long the search turns perilous, and Ruby must race against time before the plot turns deadly.

> *"In a literary world of detectives, this book offers a fresh approach to the genre. I look forward to watching Ruby grow . . . as she encounters, and solves, mysteries even more tangled than her personal life."*
>
> —Carolyn R. Scheidies
> Author of *To Keep Faith*

Sassy Cinderella and the Valiant Vigilante

A Ruby Taylor Mystery
By Sharon Dunn

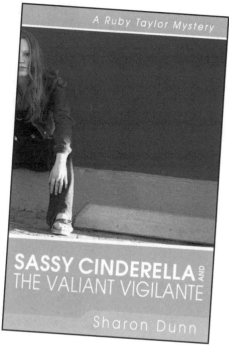

0-8254-2495-X

Once again, Ruby Taylor is thrown into the midst of an intriguing mystery—this time, she finds herself investigating the puzzling death of a local professor after she is hired to fill his shoes. This, compounded with lost love and a heated family situation, causes Ruby to rely more than ever on her newly founded faith.

> *"Interwoven in this adventuresome tale are the author's wit and humor. . . . A fun and enjoyable read. Highly recommended."*
> —CBA Marketplace

Fighting for Bread and Roses
A Novel
By Lynn A. Coleman

0-8254-2409-7

Romance, family, and politics converge explosively in a suspicious murder during the Bread and Roses Strike of 1912. These same forces now threaten to engulf a twenty-first-century woman researching the strike.

> "*Lynn Coleman wastes no time in grabbing readers by their lapels and dragging them into two complete mysteries. Sharply drawn, intricate, and interesting, Coleman's* Fighting for Bread & Roses *is a delight.*"
>
> —Alton Gansky
> Author of *The Incumbent*